W9-ARQ-235

FICTION SIMON
Simon, Leonard, 1937-
Dissociated states /
Leonard Simon.

MY 31 '94	DATE DUE	
MY 31 '94	OC 28 '94	
JE 10 '94	NO 19 '94	
JE 20 '94	SE 15 '95	
JE 27 '94	AP 16 '96	
JY 5 '94		
JY 20 '94		
JY 25 '94		
AG 4 '94		
AG 22 '94		
SE 13 '94		
OC 12 '94		

DISSOCIATED STATES

Also by Leonard Simon

DISSOCIATED

S·T·A·T·E·S

Leonard Simon

BANTAM BOOKS
New York · Toronto
London · Sydney
Auckland

This is a work of fiction. Names, characters, places, and incidents are either the product of the author's imagination or are used fictitiously. Any resemblance to actual persons, living or dead, events, or locales is entirely coincidental.

DISSOCIATED STATES
A Bantam Book / May 1994

BOOK DESIGN BY ELLEN CIPRIANO

Library of Congress Cataloging-in-Publication Data
Simon, Leonard, 1937–
    Dissociated states / Leonard Simon.
        p. cm.
    ISBN 0-553-09586-2
    1. Psychological fiction.   2. Manhattan (New York, N.Y.)—Fiction.   I. Title.
    PS3569.I4825D5   1994
    813'.54—dc20   93-26679
                                                     CIP

Published simultaneously in the United States and Canada

Bantam Books are published by Bantam Books, a division of Bantam Doubleday Dell Publishing Group, Inc. Its trademark, consisting of the words "Bantam Books" and the portrayal of a rooster, is Registered in U.S. Patent and Trademark Office and in other countries. Marca Registrada. Bantam Books, 1540 Broadway, New York, New York 10036.

PRINTED IN THE UNITED STATES OF AMERICA

RRH 0 9 8 7 6 5 4 3 2 1

To my children:

ANNY

LYDIA

BENJAMIN

ARIELLE

DISSOCIATED STATES

PART I

A young man with broad shoulders and a muscular build got off a Greyhound. He moved with the rolling gait of someone who grew up on horses. He wore no Stetson, but his jeans were the brand the men wore in this Western town, and his shirt was the same, and even his haircut once had been the same—though it had grown out now and touched his shoulders. The nylon bag he carried was a souvenir of Los Angeles. It was like a flag—a signal that, no matter where he started out in life, he now lived elsewhere.

From the cab of a decrepit pickup, an older man with a weathered face called out a name: "Felix!" But the young man seemed not to hear, or if he did, chose not to answer. "Hey, Felix! You still up in the clouds? Where the hell you goin'?"

The young man walked the narrow sidewalk. He headed one way, stopped abruptly, looked up and down the empty street, then turned back. He passed the truck, then stopped and turned and walked past it again. He ignored the man. There was hardly town enough to make it possible, but if

1

you were watching him you would have thought that he was lost. If you got up close and looked into his watery blue eyes, you would have seen fear. If you noticed his hair and the place his bag came from, you might have guessed that he was on some psychedelic drug. It was, after all, the early seventies, when it was the fashion among the young to experiment with such things. You would have been wrong.

"Hey! Felix! Where you at? You comin'? What the hell's the matter with you?"

The young man stood frozen. Too scared to run, he studied the truck as if it held explosives. Then his eyes widened as he remembered something he had long ago forgotten. His mouth curled into a scowl. "Where I been at is none of your damn business . . ."

"You a city boy now, is that the way it is? You too good for us?"

"It's got nothin' to do with any city."

The young man reached out suddenly and opened the door. He took a seat inside the vehicle. He would have said, had someone asked, that he was a hitchhiker. He would have said—in a muted voice, with extreme politeness, that he didn't know this man behind the wheel or the name of this little town. He would have said he had no plans.

The older man drove slowly through the quiet streets and onto a state highway that had no traffic. After ten miles, they left the blacktop for a gravel road. After another five miles, they left the gravel for a wagon track beside a dry streambed. They crossed barren land covered with ragged brush. They climbed slowly into a high valley, between the walls of higher hills, where the burnt brown colors of the arid landscape gave way to a surprising green. There was water somewhere. If they cared about such things, which they did not, they would have commented on the extraordinary beauty.

"So how you been?" the old man asked. "What you been up to? You aim to tell?"

The young man looked straight ahead.

"I figured—since you took it on yourself to come—that you let go the past. None of us is who we was. I know I did bad, and I'm sorry for it, but I won't grovel."

"Do what you want," the young one said. "It don't matter now."

2

The track ended at a farmhouse where a woman stood beside a barbed-wire fence. Her long hair was matted and streaked with gray, and her worn-out face had lines that made her look much older than she was. "Felix . . ." She reached out as the young man stepped down from the truck, but he pulled away.

"Your ma keeps prayin'," the old man said. "She ain't been the same since you run off . . ."

"I ain't been either."

They waited in the littered yard outside the stark, unpainted house as the one they called Felix looked off into the distant hills. Then he faced her, and she led the way inside. The house had a familiar smell of dust and sweat. He sat across from her on a sagging couch as she talked of sorrow, regrets, the punishment that God had given her. He couldn't focus on her words. The smell made him sick. His eyes followed the pattern in the peeling wallpaper, the cracks in the ceiling, the weave in the carpet that was worn through to the floor.

The woman served a meal. He knew this chair, this table, this bare kitchen, this tasteless food. Bits and pieces of a life came back. He remembered the prayer she said aloud and the look of her missing teeth and how the man gripped his knife and fork like they were weapons.

"Is it time to clear?" he asked after they had eaten.

The old man smiled and shook his head. "There ain't no chores. You're our guest today."

When darkness came, the young man went outside. He sat alone on the sagging porch and looked up into the crystal sky. He knew these stars. He had sought refuge in them once. They kept him warm and gave him life. Once he read a book that told of other worlds. He had tried to build a spacecraft, but it never left the ground.

His eyes narrowed and his scowl returned and he felt a chill. Now he knew why he had come. He went into the room beside the kitchen, where they kept the tools.

He made his way upstairs. The old people were asleep. He remembered their bedroom in the dark. He knew where the floor sloped and the walls bowed and where a protruding nail would jab him if he was barefoot. In the familiar darkness, with his heart throbbing, he remembered pain.

"Felix? Ain't you asleep?" The old man sat up slowly, trying to focus. "What do you want?"

"What do you think I want?" In his right hand, out of sight, the young man held a hammer. It was the one he used when he was little.

"We don't do bad stuff no more—I told you that."

A single blow, precise and shattering, bore into the old man's temple. He fell back without a sound. The woman slept the way she always did when she had been drinking. The young man studied her face. To him, she had not aged. She still looked beautiful. He stroked her hair. Then he pulled his hand away when he smelled alcohol.

She smiled, opening her eyes to him. "Felix, I'm so happy you came home." She didn't see the old man. She never saw anything. "I know you had to go. He hurt you bad."

"You don't mean me. He never hurt me. I can't be hurt."

"I tried to stop him. He hurt me too. I did my best . . ."

In a tight arc, he brought the hammer down onto her head. The shock of the impact ran up his arm. The woman's mouth kept twitching, but the rest of her stayed still. He pulled off the blanket and ripped away her nightgown. He rolled the naked woman onto her back and pushed the man up on top of her. They were still alive. Their bodies jerked spasmodically. He remembered more: the sound of moans—theirs and his own.

He crumpled old newspapers and set them aflame with a plastic cigarette lighter. He scattered the balls of fire throughout the house. They were his own bright stars—he created them and he held them and they kept him warm. The dry walls sucked up the flames, the burning wood cracking like an open hand on skin. The blaze rushed through the house like a hot wind in the desert. Running from room to room, the young man felt his erection swelling against his jeans.

The truck was where the old man left it. The key was in the ignition. He had never been allowed to sit behind this wheel, had been forbidden to learn, to drive across the open, empty land—but he could do it now. The old man couldn't stop him. The woman couldn't tell. She could not fail him again. He gripped the wheel. It would ease his journey, prove his strength, show the world that . . .

He stopped himself.

4

He knew better than to show anything to anyone.

You have to stay hidden. You have to protect yourself. You have to punish anyone who fails you or does you harm.

He began the long walk out of that place, down to the road, down to the bus—the walk that he had made before.

CHAPTER 1

THE MAJOR HAZARDS of Dr. Jacob Silver's life were the cigarettes some patients smoked and the leather chair he was stuck in all day long. If he was in any danger, it was of developing hemorrhoids and lower back pain. If he ever felt fear, it was of losing patients and having a coronary. Not that these were serious concerns; his practice thrived and he exercised regularly, and except for too much alcohol at times, he watched his diet. Dr. Jake Silver was even prepared for the possibility that a patient would want to hurt him. He didn't own a weapon, but he had words. As a psychiatrist and psychoanalyst, he knew how to find the roots of hostility in early childhood and how to help someone work it through. He knew a great deal about the Oedipus complex, but next to nothing about how to deal with someone who meant real harm. In seven years of practice, no matter how disturbed his patients sometimes were, no matter how full of misdirected rage, his life had never been on the line. The possibility that it might be wasn't remotely in his mind when he was first consulted by Arthur Moss.

After he told the doctor his name, he sat and waited.

"We might begin with your telling me what brings you here," Jake said.

"It isn't me, Doc, it's my head."

"What about your head?"

Moss pressed his fingers hard above his eyebrows. "The damn thing kills . . ."

He was tall, athletic looking, a businessman of forty who said his headaches sometimes kept him in bed, curled up in a ball, for days.

"What makes you think you need a psychiatrist?" Jake asked.

"I've seen internists and allergists and neurologists up the old wazoo. The only thing they all agree on is that I need a shrink."

"The question is whether *you* agree."

Moss looked surprised. "You're the shrink—don't you tell me?"

"I can tell you my opinion, after I get to know you, but it's important to know what *you* think."

"What I think, Doctor, is that I'm living a fucking nightmare . . ."

Not a good sign, Jake thought; not someone who is ready to look inside. "You've had these headaches for a while?"

"I was born with them."

"Well, maybe that's where we begin."

"I don't go back that far."

"How far back do you go?"

"Except for work, where I deal with numbers, my memory is pretty bad."

Moss told Jake that he lived alone, that he was never married, that he had no siblings or other relatives, and that his parents had been dead for years. He said his work was in the market. And it seemed, from the look of his expensive suit and the fact that he didn't blink when he heard the fee, that he was good at it. The way Arthur Moss described himself—from his earning power to his tennis game to his performance in bed—one might have thought he was good at everything.

"The place where you have trouble," Jake said, "is knowing what you feel."

"I don't get you, Doc."

"You know when your head hurts and when you have an erection, but there's more to life than that . . ."

Moss grinned. "There is?"

It wasn't a joke. The more Jake questioned him, the more he found that Arthur Moss had no access to his inner life at all—no feelings, no fantasies, no dreams—none of the stuff that psychotherapists work with. By the time they were halfway into the consultation, Jake was convinced that the pain in Moss's head came from powerful emotions he was trying to suppress. "What made you decide now, after all the years you've had these headaches, to see a psychiatrist?"

"Doc, this is New York! Everyone and his mother has a shrink. You're a freak if you don't have one." He put his hand on his head again. "On top of that, the pain is worse—much worse."

"Do you have any thoughts about why there's been a change?"

"I thought I pay you and you tell me."

Jake Silver sat in silence. His face was expressionless, and his eyes were narrowed into slits. He was a dedicated poker player, and the look was one he might give someone when he thought they were bluffing. "I can't do it alone—no shrink can. Psychotherapy involves two people."

"What do I do?"

Did he really not know? Jake controlled his urge to say something sarcastic. "Mostly, you talk about your thoughts and feelings. I would guess you know that sometimes, if a person doesn't deal with what he feels inside, it can lead to physical problems."

"Doc, if you can show me I'm making my own head hurt, I'll do everything you say and I'll pay you anything you want. I can tell you honestly, I have nowhere else to turn . . ."

It was more or less a start, though not exactly a flying one. Moss was not the kind of patient Jake enjoyed working with. The man was empty, a movie screen without an image on it. He had no humor and no imagination, nothing to make the work more than drudgery.

Jake concluded that his job would be to show this man that he had insides. Moss would have to learn that it didn't make him less of a man to pay attention to his feelings, that he could even learn from them. It was likely to be a long, slow process. Jake Silver didn't sit through ten years of training to treat men with the limitations of Arthur Moss. He became a psychoanalyst because he wanted to help poets who couldn't write, artists who couldn't paint, philosophers who couldn't speak their thoughts. But his practice too quickly filled with lawyers, brokers, periodontists and their unhappy wives—the only ones who could afford him.

Hoping for the best, Jake put aside his reservations about Arthur Moss. Jake was experienced enough to know how often his first impressions turned out wrong. His work had plenty of surprises, and he knew enough not to put too much weight on any single interview. He proposed that they meet twice weekly for a month. At the end of that period they would decide if psychotherapy was helping.

Jake took the names and addresses of Moss's three most recent doctors, all in California, and wrote to them that afternoon. He gave Moss the name of a trusted neurologist for another workup. A week later, the neurologist told Jake that Arthur Moss was in perfect health. There were no abnormalities. The patient's headaches were almost certainly psychosomatic. More intrusive tests weren't worth the risk. Jake never did hear from California.

In the form of psychotherapy Jake Silver practiced, the patient chose what to talk about. This was supposed to lead to important subjects. But Jake soon discovered that if he left Arthur Moss to his own devices, they got nowhere. He talked, more or less continually, but it was superficial at best; there was no depth, no introspection. He described one disconnected incident after another without the slightest hint that there might be a thread worth looking for: who he slept with; how he invested his money; how he spent the weekend past; how he planned to spend the weekend coming; the status of his pain. Though Moss was clearly intelligent, his mind was the most literal and profoundly boring that Jake had ever encountered.

After three weeks, Moss was still stuck on the surface, and there was no hint of anything other than a surface.

"Maybe it would be useful if you told me what you think about while your mind just wanders."

Moss looked at Jake as if he had made an indecent proposal. "Doc, I don't let it wander."

"What about fantasies?"

"What about them?"

"We all have them."

"The only one I have is of a life without this fucking pain."

"What would that be like?"

"I don't know. I still have the pain."

When Jake said *everyone* had dreams, Moss acknowledged that he'd read that somewhere, but could not recall a single one. Ever. When Jake asked if there was anything in his life beside the head-aches that he considered a problem, Moss told Jake about the problem with his backhand.

"I know how important tennis is," Jake said, "but that isn't what I had in mind."

"Doc, my life is great. It's perfect, except for these damn pains . . ."

"Do you ever feel guilty?"

"Doc, to be honest with you, I don't know what the word means."

Arthur Moss came to his appointments punctually, but the pain in his head persisted along with his utter lack of talent for self-examination. As the sessions wore on, Jake began to think of him as a kind of curiosity. He had seen plenty of patients who were hard to work with and had even gained a reputation for being good at getting to them. But Moss was unique. Jake had never heard of a functioning person who lived so much on the surface. And there was just no going deeper. Whenever he pushed, Moss came back for his next appointment and said his head hurt worse. Even when, in desperation, Jake asked superficial questions about the details of Moss's past, he ran into a wall. Moss said that he'd done well in school, that he had a B.A. and an M.B.A. from Stanford, but he never had a friendship with a man or a long-term relationship with a woman. This was clearly significant, but every question Jake asked went nowhere.

"That's it," Moss said.

"I don't understand."

"That's the way it was."

"But you haven't described the way it was."

"I don't remember more."

The phrase became a litany that covered every aspect of Moss's life: his family, his early schooling, his friends and enemies. "I don't remember. I don't remember . . ." To Jake's amazement, there was *nothing* before his late twenties that Moss could recall with any clarity, and not much that came later.

Jake's inability to penetrate the man's defenses made him feel bored and impotent and irritable. He got through potentially excruciating sessions by telling himself that there were things to learn. He told himself that he was asking the wrong questions. The trouble was, he didn't know the right ones. His goals became more modest. In his own puzzled way, Arthur Moss was doing his best. If he needed time, the smartest and kindest thing a therapist could do—maybe also the only thing—was to let him have it.

There was one redeeming feature, a side to Moss that Jake admired and even envied. When he was free of pain, Moss immersed himself in one physical challenge after another: He'd been helicopter skiing, white-water kayaking, wind surfing, rock climbing—all activities that Jake just dreamed about. Moss said he played tennis twice a week and told Jake he had energy left over for a succession of gorgeous women with whom he performed spectacularly.

Instead of thinking or feeling or analyzing, Arthur Moss lived in a world of action. He was a real Westerner, not a New York Jewish shrink who could have been plucked from a Woody Allen movie. Moss once said his mind was "shit," and he was perfectly content— except when he was in pain—to leave it that way.

After five weeks passed, Jake asked him how he felt about their work.

"I'll be honest, Doc. My head's as bad as it ever was, maybe worse, but I like this . . ."

"You like therapy?"

"You're showing me all kinds of things I never thought about."

"I am?"

"I want to stay with it."

The man was trying. If nothing else, at least that much was clear. The fact that he had limitations was hardly a reason to reject him. Besides, like every therapist, Jake had cases where it took six months or longer for the real story to emerge . . .

All of this was hardly diving into the analytic depths. It was more like digging with a teaspoon into a massive dune. But Moss paid in cash at the end of every session, and they went on. The cash was useful in Jake's poker game. If his streak continued, as it had for longer than he cared to remember, he might as well lose money that would never show up on his tax return.

CHAPTER 2

A PSYCHOLOGIST NAMED Harry Harlow conducted a famous experiment in which infant monkeys were raised in isolation and fed by artificial mothers made of wire mesh. As even a layman might imagine, it drove them crazy, in ways that ranged from an inability to copulate to an inability—when they were artificially impregnated—to raise their young.

When Jake drank too much at parties, he used to say that the only thing worse than a wire-mesh mother was a wire-mesh wife. His wife, predictably, was not amused.

Dr. Claire Baxter, like her husband, was a psychiatrist and psychoanalyst. They had met ten years ago, during their training at the same midtown hospital, but they went on to different institutes, where they became psychoanalysts of very different persuasions. She was a classical Freudian who used traditional techniques; he called himself an eclectic and said he was open to whatever new ideas would work.

She said he'd try nude sessions in a bathtub if someone claimed they'd help. He said he had already, but found he couldn't concentrate.

She asked if the patients were men or women.

He said they were . . . men or women.

In Jake's view, once he and Claire got past the surface, they prayed to the same analytic gods. He said the only difference was ritual. Claire insisted that the gods themselves were different. She was a purist who believed that the exploration of a person's inner life was a worthwhile project in and of itself. The goal was understanding, not always improvement. He was a pragmatist who cared more about helping people than creating theories about them. She thought his work was superficial and that his approach lacked rigor. He thought she was detached and doctrinaire. Most telling of all, they each believed the other's own analysis had failed in crucial ways.

Five years ago, when they married, Claire turned her old apartment, three blocks from the building where they now lived, into an office. Claire needed walls and fences and her own defined space. She was good for certain kinds of patients because she knew how to set clear limits. Jake was good for other kinds because he was willing to be confused.

This is not necessarily the best combination in a marriage.

On a Saturday morning in early May, with the sun shining brilliantly and the air cool and clear, Jake and Claire took to the tennis court. Their club was a low-key place for serious players, a mile from the house they owned outside the Village of East Hampton. They had bought the house three years ago, and they spent every weekend there no matter what the season or the state of their relationship.

They had been rallying for half an hour, relaxing and trying to loosen up. Jake had a match with one of his poker buddies at noon. He was out for blood. Claire was scheduled to play doubles with a group of women doctors as a favor for a friend. It was a big favor: She had better strokes than any of them, but she always played poorly in such company.

15

When they paused, Claire rubbed her forearm.

"Does it hurt again?"

"I think I'm cursed." She'd been suffering all year with tennis elbow. "I must have done something horrible in some past incarnation."

"Why blame the past?"

"Very funny."

"You took aspirin?" he asked more gently.

"Advil. I'll take more now."

He poured water from their jug. "I have a patient who said that he was cured by some new thing that's on the market. It's a kind of strap—you wrap the muscle with it."

She looked surprised. "It must be good. The other day I heard something similar."

He had to grin. "I'm shocked. *You* let a patient talk about tennis! I thought you only dealt with deeper things."

"Give me a break. I'm really in pain."

They walked together toward the clubhouse, where he saw Calvin Wiggens waiting. The beefy lawyer waved.

"I'm going to the pro shop," Claire said before they reached the porch. "I'd just as soon not meet this asshole."

"How do you know he's an asshole?"

"He plays poker, doesn't he?"

Jake watched his wife walk off, still rubbing her arm, never looking back. Her clothes were sweaty and the fabric clung to her, and the sight of her body filled him with tenderness. He was sorry he had teased her. The joke was automatic, something left over from his distant past. All it ever accomplished was to make Claire pull away.

Jake's game was on, his strokes as consistent as they always were, and his serve went where he wanted it to go. But Calvin Wiggens was overpowering—his tennis game indistinguishable from the aggressive way that he played cards. He went all out, always. He bet the limit no matter what, and even if predictable, he was unstoppable. He'd come charging to the net behind his serve or his return of serve, deep or not, strong or not, flailing away like a windmill that had come to life.

16

Somehow, he'd reach the ball. Even when Jake got all his power into a stroke, Wiggens would just extend an arm and tap a winner.

Claire's doubles partner dropped her at the house when their match was over. She was napping when Jake got home. He peeled off his soggy clothes and spent ten minutes in a scalding shower washing the gritty green clay off his tired legs and loosening his back. Then he got into bed beside her.

She reached for him so quickly that he jumped.

He looked into her blue eyes. He ran his hand through her straw-colored hair. She looked like a child to him, a mixed-up adolescent who was smart and pretty and more than a little confused. She could have been a cheerleader, but she had suffered; her eyes had soul. She was the kind of girl Jake always wanted in high school but could never get. Now he was married to her, though he was far from sure that she was his.

"I thought you were asleep."

She bit his neck. "I was waiting for you."

"I wish I knew—I would have thrown the match."

"You beat the asshole?"

"No."

She wrapped herself around him. She was warm and welcoming. "It doesn't matter. I love you anyway."

"Even though I'm a creep?"

"You're not a creep, you're just a prick sometimes."

"And you like pricks?"

She took him in her hand. "They have their uses."

"That's it? You want to use me?"

She stroked him gently. "Of course I do, but I love you too."

They fit together. It didn't matter if they agreed or disagreed or argued or got along. It didn't matter if it was chemical or psychological. Their bodies were a perfect match, and they had the wisdom not to analyze it. The only thing that mattered was the way they fit.

"And I love you." She led the way, and he settled himself inside her. He felt her open up to him, let down the wall. It was more than sex. It was more than her body.

17

.   .   .

Later, they had dinner with friends and saw a movie.

They left East Hampton as late as possible, but the ride back into the city was still a crawl.

"So why don't you write an article?" she asked. "Helpful hints for life and tennis elbow from kindly Uncle Jake . . ." It didn't matter what they felt that afternoon, this was a law of marriage: Claire always gave back in spades whatever he dished out.

"And your patient—what's she into? Will you tell me how *profound* her treatment is, how deep into her unconscious you've already *penetrated?*"

"What makes you think it's a woman?"

"It's not a woman?"

"A man," Claire said. "A very strange man. I haven't worked with anyone this sick in years. Serious pathology, major ego defects." She shook her head sadly. "He's a sculptor. He developed tendonitis while chipping a block of wood. For a while he wore an elastic band around his arm. We didn't talk much about it. The major issues of his life are a lot more serious."

"I envy you," Jake said. "When my patient told me he had tennis elbow, I considered it a therapeutic triumph. At least he had a problem. Of course, as is typical of him, it was solved already."

Claire was sympathetic. "Tell me a dream. I'll supervise you."

"There aren't any dreams. There aren't even fantasies. All this guy talks about are his headaches and his money and his penis. Another of our great business minds."

"Where do you find these people? How do they find you?"

"That's how men are, isn't it? That's what the women tell me."

"You're not like that," she said, "despite your aspirations. You do your best to be among the assholes, but at least you don't succeed."

"Should I say, 'Thanks'?"

"I mean it as a compliment."

The traffic was bad, but not bad enough to change the way they felt about East Hampton. They talked about trying to shift their schedules and drive in on Monday mornings. They made jokes about

18

whether to get divorced, and then more jokes about whether to have a child. They analyzed, very differently, the movie they had seen. They went over their plans for the coming weekend. There was a mixed-doubles tournament at the club; but they decided, no doubt wisely, not to enter it.

They talked about whether to see a therapist together. They knew perfectly well their marriage was in trouble. They talked about the kind of therapist who would be right for them and even managed to avoid a theoretical dispute. It was a constructive conversation, maybe the best they'd had in months, but it didn't lead to action. For some reason, they both held back. Neither said, "Let's do it." Neither said, "I'll make the call." The timing was wrong, their pain not great enough. They still needed to be alone, in their separate offices with their separate names, working with their patients in their separate ways.

19

CHAPTER 3

THE PATIENT JAKE saw at seven-thirty on Tuesday mornings was an architect named Alice Quinn. She was one of his first analytic cases and one of his success stories; a woman who had transformed her life entirely through the course of their work together. She was brilliant and beautiful and unaware, when she started analysis, that she had either looks or talent. In eight years of treatment, she had gone from a secretarial job at a city agency to college and architecture school and then on to a fine career. Her graphic talent had first revealed itself in a drawing she made of an intricately detailed dream. Now her analysis was winding down. The long treatment was ending, and Jake felt a certain sadness at the thought that she was leaving soon.

Before the session with Alice was over, he heard the outside doorbell. With a feeling of weariness and irritation he knew he'd have to analyze, Jake buzzed Arthur Moss into his waiting room. How depressing it was to give up Alice for Moss. How depressing it was to give up Alice at all. A few minutes later, after she left, he opened his office door. Moss was standing in the center of the waiting room with a cup of coffee in one hand and a half-eaten Danish in the other.

"You want a bite, Doc?"

Jake shook his head.

"You're not hungry?" Moss stepped into the office and took his chair. "I'd be *starving* after a piece like that."

Jake kept studying Moss. Alice had been talking about the new man in her life. Had Moss been eavesdropping? Was Moss that low?

"Would you like to screw her? I hear it's easy for you guys . . ."

Jake did not respond.

"Nice ass," he went on. "Nice long legs. Nice head of hair. A little small in the tit department."

Jake stayed silent.

"Does she tell you what turns her on?"

Jake shook his head with irritation. "I really prefer to hear about people's *problems*," he said sharply.

Moss looked surprised. "I thought you shrinks were into sex . . ."

"You're not talking about sex. You're talking about some power trip you're on." Jake's tone was harsh. "What I'm *into* is what goes on inside a person. I don't give a damn about the way they screw unless it's a problem." He studied Moss and decided there was more to say: "You know, this macho stuff is all an act. You put on a good facade, a smoke screen, but I think you're terrified of something. I don't know what it is, and maybe you don't either, but it's time we tried to look at it. We won't get anywhere if you just keep proving what a stud you are."

Moss rubbed his cheek as if he'd just been slapped. He blinked repeatedly. His voice turned high and quavering, like a child about to cry, and he began to rock back and forth on the edge of his chair. "Doc, you got it wrong . . . I don't know . . . *please*, Doc, you got it wrong . . . I really don't know . . . please don't throw me out . . . I *need* you, Doc."

21

"I got what wrong?" Maybe he said too much, maybe he was defensive about the things he felt for Alice, but Jake never thought that Moss would melt.

"I don't know! I don't understand. This is bad. You're scaring the shit out of me!"

"What makes you think I'd throw you out?"

"It popped in my head. It was like I was a kid."

Moss looked frantic, even close to panic, and Jake tried at once to calm him. "Look, I have no intention of throwing you anywhere. All I want is to understand. I already know what turns you on. I know how good you are at the things you do. The trouble is, I sometimes feel I don't know anything. What I said a minute ago was an expression of frustration. It was not a threat."

Moss looked at Jake sadly. He seemed to relax a little. "Someone else said that. I was young. I remember the words. I don't know why she said it." To the surprise of both of them, he began to weep.

After a while, Jake gently asked: "She?"

"My head is spinning . . . I never felt this way before . . ."

"One thing we've learned is that there's sadness in you."

Moss cried again. His coffee cup was on the floor beside his chair, his expensive suit was rumpled, his shirt wet with tears. Moss wiped his face with a wad of tissues. He looked dazed, out of contact, as if he'd had a seizure. Jake chose not to ask more questions. He let Moss use what time was left to pull himself together, which he managed with surprising speed. By the end of fifty minutes, Moss was his old smooth self. He wanted to recommend a stock for Jake to buy. Under other circumstances—ethics aside—he might have been tempted. Now he told himself: not with this man, not after what you just put him through. For all you know, in his unconscious, he'd like to murder you.

After Moss was gone, Jake got rid of the coffee cup and the remains of the pastry and sat back slightly shaken. The session worried him. He had never seen someone fall apart that suddenly. It was obvious that Arthur Moss was sicker than he'd thought.

The rest of the day went more or less as usual. People came in, sat in a chair or stretched out on the couch, talked, cried, laughed, sometimes slammed the furniture in anger. Two patients said their lives were getting better; another denied it when Jake made the observation. A man said nothing ever changed; a woman told Jake she loved him; another woman said he was a fraud and a charlatan— exactly like her father. In one way or another, successfully or not, with insight or without it, they all talked about the past and struggled to find a way into a different future. In one way or another, Jake was helpful.

At seven o'clock, when his last patient was gone, Jake dumped the ashtray and opened the drapes and looked out the window at his tiny fragment of a Hudson River view. It was a lovely evening. The sky glowed brilliantly in shades of pink and purple. On the street outside, there were men in shirtsleeves and women with bare shoulders, and he felt a longing to walk among them. He took the elevator to the lobby and stepped into the twilight. A smooth breeze brushed his face. He felt enveloped, warm and comfortable, turned on. It was a world apart from the cool dry air-conditioned cell in which he'd spent his day. He walked along Broadway and looked at all the couples, young and old, their fingers intertwined, their arms wrapped tightly around each other. It was a night for making love outdoors, and it made Jake sad.

On impulse, he decided to surprise Claire at her office. He knew she was due to finish in ten minutes, and he thought he'd show up there and take her for a walk and maybe someplace new for dinner. He wanted to be like these people in the street; ordinary, unanalytic, in love—to be the way they were before their lives got locked behind the couch.

Jake stopped at a florist's shop on Broadway and bought a dozen roses. When he reached Claire's building, he stood on the sidewalk across the street and checked his watch. It was seven-thirty-five, and he knew she was done. She finished at seven-thirty, and she was always precise. To be sure, he waited another few minutes and then started across. He stopped suddenly. Not twenty yards away, Arthur Moss was walking out of Claire's lobby. Jake backed up quickly and ducked behind a car as Moss stood waving for a cab. At first Jake was confused. The clothes were different. The conservative suit was gone and Moss's muscular physique was on clear display. Moss was wearing faded jeans and a black T-shirt emblazoned with a brilliant orange ball. It was a striking shirt, quite beautiful, completely out of charac-ter for the man Jake was treating. Could he be gay? Bisexual? Was *that* what he wouldn't talk about? Jake looked him over carefully and knew without the slightest doubt that whatever his secret, it was still Arthur Moss.

Claire was touched by the flowers. She hugged Jake tightly and kissed his neck. "You mean it's a date? We can go out for a nice long walk?"

"We can walk and eat and then, who knows, I might get lucky . . ."

"Maybe we'll both get lucky." She moved around her office, tidy-ing the room, eager to be out of there with him.

"Our profession is so strange," Jake went on. "Patients always show up where you least expect them. I just saw my newest patient come out of this building. I assume that one of his ladies lives here, or maybe not a lady."

Claire was turning lights off.

". . . I would never, in a million years, have thought he'd look the way he did . . ."

"Was he wearing a dress or something?"

"He looked relaxed," Jake went on. "When he comes to me he's an uptight businessman in thousand-dollar suits. Tonight he was wear-ing jeans. He wore this T-shirt with a ball of fire on it—hand painted. I should take it as a good sign. We got evidence today that he actually has insides."

Claire looked at him sharply. "A black T-shirt with a big orange ball?"

"You saw the guy?"

"My patient wore one."

They were both confused. There could be no two shirts like that. "His name is Arthur Moss," Jake said. "Forty. Financial something or other. Big bucks, apparently. A macho stockbroker, but empty on the inside. I thought *really* empty until today."

She was relieved. "My patient is thirty. He was wearing a black T-shirt with what I thought looked like the sun. I took it to mean he was becoming less depressed. The rest of what you said has nothing to do with him. He could never survive as a businessman. He's an artist, the sculptor we once talked about."

Jake's mouth dropped open. "Mr. Tennis Elbow."

They sat on her couch together.

"Light brown hair?" she asked. "You're sure of this? Blue eyes. A kind of wounded look. Confused. A little helpless. Seriously depressed."

He kept shaking his head. "The looks are right, but not the rest. I saw the guy this morning on his way to work. He was wearing a suit. He must have changed to jeans and to depression before he came to you."

"He *never* wears a suit," she said. "He works in a loft downtown, in total isolation." She studied Jake carefully. "I'll kill you if you're playing with me. I really mean it . . ."

"I wouldn't play this way. I don't much like this game."

"I can't stand it!"

"Arthur Moss." Jake said.

She shook her head. "Alan Maliver."

"Yeah," he went on, "and he's got a brother named Andrew Mellon."

The mood was gone. Romance and sex were out of the question. Now there was work and worrying to do. She put the roses into a vase. They gave up on the walk down Broadway and went instead to the boring Chinese restaurant around the corner. It was where they used to go before they were married.

"I don't like this feeling," he said.

Claire's brow was furrowed, her eyes searching. "What does he want? What does he know about us? He's gone too far . . ."

"How far is too far?"

Among the things Jake hated about his work was the fact that he

_____

could never quite escape it. Patients and their problems always managed to find a way inside him, to be carried around and thought about at the most unlikely moments. Claire was better at keeping a distance, at holding on to her own space, but this time he saw something else in her frightened eyes—she had no defense at all.

CHAPTER 4

"HE CAME TO me in March," Claire said.

"He came to me in April—April Fools' Day from the look of things."

"He said he called my Institute," she went on. "He said they gave him three names and he picked mine randomly."

"It's exactly what he said to me."

"I'm really upset about this."

"I'm not too thrilled myself."

"I thought we were making progress. To tell you the truth, I thought I had an amazing patient I might write about some day."

Jake shook his head. "I thought so too—I suspect for different reasons."

He sipped his beer and listened attentively as Claire told him what she knew:

"Alan Maliver is all in pieces. I mean this quite literally. He lives without memory, if you can imagine that. It's as if he has Alzheimer's, which is what I thought at first, or seizures, which is what I thought next. He knew a couple of isolated facts about himself and a couple of things about the city, and that was *it*. He said he sometimes found himself in places with no idea of how he got there. He said he sometimes woke with new clothing in his closet or strange food in his refrigerator. He often couldn't tell me the smallest thing about the day before."

"When he comes to me he mostly brags about how great a stud he is."

"As far as I know, he was never with a woman."

"How could you work with him?" Jake asked. "I'm amazed you even tried. He's not exactly the perfect candidate for psychoanalysis."

She shook her head. "I know better than to do analysis with someone like this."

"I'm not criticizing. I'm impressed. He sounds like he should be in a hospital."

"I raised it right away, but he refused. He insisted he could get along. He agreed to see a neurologist, and I sent him to Martha Billingsly."

"I sent him to Morrie Parker. He didn't find a thing."

"She didn't either. The thing about Alan," Claire went on, "the reason I felt I could work with him, is that he remembers all his dreams . . ."

"He told me he never had one."

They were seated in the booth they used to think of as their own. The place was empty and the waiter, who still remembered them, gave them all the time they needed. Claire reached across the mica table and took Jake's hand. She was drinking tea; he was finishing his second beer.

"They're not like other dreams," she said. "They're more like movies in his head. I thought they told the story of his life."

"They're not disguised?"

"They're more. All the things he ever saw and felt show up."

"The missing memories?"

"I thought they made it possible to reconstruct the past."

Claire told Jake the history that she and Alan Maliver had constructed from his dreams. She had no idea if any of it was true.

"He grew up in a cattle-ranching area in eastern Nevada. His parents owned some isolated land that barely supported them. He kept dreaming about a horseback rider with his boot stuck in a stirrup. I finally put aside the symbolism and found a place named 'Stirrup' on a map. When I asked him about it, the memory came back—and with the memory, more dreams. There were dreams of being pushed into one physical ordeal after another—lifting heavy bales of hay and tugging at huge coils of barbed wire. And then he had a terrifying dream in which he was stuck on the saddle of a wildly bucking horse."

"We know what *that's* about . . ."

"I think his father was a sadist and his mother a lush. He kept having dreams of women who were ineffectual and helpless. There was one in which a woman suspiciously like me was sprawled across a burning couch and couldn't stand. The most compelling of all was of a naked woman drowning in a crystal pool. It was clearly his mother —he knew it in the dream—and the reds and blues around the pool were those on the label of her brand of vodka." To her patient's horror—and Claire's as well—at some point in the middle of the dream the liquid turned to blood.

"The other thing about him is that he's an isolate," Claire said. "Outside of his immediate family, he's never had a close connection with another human being. People have reached out, but he could never respond. He said he never had a sexual experience, not even a kiss. He remembered a young woman who made a very direct proposal —but he ran away. His work with me, brief as it has been, is the longest relationship he's ever had outside his family."

"I have to tell you, I'm really impressed," Jake said.

"I was impressed myself until tonight."

"He sounds like a person. With me he's an empty shell . . ." By then he was more than halfway into his third beer. "Does he know what he's doing with us?"

"That is the question."

"Could it be a game he's playing?"

"It doesn't *feel* like that," she went on. "I would bet my life he's telling me the truth."

Jake looked at Claire intently. "Don't play for those stakes."

They finally ordered, and almost instantly the food arrived. There had been a time, while they were in training, when they had lived on Szechuan food. Now it seemed repulsive, loaded with sugar and MSG, the spices tossed on as an afterthought, all of it bathed in grease. They ate the rice instead, and Claire drank more tea. The waiter looked offended.

"Let's assume it's not a game," she went on. "Let's assume he's telling *both* of us the truth. It narrows the diagnosis down."

"Multiple personality," Jake said.

"There's nothing else possible."

"Have you ever seen one?"

Claire shook her head. "Only in the movies. I read an article not long ago. They're not as rare as people used to think."

"Would a multiple behave this way?"

"I have no idea."

It was no surprise that in the morning, over coffee, they disagreed. It was their familiar battle—different theories, different ways of thinking about people's problems, different ways of thinking about each other. This time it mattered.

"We do what we've been doing," Claire insisted. She'd been up half the night and looked worn-out. "We treat him separately, exactly as we have been treating him. If he needs two therapists, it's his own choice. We've both been helping him—each in our own way. We wait until he's ready to tell us more." Jake shook his head slowly as she went on: "If you see a patient in the street, you don't just bring it up. You wait for him to tell you what he felt."

"What if he was wearing a dress?" Jake asked.

"That's not what happened. If you want to get somewhere, you accept your patients' terms. You respect their defenses. You don't jump in where they don't ask."

"If he came to *us*, he's asking," Jake said.

"Not in session. If and when he's ready to bring it up, he will."

She had a point, though Jake still thought she was wrong. "He knew that sooner or later it would come out. He wouldn't have picked us if he didn't want to face this."

"We deal with inner lives," Claire went on. "We're not social workers. We don't manipulate. We can't change a person's circumstances. The only thing we can affect is what's inside."

"We deal with total lives. We deal with real people, not Freudian abstractions."

They sat in helpless silence.

"We don't have to agree," she said finally. "We're separate people. We can be ourselves. We can work in our own ways."

He took her hand. "He wants to keep us separate," Jake said. "He wants us locked in little boxes. He wants to be the only one who knows what's going on."

She squeezed his hand.

"We have to deal with this together," he went on. "Thank God we have a little time."

Claire looked confused. Their bags were packed, their tickets on the dresser, but she had managed to forget that they were leaving after work for a conference in Palm Springs.

He struggled hard not to interpret or needle her.

CHAPTER 5

THE SPRING MEETING of the Association for Classical Psychoanalysis was a major bore, but that was no surprise. The surprise was that Claire had managed to forget about it. These were *her* people—the ones who claimed the purest truth and the deepest insight. They had convinced some English professors and *New Yorker* writers that they were closer than their colleagues to Freud or God, but Jake felt otherwise. He knew what their lives were like. They were as far from Freud or God as everyone else, and he had no interest in their arcane papers and esoteric theories. As far as he was concerned, the duller the conference, the better. The thought, out on the tennis court, that someone in some frigid auditorium was saying something useful would hardly help his game . . .

Jake spent most of the first two days in the tennis program: three hours of drills, a small lunch, two hours of competition, a swim, a massage, then time in the whirlpool. Claire went to hear the presentations, though she found it hard to stay focused. She kept worrying about Alan Maliver and seemed to be functioning in a kind of daze. On the third day, with Jake's back sore, they drove across the desert for a day in Las Vegas. Claire fed quarters into the slots and then struggled to swim laps in a huge crowded pool while Jake tried his hand at the poker tables. He quickly learned that any fantasy he had about his skill was merely that. He played against seedy men and chain-smoking grandmothers who knew exactly when to call and when to raise and when to fold. His losing streak continued, and Claire made no secret of the fact that the debacle pleased her. If there was just one thing about him she could change (there were plenty) it would be poker.

It wasn't a happy trip. Much too quickly, they fell into their old pattern. The crisis that brought them closer was too far away. What Jake's first few days amounted to was the poker fiasco and some unwelcome information from the tennis pro about the deficiencies of his serve. He ended up with a muscle spasm, unable to play at all, stuck ruminating on how bizarre it was to be in this place he called Palm Nothingness, with this crowd of paunchy fellow shrinks, immersing their bodies in the tepid, overchlorinated pool, nursing their aches and pains, talking about stocks and real estate and their backhands. It was hard to imagine that psychoanalysts were once interesting people and psychoanalysis a revolutionary discipline. They used to think that they would turn the world into someplace more rational and caring. Now they were indistinguishable from the fat gurus who flourished in the dry brown air.

It turned out that Arthur Moss or Alan Maliver—whoever or whatever he really was—was the most interesting subject within three thousand miles.

Jake was alone while Claire dutifully attended another presentation. He took the telephone onto the balcony and sat in the afternoon sun with a glass of wine. He'd been methodical enough to bring along the names and addresses of the doctors Moss had seen. The first on the list was a Dr. Jason Parness, with an office on Wilshire Boulevard. He found an L.A. phone book in the dresser, but there was no Jason

33

Parness. He called Information and the operator said there was no listing for an office or a home. He asked her to check the surrounding counties, but she found nothing.

He told himself he should have known.

The second name on the list was a Dr. Sheila McGarty, who had a Beverly Hills office. She did exist—at least in the directory. The phone rang three times before he heard a click and then a metallic voice that said the number had been changed. He called the new number and got a service. He told the operator that he was a doctor who needed to speak with McGarty as soon as possible. "I'm sorry," she said. "Dr. McGarty is deceased. I can give you the number of Dr. Ambrose Gannon or Dr. Elizabeth Blair or Dr. David Goldenberg." He asked how long ago McGarty died, and got the woman's own sad California story: "It happened before I got here, and I've been here four years. I never dreamed I'd be doing this that long. I'm an actress, like everyone else in town. She doesn't get many calls. They keep the number going because it brings in people who saw her on television. You could ask Dr. Gannon. He's really nice . . ."

Jake went back into the bedroom and refilled his glass. Then he went outside again and stood in the blazing sun and leaned over the rail and worried. On another balcony, across the way and two floors down, a woman had removed the top of her bathing suit and was sleeping in a lounge chair with her breasts exposed. She opened her eyes and saw him looking at her and made no move to cover herself. His first thought was to tell her that taking the sun like that was not a smart idea. Then he realized they had met at a cocktail party the night before; she was the wife of a well-known Freudian theoretician and an analyst in her own right. He smiled and she smiled back. Then he shrugged and waved and went back into the room. He told himself that if circumstances were a little different, he would have offered her some wine.

Jake dialed the number of the last doctor on his list: Dr. Sanford Schwartz, Culver City. It rang a bit too long but eventually a real receptionist in a real office answered. "Oh, you mean Dr. *Sanford* Schwartz," she said. "He's been gone three years." It was obvious that

34

gone meant dead. "This is now the practice of Dr. *Philip* Schwartz, his son." Jake made an appointment to see the man as soon as possible. The next day. His head was killing him.

Dr. Philip Schwartz was seated at his desk eating a tuna fish sandwich while a waiting room full of patients, most with serious neurological diseases, twitched and trembled and stared into space. He was short and very thin and he made grunting noises as he chewed.

"Doctor, what can I do for you?" Schwartz asked through bites of tuna.

"I'm following a patient who was seen here some years ago—by your father, I take it. The history is kind of spotty. The patient has serious memory loss, and the whole case is very confusing. I was hoping there might be something in the files . . ."

Schwartz looked at him skeptically and kept on chewing. "Quite the dedicated healer."

"I wrote about a month ago, but got no answer. I have a signed release," Jake went on. "The trouble is, it's in New York. I never expected to follow up on this, but I got bored with a conference I'm attending."

"All for some old *notes?*"

"I'm doing a paper. The patient is really quite unique."

"What's the diagnosis?"

"Multiple personality, most likely. I'm trying to rule out neurological abnormalities and get a picture of what he was like before he came to me. The main complaint is headaches."

"I take it you're a psychiatrist. Half the cases in my practice need a decent shrink. The ones around here mostly do massage." Schwartz put his lunch aside and led Jake through a maze of hallways to a door that opened on a dusty flight of stairs and the smell of ashes. Jake followed him down into the basement, where he could see old signs of fire and water damage. "I don't even look at this shit any more," said Schwartz. "When I get one of his old patients I just start from scratch."

"You had a fire?"

"Damn right we had a fire." He studied Jake, then shrugged. "Along with his other appealing attributes, my father was a drunk. He lived and practiced here and one day he burned half the fucking house down. The bastard killed himself and took my mother along with him . . ."

"I'm sorry . . ."

Schwartz shrugged again. "Do you know the song from Gilbert and Sullivan—'It sometimes is a useful thing to be an orphan boy'?" Then he left Jake alone.

He started looking through the files and soon began to feel tremendously elated. Jake hadn't seen notes like these in over twenty years—not since he had worked one summer for his family doctor and spent half the time reading private records. Every patient of Dr. Sanford Schwartz had a folder in which every visit, every symptom, every conclusion was precisely noted in a tiny, clear script. He may have drunk too much, but the senior Doctor Schwartz was a very careful man. Jake had read that first collection in the hope of discovering sexual secrets. By now, he'd had enough of those and was much more interested in following the cool clear logic of neurology. Every symptom means something specific. Every symptom in combination with every other symptom means something more. Every meaning takes you further. It's like mathematics, except that lives are on the line. Eventually, you can put the pieces together and make the diagnosis. The trouble is, after you've done it all, half the time you can't fix anything.

Jake could have spent the rest of the week alone in that basement, reading those ancient files, remembering when he was young and ached to be a doctor. But no matter where he looked, there was no Arthur Moss and there was no Alan Maliver. There were three patients with the initials AM but two were women and the third an elderly man. He reversed the letters and tried MA, and even made one stab at the code Freud used. But no matter what he tried, he came up empty.

A short while later, Jake climbed out of the basement and wandered through the corridor upstairs. His head was spinning and his chest was thumping and it had nothing to do with climbing a flight of steps. Who was this man who pretended to be a patient? What did he really want? He met Schwartz in the hallway, and the neurologist took his arm and pulled him into a bare examining room. An attractive young woman was sitting with a white gown wrapped around her, looking dazed. "This is Dr. Silver, honey. He's a specialist from New York. I'd like him to have a look."

She let go of the gown and waited calmly, her creamy breasts exposed, the pink nipples pointing up at the men. Jake was swimming in a sea of breasts. The trouble was, there was no way he could enjoy it.

"Look here," Schwartz said, running his hand across her back and winking lewdly.

She looked at Jake, not shy at all, more hopeful than anything, and smiled a small, sad smile. Her back was a mass of tiny twitches— it looked like something alive was crawling underneath her skin. "You can get dressed now, sweetheart. I'll be right back," Schwartz said. Now he steered Jake out the door and into his private office.

"You know what she's got?" he asked. "Over and above the gorgeous tits . . ."

"She's got a pig for a doctor and fasciculations."

"Which would you say is worse?"

"You can always fire your doctor."

"I take it you know what they're about."

Jake shrugged. "I'm a shrink, remember."

"She's got the worst," Schwartz said. "ALS. Lou Gehrig's disease. She's young for it, but that's the story. Tits like that and in the not too distant future the rest of her is gonna turn to jelly."

It dawned on Jake that Schwartz was really upset. The crass facade, whether he knew it or not, was all defense.

"You know what I want to tell her?" Schwartz went on.

Jake was in his element. He waited.

"She should find some decent guy and fuck her brains out while she's still got the chance."

"You could say worse," Jake said.

"Sometimes I can't *stand* this shit!"

When Schwartz recovered enough to see his next patient, Jake called the Los Angeles Medical Society. Jason Parness was also dead. The woman on the phone tracked down the dates of all three doctors' deaths. Schwartz's receptionist gave him directions to a nearby public library. In half an hour, he was scanning microfilms of the *L.A. Times*. Each story made the paper. Each of the articles left him feeling worse.

On the morning of July 7, 1980, while backing out of his drive-way, Dr. Jason Parness and his wife Maxine were killed by a truck that crashed into their convertible at a high rate of speed. The driver of the stolen vehicle was believed to have escaped on foot. No trace of him was found. Dr. Jason Parness was the highly respected chief of the neurology service of University Hospital; Maxine Parness was an ex-ecutive vice president in charge of data processing at Merrill Lynch. Both were in their late forties; they were active in the Republican party; they had no children.

On October 4, 1983, in the middle of the night, the Malibu home of Dr. Sheila McGarty-Pederson and her husband Brian Peder-son burned to the ground. The alarm had failed. The fire was thought to have been caused by a defect in an electrical circuit. Dr. McGarty was a prominent internist, renowned for her wit and beauty, who gave medical commentary on local television. Brian Pederson was a vice president at the brokerage firm of Potter, Weeks. He specialized in technology and had been the firm's top salesperson in the Pacific division for three years running. Both were in their early forties; they had no children.

Jake's stomach had worried itself into a knot. He could hardly believe what he was reading.

On Christmas Eve, 1987, Dr. Sanford Schwartz and his wife Bette died in a fire that ravaged sections of the Culver City structure that served as the doctor's home and office. The remains of Mrs. Schwartz were found in bed; the remains of Dr. Sanford Schwartz were found on the living-room couch, in front of the television set, where the blaze apparently began. Fragments from a bottle of Scotch

38

—the green glass melted until it was almost unrecognizable—were found on the floor beside the doctor. The fire was believed to have been started by his lit cigar. The couple was survived by their only child, Dr. Philip Schwartz.

Jake found a phone in the lobby and made a call to Claire. "I'm in the library. I saw the son of one of the doctors and tracked down the other two."

"I can't believe you're doing this," she said angrily. "You have no right."

"Of course I have a right. He gave me the names himself. All I did was consult his doctors—or try to consult with them."

She was furious. "You're fucking up. You're too involved. I don't even want to know about this."

"I think you'd better hear . . ."

"Don't you believe in respecting someone's boundaries? You're going too far. I can't believe you'd do this."

"We're separate people," he said bitterly. "Remember? We do our own things. We work in our separate ways."

"It doesn't matter what you say—there's no defense."

"It matters that they're dead," he told her then.

"What?"

"Six people. All the husbands and all the wives. The ones that got along and the ones that didn't. The ones that slept together and the ones that slept apart."

"Oh my God . . ."

"Yeah, right—have you got anything else to say? Have you got some stupid analytic rule that I should follow now?"

"Oh my God . . ."

He spent the night in Los Angeles. He found a motel near the beach in Santa Monica, bought a six-pack, saw a movie, drank himself to sleep. She wanted separateness and that was what he'd give her. In the morning, he parked outside the headquarters of the Los Angeles Police Department and told his story to Detective Vince Moran. The man was polite, respectful, appropriately concerned, completely professional, and convinced that Jake was overdoing it. He wrote the doctors' names on a yellow pad, taking care to spell them all correctly. Beneath the list, he drew a line and wrote Jake's name and address. "Give me a couple minutes," he said when he had it all. "I have to talk to this machine."

Jake waited at Moran's bare desk. The bustle in the large, open room appealed to him. Assorted officers moved briskly; telephones kept ringing; men were involved in animated conversations—they laughed and punched each other's shoulders and slapped each other's backs and looked pleased and worried and fulfilled. It was all so different from his own life. He saw the guns they wore and told himself that the first thing he would do when he got home was get his own.

Detective Moran held a printout. "According to the computer, these deaths were never tagged as suspicious and were never connected in any way. There were no criminal investigations—except for the hit-and-run. No one saw a pattern. There's a lot of crazy drivers and a lot of drunks and a lot of doctors in this town. If you want me to go further, I would need your patient's name. Both names. Maybe the computer knows the guy."

"I'm not sure I can do it," Jake said. "There's an issue of confidentiality."

"Doctor, you're not giving us a lot to go on here."

"I can't use his name unless someone's in danger. According to your computer, there isn't any danger."

"Computers fuck up," Moran said flatly. "As do coroners. I imagine shrinks do too . . ."

"What about detectives?"

"Never happens."

Jake wrote *Alan Maliver* and *Arthur Moss* on a sheet of paper that he then slid across the desk.

Moran shook his head when he returned from the computer. "Never heard of 'em. They don't even have driver's licenses."

"Is that good or bad?"

"Depends on where you drive." Moran winked. "My advice is that you talk to someone in New York."

"You think that this is real?"

"Everything is real. Isn't that what you people say? Even if it's crazy, it's based on something real." He handed Jake his card. "The paranoid who says people are after him is onto *something*. I took abnormal psych last year, and the guy who taught the course made a real big point of that."

"Was he a paranoid?" Jake asked.

CHAPTER 6

THE NEXT MORNING, with the conference plodding uneventfully into its final days, Jake and Claire checked out of the hotel and drove across the desert to Las Vegas. There was no bitterness now, no disagreement, just a tense and silent ride through the unearthly landscape. Jake drove Claire directly to the airport, which they reached an hour before her flight was due to leave. He had other plans. They found an empty cafeteria and drank weak coffee.

"This is crazy," Claire said. She was more afraid than angry.

"We can't pretend that we know nothing. That would be more crazy."

"There's no proof," she said. "Maybe he got their names out of the newspaper. It could be some fantasy he's playing out."

"Will that help you sleep?"

"I've given up on sleep."

He took her hand.

"We could just get rid of him," she went on. "We could tell him we can't help him."

He shook his head. "For all we know it's what *they* told him."

"Please be careful. I don't want to lose you."

"You're sure of that?"

She squeezed him hard. "I really am . . ."

"No matter what?"

"No matter what."

"Even if . . ."

"You're really pushing it!"

He walked beside Claire to the gate and kissed her forehead just before she boarded. She held him tight and they looked into each other's eyes. "You be careful too," Jake said. "He isn't *here*. Remember where he lives."

Jake waited until the plane took off. Then he crossed the torrid parking lot and got back into the rented car. The seat was on fire. With the air conditioner turned up high, he drove to the interstate and started east. Soon he was back in the desert and a short while later at the exit to the state highway that would take him north across a vast, empty quarter of the state. The road was free of traffic, and he pushed the car to eighty-five, but he had to slow when the thermometer began to climb. Did he need water? At sixty-five the car stayed cool and everything was fine. He drove through rock-strewn valleys and fields of cactus and scrub brush, a harsh landscape that fit his mood exactly. On his left, extending mile after unending mile, was a barbed-wire fence and sickly yellow signs imprinted with a skull and crossbones. It was a military area. He imagined clouds of nerve gas, dead cattle and dead buzzards and dead people in crashed cars. But there were no cattle, and, except for his, there were no cars. He was the only one to see the sun go down and the sky transform itself like a sudden sigh into the deepest blue.

For better or worse, Jake was out from behind his couch. He played cowboy music, the only kind there was, on the radio, and toyed with thoughts of what it would be like to ride across this dead land on a horse. He came to a gas station where he filled the tank and emptied his bladder, and went on again. In the distance, as he drove through miles of emptiness, he saw strange flashes of colored light. He pulled off the road and turned off the engine and stood alone in utter silence. It was cold. There was no moon. The stars glowed brilliantly, making every cliché about the desert sky an understatement. He saw another flash of light, and many seconds later he heard a distant rumble. It was far away. But what was it? Artillery? Bombing practice? A UFO? A storm? He had no idea. What he knew was that he suddenly felt fear. He got back into the car and gunned the engine and shot stones out from underneath his wheels.

A seedy town arrived as a blessing. It was almost ten. Jake hadn't eaten, and he was close enough to Stirrup to leave the rest for morning. The town consisted of a row of dark stores and a small casino with a flashing sign that advertised its action. He checked into a motel where the elderly clerk held his credit card as if it were a large, dead insect.

The casino beckoned—the only place where it still was possible to get a meal. He drove to the parking lot of the two-story building with a wooden facade and an authentic-looking wooden sidewalk. Inside, there was life and light and action—a crowd of soldiers from a nearby base and a smattering of hookers and more country music. A haggard waitress served Jake a surprising steak—large and tender and broiled exactly the way he asked, with crisp French fries and ripe tomatoes and icy beer. The perfection of it shocked him. When he was done he fought the temptation to buy a pack of cigarettes, briefly considered a cigar, then ambled instead to the side of the room reserved for gambling. A middle-aged woman stood dealing at a half-full blackjack table. He watched as three young men played crazily, one of them pulling to sixteen when the dealer showed a five, all of them losing steadily, one dollar at a time.

"You want a seat?" she asked.

He pushed a twenty toward her, and she slid a small stack of chips right back at him. He bet a single dollar. She turned blackjack for herself. He bet two dollars and lost with nineteen to her twenty. He bet four dollars and busted. He bet eight dollars and pushed. He bet the eight again and lost with twenty to her twenty-one. He took another twenty from his wallet, put it on top of the five he had remaining, and bet it all. She showed a six to his thirteen.

"I'm good," he said.

She showed her ten and then dealt herself a trey.

"Tough goin'," she said as Jake began to back away. "You caught a bad spell. It only happens once a night."

"Once a night is enough for me."

"Shit, you ain't *that* old," she said, winking.

He went to the bar and drank another beer. He avoided the eager eyes of a friendly hooker and stood behind a poker table where five men and a woman were playing hold 'em. "Seat's open," the dealer said.

Maybe it was the friendliness he wasn't used to. Maybe it was the day or the night or the flashes in the sky. Maybe everything he'd learned had come too fast. Whatever the reason, Jake had a momentary hallucination, a waking nightmare that popped suddenly into his head and almost overwhelmed him. No thinking was involved, no rationality at all, just a sudden perception that everyone inside the room was linked together in some evil plan. It was all a scam, an act, a staged attempt to get his money. They were thieves or con men or nameless somethings worse. They waited in this lonely place for innocents like him to fall into their hands.

"You lookin' for action?" a man at the table asked.

Jake stood motionless. "No thanks," he said. His heart was pounding as his thoughts became more terrifying: They were killers, out for more than just his money or his credit cards—they wanted blood. His voice was tight and barely audible. "I've been on the road all day. I can't see straight. Maybe tomorrow, after I get some sleep, I'll come back after you folks . . ."

"You from the East?" the dealer asked.

Jake nodded.

"Here on business?"

"More or less."

"You can always get good action here," the dealer said.

Jake left the casino and crossed the parking lot as quickly as he could without breaking into a run. He locked the car as soon as he got inside. His hand shook as he turned the key. He locked the motel door with its useless little chain and then jammed a chair under the knob. Exhausted as he was, he had difficulty sleeping.

The town of Stirrup, Nevada, home of Alan Maliver, according to Claire, was surprisingly pleasant. The low hills were dotted with green, and the town was less dusty and less sleazy than the one where he had spent the night. The place appealed to him. It felt authentic, like the first real Western town that he had ever seen, but the sheriff's office looked like a schoolroom.

"Moss? Maliver?" The officer behind the desk was puzzled. "How long ago you say they left?"

"I don't know that they did leave. My information is that the family has lived in the area for many years."

The officer shook his head. "I grew up here. I never heard those names."

"The parents would be pretty old. The son is pushing forty."

The man shook his head again.

"Are there records I could see, someplace where I could look them up?"

"Maybe City Hall . . ."

Inside a tiny, ancient building with a painted marker out in front that identified the structure as a "Historic Edifice," Jake spoke with a birdlike woman who tried her best to help. She used a computer to scan through voter lists and lists of people who paid real-estate taxes. Then she looked through an ancient cabinet that held old deeds. No matter where she looked, she came up empty. The names Maliver and Moss did not exist and never had existed in this town.

He tried the local paper, *The Stirrup Stockman*, housed in a dusty storefront where two women sat at ancient typewriters. He guessed they were about Claire's age—though they looked older.

They glanced at each other after he asked his questions. The pretty one took charge: "My folks might know, but they retired to Arizona. If I were you, I'd head down the street about fifty yards to the office of Willard Barret. He's the real-estate agent and the insurance agent and our unofficial historian. If anyone knows them, it would be Will." Then she grinned coquettishly. "If that don't work, you bring your butt back here and I'll treat you to a beer . . ."

He thanked her warmly.

He found a brick-front building with a faded sign. To the jingle of a bell above the door, he stepped into the office of Willard Barret and was instantly transported into the nineteen twenties. He saw an ancient rolltop desk that would have sold for thousands in New York, and then Will Barret himself, in his vigorous late seventies, wearing garters on his sleeves and drinking coffee. "Hey there, young fellow."

Barret offered a cup to Jake. He listened carefully as Jake explained: "The names I have are Moss and Maliver, but I'm beginning to doubt if either of them is right. I believe they had a son who left the area for California. He'd be about forty now. My guess is that it was a family with its share of troubles . . ." He waited for a sign of recognition.

To his surprise, there *was* one.

"That could only be one bunch." Barret rolled his chair across the room to a wooden cabinet. "Wrote the policy myself." He pulled a folder out and flipped some pages. "Not Moss. Not Maliver either, don't know where that comes from. The name is *Kiehl.* Hugo and Mary Kiehl. Boy named Felix. They lived in a canyon twenty miles due west. Had this farm that never should have been a farm. Tried all kinds of things this land was never meant for. Dairy cows! Vegetables! Kind of crazy if you want the truth. Kept to themselves. Got religion, but wouldn't come to church. They lived hand to mouth, but they had strong ideas. Came in for insurance—I didn't have to sell a thing. Turned out they were smart. Couple years after they bought their policies, the house burned like a torch. A herder saw it from across the valley. All they found of them folks was a pile of bones." He shook his head. "I remember the boy. Hardly ever spoke. He got sent away to school and never did come back. Had to track him down at

47

some big company in California. Few months later he showed up. Never asked where they were buried. Not exactly sad, not exactly grateful. Sat there all polite in his city clothes, just where you're sittin' now, and never asked one thing about 'em. Happy with the check, though."

"Do you have the date when this all happened?"

Barret looked into the folder. "Long time ago. August eleven, nineteen-seventy-two. He was just a kid, twenty-two years old, and he walked out of here with fifty thousand dollars, lot of money in those days, lot of money in this town, lot of money for a kid—I don't care that he was supposed to be some kind of genius." He put the folder back into his cabinet.

"What did he look like?"

"Tall, strong. The gal who worked for me thought he looked mean."

"Can I make a copy of what you have?"

Barret shook his head and smiled politely. "Not without a letter from the boy or an order from a judge or a weapon in your hand."

Jake returned to the office of *The Stirrup Stockman*, where the woman he had spoken to looked happy and then disappointed. She said old issues of the paper were stored in the public library. He drove a short distance to a modern glass-and-concrete building. The newspapers were kept on open shelves in neatly labeled boxes. The box he sought was there, with all the issues yellowing, with stories on the price of beef and the price of fuel. There was no mention of Vietnam or Richard Nixon or what was happening in the country. The week before had rainy weather and the week that followed was pleasantly cool and the week that he was looking for was gone.

He almost went back. There had to be a copy somewhere, but he didn't have the heart to face the woman again.

After he drank a beer alone, Jake drove out to the ranch. Eventually, he found himself on a narrow wagon track, trailing a plume of dust, the low hills pressing down around him. The track followed a dry streambed and was often indistinguishable—at least to him—from the stream itself. The land was unused and the track itself was slowly disappearing. The trip took almost two hours, with Jake pushing the car as hard as he dared, knowing that if he broke an axle he would have to walk. He finally emerged from between two hills, and the country opened into a broad, pretty valley where he saw the chimney and the remains of what must have been the house.

He parked his car and slowly walked across the land. The ruin had been stripped bare years ago. If there ever was some clue, some hint of what had happened, of who had lived here, of why they died, it was long gone. Brush was growing inside the borders of the house, and, except for the chimney, which still looked solid, all signs of habitation were disappearing. There had been a barn. It hadn't burned, but had collapsed of its own weight, and its rotting boards were melting into the earth. There were broken fences and rusted wire and three stripped, rusted hulks of vehicles: a Studebaker, a DeSoto, a Ford truck of nineteen-fifties' vintage. There was nothing more, nothing recognizable, nothing—other than the silent landscape itself—that could tell him anything about this man named Felix Kiehl.

If he had hope before, some dream that things were not as bad as they appeared, some wish that when they sorted out the puzzle it would somehow turn benign—the fantasy of every therapist—he had none now. He knew that what he had to face was a great deal worse than anything that he had ever known.

CHAPTER 7

J AKE MADE THE long drive back to the Las Vegas airport and got rid of the dusty car. He was lucky to catch a nonstop flight east, a midnight plane crammed full of returning junketeers, all of them depressed and chastened and exhausted, not a winner in the bunch. They reached New York shortly after dawn. The plane banked sharply, and he could see up the harbor to the Verrazano Bridge and the Statue of Liberty, and the morning sun reflected off the walls of glass. By the time they were on the ground at JFK, it didn't seem so pretty.

But Claire was waiting.

"You didn't have to."

"I *wanted* to," she said. "I can't tell you how much I've been thinking about you."

It was Thursday, and they weren't booked to work until Monday morning. Instead of fighting traffic into the city they drove due east, out toward East Hampton and their beloved house. It was exactly what they needed now—solitude, a respite, more time to think. Claire drove. They took the Sunrise Highway, aptly named for the morning light that poured into their eyes. There was a soft spring sun, completely different from the harsh glare of the West, but that didn't make it any easier to see the road. She flipped the visor down and he found dark glasses in the glove compartment.

"We've got to deal with this," Jake said.

"I totally agree."

She'd spent yesterday in the library, devouring every book and article she could find on the subject of multiple personality. There was now a serious scientific literature. Study of the disorder had gone far beyond the ancient case descriptions she had read during her residency. The incidence of multiple personality disorder was much greater than had ever been recognized before. Though there were skeptics, psychiatrists who thought it was created by suggestion, the disorder had spawned a sub-specialty with its own professional organization and its own journals and even—a sure sign of its rising status— its own abbreviation: MPD.

They reached the house at nine in the morning. It was hidden behind a lush green wall of early summer foliage that could never exist in the arid West. They opened the blinds and the sliding doors and brewed a pot of coffee. A short while later, Jake sat beside the phone. "I have to call Spicer. You may not like poker players, but I'd trust him more with this than anyone I know."

John Spicer was by far the strongest player in Jake's poker game and among the best in the city. He played three times a week in three different high-stakes games and won consistently in each of them. He was a lawyer and a C.P.A., though he didn't look or sound anything like either. A smooth black man who worked as a prosecutor in the Securities Division of the U.S. Attorney's office, he never spoke about the cases he handled or anything else in his current life. Instead, he liked to joke about two long-ago divorces, both of which were messy and expensive and had left him scarred.

Jake got the answering machine at Spicer's apartment. At nine-fifteen he tried his office but there was no answer. At nine-thirty a woman with a Brooklyn accent said he hadn't yet arrived. "He ain't on trial, sweetheart. Not likely he'll be in till something like eleven. You know these lawyers . . ."

Spicer's call came at ten exactly. True to form, he started with a joke: "So what's happenin', my man? You strapped for cash? The shylocks after you? You need a shrink?"

"I wish it was that easy," Jake said.

Spicer listened silently to the story of their patient. He grunted softly after Jake told him about California and then more audibly when Jake described Nevada.

"You did good work," he said. "If you're thinking about a new career, I might have something."

"What I'm thinking about is how to stay alive."

There was a momentary pause. Then Spicer spoke rapidly: "The NYPD won't do shit, I guarantee that. They'll jerk you around a while and then tell you it's all supposition. You have to call, but I wouldn't waste much time with them. What I *would* do is call the FBI. They won't protect you, no way on this, but they'll check it out. At least it's interstate. I'll make a call myself and let them know you're not a nut. . . . I assume you're not a nut."

"That's it?"

"Is *he* some kind of nut?"

"Some kind."

"Does the guy know where you are?"

"No one knows. We're still supposed to be out west."

"So stay out east, my man."

"And what happens Monday? What do our patients do? How do I make a living?"

"You could try poker . . ."

"Not with you around."

"Give me a little time," said Spicer. "Let me see if I can come up with something."

·   ·   ·

At six-forty-five on Monday evening, Claire was scheduled for her regular appointment with Alan Maliver. Jake was in her office, seated on the analytic couch.

They had protection, of a sort. Spicer had come at six-fifteen. He'd brought along a rat-faced man who didn't say a word as he sized up Claire and then her office with his darting eyes.

"I'm impressed with how you worked it out," said Spicer. "Maybe shrinks know something after all."

Their argument had gone on all weekend. Jake pushed hard—insisting that the only option was to confront the patient—and Claire eventually agreed. There really was no choice. They couldn't wait for the treatment to evolve. Claire was already too terrified to sit in a room with him. The likelihood that it would evolve into an even worse nightmare was all too obvious and all too overwhelming.

Everything was carefully arranged. Spicer and his man would wait in the outer lobby. The rat-faced man unbuttoned his jacket and showed his shoulder holster. In case of trouble, all Claire had to do was press the button that controlled her door. They would hear the buzz and come at once.

Her bell rang at six-forty. Claire pressed the button, and they heard the door slam as Alan Maliver entered her waiting room. She looked at Jake unhappily. "This really smells of Oedipus. Why didn't we see it?"

"We should have seen lots of things . . ."

"He's the son; we're the parents," she went on.

"It won't help now."

"I'm not so sure. Sometimes the best thing you can do is give someone the right interpretation . . ."

"We need more than words."

She opened the inner door, and Alan Maliver stepped from her waiting room into her office. There was no way to prepare him, no time to say one word. He was all the way inside before he noticed Jake. His head jerked back as if someone slapped him hard. He looked stunned, terror-stricken, more frightened than they were. He turned from Jake to Claire and then back to Jake again. Then he stood motionless. The only movement was the rapid blinking of his eyes.

"I know that you know Dr. Silver," Claire said softly. She took her chair as Maliver stood alone. "We didn't want to shock you, neither of us did, but we had to deal with this, and there was no other way." She kept on talking, hoping the sound of her voice could help him settle down. "We know you've been seeing both of us. We understand that you may not remember, but it's been going on for quite a while. As you and I discussed, you have serious problems with your memory."

Her patient stood frozen. He was the same, yet completely different from the man Jake knew—not just his clothing but the way he held his body and the shape of his mouth and the slackness of his jaw. There was none of the aggressive cheerfulness of Arthur Moss, none of his macho cockiness. This man was made of wood; of wax; of stone. He gazed at Claire and then at Jake and then back at Claire. Then very slowly, his body came to life. His head rolled back and forth. He had turned into someone neither of them knew.

"It's all right," Claire went on. She could hear the tremors in her voice and each breath she took caught in her throat. "You don't have to be afraid. This is a very unusual situation, but we can deal with it. Dr. Silver and I are in agreement. We want to help. We want to talk with you about what's happened . . ."

His lip was raised; it might have been a schizophrenic grimace; it might have been the mask of death. His words came with a snarl. *"You'll pay. I swear you'll pay for this!"* It was not Moss or Maliver but a voice they had never heard.

"Who are you?" she asked, looking into his eyes.

His hands balled tightly into fists. His raspy voice went on: "It's not for you to know."

"Are you Felix Kiehl?" Jake asked.

"Who said it was your business?"

"You asked me for help, so it is my business."

"We want to help," Claire said. "Really."

"Too late. You're a hundred years too late. He didn't hurt you. You should have let him be."

"Who *are* you?" Jake asked again.

The patient looked at Claire. "He would have talked to you. One day he would have talked. You should have let him be."

"I couldn't do that . . ."

"You failed him." He strode across the room and grabbed a glass ashtray from a side table. He tossed the heavy glass from hand to hand as Claire raised her arm to protect her face. "You're a fool, a fucking fool, a stupid woman, a useless bitch . . ." Before Jake could act, the patient flung the ashtray at the wall behind Claire's head, where it shattered into splinters that sprayed across the room. He opened her office door and crossed her waiting room and then opened the outer door, leaving them both wide open. He never looked back.

"I think we fucked up," Jake said.

There was a pause before she spoke. "At least we know what he's been carrying around."

"You guys all right?" Spicer came in through the open door.

"Not really," Jake said.

"*What?*"

"I don't know what we are." Claire's false calm faded and her hands began to shake. She saw the dent in the plaster wall.

Spicer saw it too. He looked at the splinters on her couch.

"It's his gift to us," Jake said.

"What?"

"He went into a rage," Jake went on. "It was pretty intense. I hope we've seen the last of him."

Spicer smiled slyly as he shook his head. "He ain't seen the last of us."

But the rat-faced man was back within ten minutes and hardly able to look Spicer in the eye. He was one of John Spicer's most trusted people, a human bloodhound who could track a drunk across

Times Square on New Year's Eve, but the patient was gone. As soon as he reached the street, he disappeared.

Jake picked glass splinters off the couch as Claire sat numbly in her chair.

"What a mess," was all she could say. "What an awful mess . . ."

CHAPTER 8

O<small>N THE FOLLOWING</small> morning, John Spicer's man was hidden on the landing outside Jake's office, but Arthur Moss never showed up for his scheduled session. Nor did Alan Maliver appear for his Wednesday morning appointment with Claire. Jake called the number Moss once gave him, but he got a recording from the telephone company stating it was not in service. He tried to remember where Moss said he worked, but he was unable to. Moss may never have told him. He wrote a note to Moss suggesting that he come in and talk, but before he mailed it Spicer found that the address did not exist.

The man was gone, though it was hardly a relief. As each day wore on they worried more. Who was he? *What* was he? They had seen his rage and knew too well where it could lead. What echoed in their ears was his raspy, snarling, otherworldly growl. Claire heard it in the middle of the night and didn't know if she was dreaming. She woke Jake often, and they lay together in the dark, listening to the traffic and the drunks who prowled along Broadway. Was he psychotic? Was he out there on the street among the homeless? Did he have some crazy plan? Were they figures in some fantasy that he was playing out—a fantasy they only dimly grasped? Were they doomed to be the victims of an accident or fire?

The days passed in a fog. After the first night, they stayed off Valium and Xanax and assorted other psychiatric remedies. They needed to keep their wits about them. They tried to follow the advice they sometimes gave to patients: The deed was done; the disaster in the past; all they could do was make sure nothing worse transpired. When Friday came, they drove out to East Hampton. They were always happy on the way out there, and this time, feeling the city fade, along with the ghost of their patient and the terror in his wake, it was close to bliss.

The sun was shining and the June day was very hot. When they reached the house a rabbit darted across the driveway. They took it to be a lucky sign. They looked up at their house, perched on its little dune, in the center of their little woods, with its cedar siding glowing silver. There was no need to plan—they knew exactly how to spend the remainder of this day. After they unloaded the car, they would go straight out to the garden to harvest their lettuce and their peas—assuming that the rabbit hadn't been there first. They would pull weeds out of the garden's neat rows and gradually get covered with clean, East Hampton designer dirt, which would displace the dirt they'd brought out from the city. Eventually, they'd get back into the car for the short ride to the beach. He would plunge into the frigid surf while she would wet her toes. If anything could wash the week away, it would be that.

They carried bags of groceries up onto the deck. Claire breathed deeply, filling her lungs with the smell of pine trees and the ocean and the sun on cedar walls. Jake unlocked the door. The sight that greeted them was one of utter horror.

They stood frozen in the entrance as the door creaked on its hinges. The place was in shambles. Everything—from the furniture to the appliances to the inner walls themselves—had been hacked and ripped and chopped apart.

He must have had an axe. His rage was so profound that nothing he could do, no damage he could inflict, had been enough to end it. Claire's piano looked like firewood, the keys all scattered, the broken strings splayed out in all directions. The TV and the stereo were smashed, and glass covered the floor. It crunched beneath their feet as they stepped inside. The couch was upside down, its stuffing strewn across the room. The dining table was on its back, each leg broken off. The door was torn off the refrigerator, and the floor was smeared with food, rotting in the heat.

Jake felt Claire's body sag. He put his arm around her and felt her skin turn clammy. "I'm going to vomit," she said weakly. He helped her toward the bathroom, saw that the bowl was smashed, then grabbed a plastic pail that had survived. He held her there, one arm around her waist, until the moment passed.

It dawned on Jake that they should not stay where they were. He got Claire out as fast as possible, shoving her into the car. Then he drove the mile to the general store and the public telephone more quickly than he ever had before.

She sat in the car, crying hysterically, as Jake called the police. They told him to wait exactly where he was. Then he called Max, an old friend and mentor who owned a house nearby. The police arrived in about three minutes and followed them back to the house, and not much later, Max drove up. He held on to Claire as Jake answered questions and more and more police appeared. A detective dusted for fingerprints without success. A photographer took pictures that reminded Claire of photos of a corpse.

The detective saw the M.D. plates on their Saab. "What kind of doctor are you?"

"We're both psychiatrists," Jake said.

The man nodded sagely, as if all his questions had been answered. "I get it now." He looked around. "This wasn't kids or locals. This ain't your usual break-in. You must have someone pretty pissed."

"I imagine I do," Jake said.

"You work with psychos?"

"Psychos don't do this kind of thing."

"Doctor, whatever you want to call him, is there someone out to do you harm? It would be in your interest to give us that person's name."

Jake looked at Claire, who was in no condition to speak. He pulled Spicer's card out of his wallet. "I have someone for you to call."

"*Federal?* What is this, drugs? Some kind of warning?"

"There are complications. Certain information may be confidential. I'm not sure what I can say. The best thing would be to talk with him. He'll tell you everything you need to know." He knew as soon as he used the phrase that it was wrong.

The detective shook his head and looked disgusted. "He *will?* He's that smart?" He wrote Spicer's name and number in his pad. "You want your people in the city, a hundred miles away, I guess it's up to you. You keep your little card and you hand it to this creep when he comes to cut your nuts off."

Max wrapped his free arm tightly around Jake's shoulders as he propped up Claire. He exhaled gin and stale cigar. "You have had enough," he said to Jake. "Let me take care . . ." He turned to the detective. "This has been a trauma. You may not realize how severe. I believe these people need a respite now."

The detective looked at Max's big black Mercedes and saw more M.D. plates. He rolled his eyes. "What are you, the shrink of the shrinks?"

"My good man, have you heard of friendship?" His accent was Viennese.

"Don't matter to me. If they're in no hurry, why should I be? They don't want to file charges, it's their business. They can say they had a domestic dispute. I won't have to write a report and the insurance company will be real pleased . . ."

"You can write it," Jake said. "We just need a little time."

It was true. Claire was in no condition to make an inventory. When she wasn't crying, she was standing motionless in a silent fog, as if she had been drugged. They arranged to meet the detective at noon on the following day. They would come back in the morning and go through the house and prepare as complete a list as possible of all the damage.

Then they went outdoors. Amazingly, the world was still the same—the sun still shining, the air still clear, the day as lovely. They got back into the car and followed Max through the winding roads to his place.

He set them up in deck chairs and mixed martinis. They watched birds fluttering around his feeder. He put Mozart on the stereo, but Jake asked him to turn it off. Then Max sat in his chair. "Please, tell me *everything* about this patient."

They went along as much for Max as for themselves. It brought back the days when they were his students and would hang on every word. The trouble was, those days were gone. Now it was irritating— to Jake especially. In his opinion, Max Dorfmann had reached the classic end-stage of a psychoanalytic career: He was overweight, self-centered, more or less a lush, so used to his patients' gratitude for the pearls he dropped that he had lost the ability to judge if they were pearls or turds. He rambled on, between swallows of his drink and puffs on his cigar. He spouted accented nonsense without for a moment doubting that it was profound: "A convincing analysis of multiple personality disorder has yet to be accomplished. What we see are stories for the television, case histories by poorly trained psychiatrists who know nothing of the psychic depths. It is a pity. The phenomenon itself is truly fascinating. It raises extraordinary questions about the nature of the mind."

Jake knew from endless afternoons and endless arguments beside the ocean that his words would be ignored, but he spoke anyway: "Max, give the profession a little credit. Maybe they're not as brilliant and insightful as you are, but they try. There *is* a current literature. There are more people diagnosed as multiples right now than there ever were in history. There are more people trying to understand them. There's even a professional society that's been organized to . . ."

Max sailed on. "I regard the entire concept of dissociation to be theoretically inadequate. It lacks dynamics. It lacks a developmental base. Repression, yes—dissociation, no! In thirty years of practice, I have never seen such a mechanism."

By then, Jake was feeling the alcohol. "You think people like Pierre Janet and Harry Stack Sullivan, who used the concept of dissociation, are theoretically *inadequate*? All you're saying is that you haven't read their work or don't understand it."

Max looked at Jake scornfully. "You know what I think of your great Dr. Harry Sullivan."

Claire had to stop them. Her head was clear and she was feeling a little better. "You're mixing issues," she said to Max. "We don't care about theory now. We do care about the man's dynamics. If you have some idea of what this means, I want to hear it." She looked at Jake in a way that made him keep his mouth shut.

Max Dorfmann smiled. "That much, my dear, is simple. The dynamics are transparently Oedipal. Why else would anyone seek treatment from a married couple?"

"Assuming he was seeking *treatment*," Jake said.

"Let's assume that," Claire said quickly.

"We are talking about his unconscious," Max went on. "The way to understand this act is to know the demons in this man's unconscious. Sooner or later, with every patient, we must face the inner world. His conscious rationale is not the issue."

"It is to me . . ."

"*Jake!*" Claire interjected.

He kept silent as Max continued: "So I infer that your patient harbors Oedipal desires. That, of course, hardly makes him unique, though perhaps his desires are more intense than those held by the rest of us." He relit his cigar. It didn't matter that Jake looked irritated—Max was now in gear, and no mere look could stop him. "To the paternal figure, our Jacob here, the patient presents as the son who has surpassed the father. He is unresponsive to interpretation and opaque to all attempts at understanding. He is *impenetrable*. Do I have to remind you that this is a form of castration? He castrates the therapeutic function. As with all sons, the wish is to render the father impotent."

"You score one point," Jake said. "Most of the time I felt that way."

Max puffed and grunted and kept on rolling: "With the maternal figure, this patient is childishly seductive. He tells her his dreams and all the tempting secrets of his inner world. He makes a mystery and draws her in. He creates a bond that only they can share. He becomes her perfect child and perfect lover all at once."

"You get another point," Claire said. "Now tell us why he wrecked the house."

"Perfection failed," Max went on. He fixed his eyes on her while trying to frame his thought as carefully as possible. "It's that simple. The cooperation the two of you achieved, your common front, your decision to face him together, showed his fantasy was hopeless. Despite his wish to keep you apart, you were manifestly *together*. It must have been evident, even to someone with the most severe pathology, that the woman he coveted would never be his, that the father he wished to destroy retained his phallic power. It was obvious that he had lost. Rage was then inevitable."

Claire looked upset again. "How long will it go on?"

Max studied her. "There is no *time* in the unconscious. You know that as well as I do. Feelings last forever . . ."

She turned to Jake. "I think we should tell the rest of it."

"You held something back?" Max looked offended.

Jake told him then what he had learned out West.

Max's face went dead white. "This is serious."

"We know already," Jake said.

"You must take precautions."

"We know that too."

"You must find a way to keep track of him."

"You have some bright idea?"

63

Max sat there gaping, and soon Jake had enough. "I'm going to the house," he said suddenly.

Max looked confused. "Don't be reckless. There is danger. I have all the space you need."

Jake stood. "Thanks for the offer, but I have to go. I need to spend the night there."

"*Why?*" Claire asked plaintively.

He wasn't sure, but somehow words came: "I won't be pushed—not by this bastard and his craziness or by any other bastard."

"Go in the morning," Max said. "These people repeat themselves. You might as well be safe."

"I've been safe too long. All I am is *safe*. There's work to do." He kept his eyes on Claire. "You can stay here if you want; I would understand. You can be safe with Max. Or we can both go. The bastard is gone. Round one is over. Round two won't be starting for a while."

"This isn't necessary," she said.

"Maybe not for you—it is for me."

To Jake's great joy, Claire stood beside him.

"Are you sure?" Max asked. "I don't see the point. This really is unnecessary."

They were sure.

"I'll come in the morning."

"Not too early," Jake said as they went out the door.

CHAPTER 9

THEY DROVE FROM Max's house to town, where they stopped at a hardware store and bought two battery-powered lanterns, and then at a market, where they bought beer and rolls and cold cuts. Then they drove back to the house. From outside, in the fading orange glow, the place was as lovely as ever. They didn't linger. They carried their purchases inside and began the dismal job of sorting the debris. There was no need to pick and choose; it all had to go, and they began by lugging everything that they could carry out onto the deck. They made a list of the shreds of furniture and the smashed kitchen appliances and even the damaged books and records. The work was easier than they expected, and in some peculiar way a pleasure. They didn't need Max Dorfmann for the explanation; it was the garbage of their marriage that they dragged bit by bit outside.

It soon grew dark. By then, the living room was empty, and in the cold white light of the lanterns, strangely comforting. They could have imagined they were starting over, out in the wilderness somewhere, away from Max and psychoanalysis in all its incarnations, away from endless talk and theory, creating a new life with their own bare hands.

They went upstairs to the bedroom, where their shredded mattress had been knocked off its frame. A knife had left deep gashes in the blanket and the sheets and the mattress itself. It had been slashed mercilessly, in an assault that must have gone on and on with insane repetition. The springs were poking out, and stuffing was scattered all around the room. It was Oedipus again, the clearest confirmation possible of everything Max said. There could be no escape from psychoanalysis. There could be no escape from being human.

They sat outside in the moonlight and ate their meal. At least the stars were still undamaged.

After another hour of work, they took untouched blankets from the guest room closet and piled them in the middle of the living room to make a bed. They felt like mice in a cozy nest, though Jake kept the poker from the fireplace right beside him.

The moon was visible through the uncovered windows. It brought back memories of the years before they met, when they had hitchhiked in separate crisscross paths around the country and fell asleep peacefully wherever they found a bed. They did make love. Not with great passion, not on a high, but with tenderness and the need for comfort and the need to know, no matter what, that they were still together—that whatever the bastard was trying to do to them, he had not succeeded.

In the middle of the night, long after the moon was gone, Jake heard a noise. His eyes popped open as he lay motionless. There were footsteps right outside, a soft crunching on the gravel driveway. Someone was out there. It was unmistakable. Then the crunch stopped, and Jake heard the softer sound of shoes on leaves. Where was he now? Where was he going? He heard the footsteps go around the house. Jake got up slowly with the poker in his hand and stood beside the door. He felt like a hunted animal, aware of everything at once—the smells, the sounds, even the trembling of the air.

Claire was still asleep. Her hair was spread across the pillow like a star. She looked relaxed and beautiful, but as the sound came close again, Jake saw her stir. He saw her frown in her sleep. Whoever was out there was coming back. She sensed it somehow. He saw her shake her head and struggle to rouse herself. He started to feel afraid, but above his fear was icy anger and a wish to bring the poker down as hard as possible on the bastard's head.

The steps stopped suddenly, and Claire sat upright. She reached for Jake. He heard her gasp. He saw her terror when she couldn't find him.

"Sh . . ." he whispered, and then she saw him, still standing at the door, his finger pressed against his lips.

He held the poker up for her to see.

The knob went back and forth but the door stayed shut. The door was locked, but the intruder struggled with it. Jake heard the breathing just outside. He smelled the acrid scent of another man. It wouldn't go away. It would never go unless he faced the bastard. He raised the poker and yanked the door wide open. A man stood frozen. Luckily for him, Jake saw the uniform.

"Asshole!"

"What are you doing?" the policeman asked.

Jake lowered the poker. "It's my house!"

"They sent me to check it."

"You're lucky you're alive."

Claire sat in silence with the blanket wrapped around her. When Jake came back to bed and took her in his arms, she cried again. There was a plaintive note that he had never heard before, but all he could do was let it run its course. Before he slept, he told himself that he really had to get a gun.

In the morning, they found a telephone that worked in the cellar and called the people who could make things better. The police returned for their second look and for the list that Jake and Claire had by then prepared. The insurance man came next, then a contractor they'd used before and trusted more than most. They walked through the house together as the man shook his head and punched a calculator and came up with an estimate and a work schedule. Money heals all kinds of things, though the wounds that they were feeling would take more than insurance and a carpenter to cure.

When they had finished all the arrangements, Claire called Max and told him they were leaving. The quiet summer they had planned was over. Jake's serve and backhand would have to wait, along with the tomatoes and basil in the garden and the long swims in the bay and ocean. Claire's plans for the piano would have to wait. And Calvin Wiggens would have to wait for another chance to beat Jake down. He was beaten down enough already.

They stayed in the city through July. Every morning he walked Claire to her office, where he picked her up at the end of every day. When patients rang, both doctors walked through their waiting rooms and looked through their peepholes before opening the outer door. Their patients thought it strange, but accepted the explanation that there had been a string of burglaries. On an unconscious level, life was much more complicated. Patients had fantasies that ranged from rejection by their therapist to a lover's revenge to the worry that their therapist had turned paranoid.

When they weren't at work, they kept to their apartment, eating frozen dinners or Chinese food, drinking too much wine.

They drove out to the house on a Saturday at the end of the month to look at fabrics and countertops and paint chips, but their hearts weren't in it. In contrast to their usual manner, they left the choices in a decorator's hands. It was only furniture now. It was only a house.

They told themselves that the way they felt was temporary, that they were still traumatized, but it didn't help. They knew what their patients felt when something that they said was true but useless.

Then on August 1, when every patient and every analyst gets a month of blessed freedom, they boarded a plane to Milan. They took a train to Venice and stayed five days in a lovely room that fronted on the Grand Canal. They rented a fast Alfa and started driving south. They spent time in Florence, in Rome, in Ravello. They discovered lovely towns in the hills. They spent three days in Pompeii and another in Ercolano looking at more ruined houses. They walked through ancient villas, admired ancient frescoes. They ate extraordinary food and drank Chianti and did everything they could to become Italian. It turned out to be the best month of their lives. They did their best to forget their nightmare patient and New York City and East Hampton. They made love day and night the way they used to.

PART II

The telephone rang and Maxine Parness answered in the kitchen of her newly decorated home.

The voice she heard was high-pitched and panicky. "Maxine—I have to see you . . ."

"Andrew, it's dinnertime. I was about to let the machine pick up. Jason and I just sat down. He cooked for me tonight! Can you imagine! It's our anniversary."

"Can I come over for a little while?"

"I said it's our anniversary."

"I need to talk."

"Don't you know what people do on their anniversary?" She looked at her husband and slowly shook her head as she went on talking to the young man on the line: "Baby, I told you to relax. Remember what I said? It's the nature of the market. Surprises happen. You have to learn to live with them . . ."

"But you said it was safe. You promised me." His voice squeaked and cracked like that of an adolescent.

"Baby, it is safe."

"Almost a quarter of my money's gone—my only money, the only thing I have in my entire life. I have to see you."

She heard his tears and she was gentle. *"Honey, you don't really need it now, do you? Didn't we go over all of this? Didn't I promise that if you needed cash, Jason and I would help? You know it's for your benefit. I have good information. I promise you'll get your money back and even make some."* She looked at her husband again and rolled her eyes.

"How do you know it's good?"

"I know—you'll have to trust me."

"I have to see you."

"I can't tonight. I told you . . ."

"Why should I trust you then?" The young man's voice suddenly turned bitter. She had never heard this tone. *"It's easy for you. You're rich. Your husband is a big shot. That money is all I have."*

She held one finger in the air as her husband looked at her impatiently. *"Andrew, I have to go now. I want you to listen very carefully. You won't lose a penny. Give it a little time. I told you about this stock because I want to help make your life better. I'll see you tomorrow. I promise we can talk more then."*

He didn't answer, and she thought that he was gone, but as she hung up the phone she heard him moan.

"I take it your boyfriend is freaking out," Jason Parness said.

"I feel bad for him. He's had a hard life. He's been alone since he was just a kid. He actually grew up in an orphanage! I have to hold his hand. It's not like I bought him some loser . . ."

"I'm sure you don't mind holding that sweaty hand."

Maxine Parness grinned. *"You don't have to worry, sweetheart—it's all maternal."*

"I never said I was worried." Jason placed a steaming platter of paella in the center of the table. *"If he were a man, maybe I would be. Given what he is, a freaky fucked-up nerd, I'm not worried at all. I don't know what impresses you so much."*

She poured the wine. *"He's very smart. And he's basically attractive. He just happens to be a little . . . undeveloped."*

"He's a weirdo, if you want my take. You're too used to them. Did you ever think of getting out of data processing and working with normal people?"

She just smiled. "You really found nothing wrong?"

"Not a thing."

"His headaches are so terrible."

"Believe me, I did my best. He put up with it; I'll say that much for him. I put him through every test known to modern neurology and a few known only to the Inquisition."

"And there was nothing?"

"I'm sure a psychiatrist would have something more to say."

"You didn't tell him that?"

"Of course I did. You should know by now I don't bullshit anyone."

"Not even me?"

He raised his glass. "Not even you. I only love you."

On Saturday morning, after a week in which the market stayed stuck in its recent doldrums, just a few days before it shot up suddenly and made new highs, Maxine and Jason Parness were up at dawn. They had a long drive north to Pebble Beach. It was going to be a special weekend with special friends, a celebration of their marriage and a chance to play that famous golf course, and they were eager to get out on the road. They took the small Mercedes that Jason liked so much to drive. And since it was already warm and the air was uniquely clear, they put the top down.

Jason Parness backed out of the driveway and onto the winding dead-end street where his house was perched above Laurel Canyon.

Higher up the hill, almost at the top, the engine of a pickup roared. The driver liked the feeling, the power of this truck, the wide expanse of white hood in front of him, the little cross that dangled from the mirror. He popped the clutch like an expert, let the wheels spin, and then eased up on the gas until the tires grabbed. Then he floored the thing.

He braced his legs against the floor of the speeding truck and his arms against the steering wheel. He looked over the hood into her frightened eyes. She saw him coming. At last—her eyes were open wide at last. She knew what she had done. She knew what she deserved. He saw her open mouth

73

and the panic in her face, but he felt no pity. She had let him down. She was a liar. She made promises she never kept.

"Jason!" she screamed.

The truck hit the Mercedes broadside and lifted it off the ground, slamming it into the brick retaining wall at the border of the property. He felt a shudder, as he had the first time he was ever inside a woman. He felt something yield. Did it come from her?

His head snapped forward and his face hit the steering wheel.

The little car collapsed completely, folding like a jackknife, and Maxine Parness took blows to the head and spine that killed her before the ambulance arrived. Jason Parness, who had not yet attached his seat belt, was thrown through the windshield, dead before his body hit the ground.

The driver jumped out of the truck and started sprinting down the hill. He was dressed in running clothes and appeared to be a well-conditioned athlete who was testing himself against these steep and unforgiving hills. The houses that he passed were hidden from the road. The people who lived in them were sound asleep. Except for one early gardener, an illegal immigrant who hid from the police, no one saw his battered face and his blue eyes and the blood that kept dripping from his nose.

CHAPTER 10

O<small>N THE DAY</small> after Labor Day, to a mixed reception of relief and rage, Claire and Jake were back at work. The fantasy of staying on in Italy had powerful appeal, but they were sensible and realistic—as psychoanalysts are supposed to be—and all too soon they found themselves back in the middle of the life they had left behind. There were compensations: patients who'd done well, whose lives had come together, at times in surprising ways. For some, August crystalized the subtle progress they'd made throughout the year. For other patients, it would take weeks to work through the agony of being left behind. The most disturbed of all seemed not to notice that their doctors had ever left.

The glow of Italy inevitably faded. They threw themselves into work, knowing all the while that nothing of what sent them off had been resolved. Some wheels had turned, but there was no new light on Felix Kiehl. John Spicer had been walled off from an FBI investigation that was apparently in progress, a development that left him bitter and uncommunicative. Claire and Jake were ignored. They had no choice but to go on as best they could and live with their anxiety. They couldn't read; they couldn't socialize; they could hardly think coherently on any subject. The one act possible was the nightly move from vertical to horizontal—at the end of every day they could and did collapse. They would sprawl in front of the television set, Jake with a can of beer, Claire beside him with a pack of cigarettes, a habit she'd long ago abandoned. Together, they would flip through channels for diversion. No soaps or sitcoms; their work supplied enough of that. No politics or public stations; too complicated. Best of all, for as long as it lasted, was baseball.

On an afternoon in early September, without telling Claire, Jake put ten hundred-dollar bills into an envelope and took a cab downtown to an address on the Lower East Side. It was a strangely well-maintained building in the middle of a block that was inhabited mostly by addicts and homeless people. The structures on either side were burnt-out shells, but this one looked in good repair. The garbage was stacked in cans. The sidewalk had recently been swept. Inside, the hall was clean and a bulb glowed brightly.

Jake pressed the bell to apartment 1-R. From somewhere, he heard loud jazz, the free-form variety he could never quite follow.

"Yo?" said a voice on the intercom.

"I'm looking for Jimmy," he said. He felt dumb, but it was what he had been told.

Eventually, a door opened and a tall, slender, barefoot black man with his hair in dreadlocks looked him over.

"What you want, man?"

"I was told to ask for Jimmy," Jake said. "He's expecting me. Raymond spoke to him."

The man led Jake to an apartment in the rear. The place was cheerful, the rooms all clean and bright. There were attractive paintings on the walls—scenes of Caribbean life.

"Let's see the cash."

Jake dug down into his pocket and extracted the envelope.

"This don't bring nothin' fancy."

"I'm not looking for fancy," Jake said. He knew he was overpaying outrageously.

The man unrolled a blanket. Inside, there were half a dozen handguns. "Take your pick."

Jake looked the weapons over. None were the exotic automatics he had read about, but neither were they chrome-plated Saturday-night specials that could blow up in your hand. They looked solid, old-fashioned, well made. He selected a revolver. It was the first time in his life that he ever held a pistol. He was shocked by the weight of it.

"You want that one?" The black man reached in his pocket and handed Jake a plastic bag that held six bullets. "This is the caliber, my man. Use them in good health."

"I hope I never use them."

"You don't expect that, do you?"

"I'm new to this. I don't know what I should expect."

The man smiled broadly. He had a gold tooth with a diamond set in it.

Jake put the bullets into his pocket and wrapped the gun in his folded newspaper and went back out into the street. He had to walk three long blocks before he could find a cab. It wasn't until he was safe inside his office that he looked carefully at this *thing* that he had bought. He needed no instructions. He had seen enough movies to know exactly how to load it. He put the bullets into the cylinder and the gun inside a file under the letter G.

The baseball season ended, but their routine remained the same: frozen dinner at home, lots of wine, television. They were watching the news when there suddenly appeared, blurry but unmistakable, the face of Felix Kiehl. It looked like a photograph from a driver's license.

"Oh my God!" Claire sat up quickly.

Jake pulled himself out of his beery doze, awake enough to hear the word, "Fugitive." He saw the picture and then the silly grin of the announcer. She said that Felix Kiehl had been under investigation by the SEC and the Treasury Department for computer fraud and assorted securities violations. He had been identified that afternoon at a posh midtown athletic club but had managed to escape after an exchange of gunfire. She gave no further details and moved on quickly to another story.

The first thing Jake did was call John Spicer.

A woman answered. She sounded as if she had been asleep. He would not be back until very late. When Jake pressed hard, she gave him the number.

"I know all about it," Spicer said when Jake finally reached him. "I told them to do it differently. Those assholes can't do anything."

"Can they protect us?" Jake heard voices and clicking chips.

"They can't protect them-fucking-selves."

"Aren't we witnesses?"

"Forget it. You're small potatoes. Call me at noon, in my office. Maybe I'll have some news."

"We need someone."

"Not a chance," Spicer said.

"That's it? That's all you'll do for us?"

"It's all I can do. Keep your door locked."

Jake could tell he was grinning. "It's already locked."

"So make love to your wife, my man, and get some sleep. I got three aces here," he whispered.

"Is that the truth?"

"No."

"You want them to hear . . ."

"It's a lock," Spicer said theatrically.

"I hope they clean you out. I hope they kick your butt."

"Not these turkeys," Spicer said. "This is my sucker game."

They stayed in bed. The news was still on television—the announcers on to sports and then the weather.

"I'll be right back," Jake said.

He ran downstairs to his office and then back up the stairs with the loaded gun. He sat it on the bed between them. Claire picked it up and aimed at the television set.

He was shocked. "You know how to use a gun?"

"My father taught me. He thought we ought to learn."

"Could you shoot the bastard?"

"I really don't know. Could you?"

"*Yes.*"

They tuned the radio to an all-news station. There were fires and muggings. An abandoned baby had been found outside a church. The market was up. A water main had broken in the Village. A ninety-year-old man had won the lottery. Alternate-side-of-the-street parking was in effect. The weather would be clear and warm. The Giants and Jets had games on Sunday. They managed, more or less, to get through the night.

In the morning, they watched the news again, but there was nothing new. The *Times* arrived with a clunk against the door, and Jake went to get it, peering first through the peephole into the empty vestibule. He was tempted to make another call to Spicer, but it was only six A.M.

Should they go to work? Claire and Jake discussed the issue in the gray light of morning. Nothing had really changed. If his intention was to hurt them, Kiehl had lots of chances. They were in no more danger now than they had been before. Logic said they were in less danger, and logic ruled. They made their coffee extra strong and dressed for work. They agreed to turn off their machines and answer every call.

Jake walked Claire to her office and looked through the rooms with her. Everything was fine.

He returned to the apartment and took the gun back down the stairs to his office. Twenty minutes later, a short while before Alice Quinn was due for her session, Jake's telephone rang.

"He's *here*," Claire said.

"Not funny. I'm supposed to make the jokes, and I'm not up for it today."

"I mean it," she said softly. "He's in the waiting room."

"*Shit!*"

"He's peaceful as a lamb," she went on. "He came for his session! We used to have an early hour."

"I don't believe this. Are you all right?"

"I'm fine. He's Alan Maliver—the way he used to be."

"Can you lock your door?"

"I did already."

"And your scheduled patient?"

"I called and canceled. She lives right up the street."

"I'll call the police."

"I can't just let him sit there."

"You damn well better let him sit there."

"It's only *Alan.* He wouldn't hurt a fly."

"Don't be stupid," Jake said. "You're not a fly. Keep him waiting. I'll call right back."

Spicer was asleep, but he woke instantly. His mind was focused and precise. He'd make the necessary calls. He told Jake to meet him in the street outside Claire's office. It was critical that he not try *anything.*

Jake called Claire back.

"This is Dr. Baxter," she answered with an uncharacteristic formality.

"It's all in place. They need half an hour. We'll all be out there —the fucking army. The only thing you have to do is keep the bastard waiting."

"That would be fine," she said. "If you would ask her to call me for an appointment, I would be happy to see her as soon as possible."

"He's *in* there with you?"

"I'm with a patient now," she went on. "Perhaps I could get back to you at another time."

"You're out of your fucking mind."

"I understand. This is a situation in which one has to make a decision of one's own."

"Half an hour. Just end the session in half an hour and get him the hell right out of there. I don't care if they catch him. I care that you're all right."

"I understand. I'll call you at noon," she went on. "I'm booked up solid until that time. I may run a little late."

"If there's any change, you'll get another call."

"I understand."

"I love you."

"I'm very glad to hear that," she said. "And thanks for the referral."

Jake thought about taking the gun along, but he knew it would be stupid. He told the elevator man to tell his patients that he was called away on an emergency.

"Dr. Silver!" At the entrance to the building he was suddenly face to face with Alice Quinn. It was a shock to see her outside his office, off the couch.

"Miss Quinn, I have to cancel. I have an emergency to deal with."

She looked alarmed. "Are you all right?"

"I'm fine—I just can't talk now." He started down the street, but she reached out, and he almost took her hand. "I'll call you later. I'll try to find another time."

"Is there anything I can do?"

"Thanks, but I don't think so."

"I wish you well." She looked at him intently. "I don't know what this is all about, I know you won't tell me, but I'm going to church for you . . ."

"Thanks." He jogged away. He could have hugged her.

Barely fifteen minutes had passed, and the street outside Claire's building looked completely normal. He saw no sign of police activity. Businesspeople carrying briefcases waved at cabs. Kids walked to school, while others waited for the yellow buses. They stood in little groups with their parents beside them and looked up the street with an eagerness that he had never known.

An excruciating ten minutes later, a cab pulled up and Spicer jumped out. His eyes were red. An unlit cigarette dangled from his mouth. "He's still inside?"

"The lady's expensive," Jake said. "He can't afford all day."

"From what I hear, this dude can pay for all the shrinks he needs."

"From what I hear, he may have to."

Slightly more than forty-five minutes from the time Claire telephoned, the man who called himself Alan Maliver stepped out of her building and stood blinking in the morning sun.

"That's him," Jake said.

Spicer nodded.

A man holding a briefcase dropped it next to Maliver. The patient bent reflexively and the man tackled him around the waist. An instant later another man ran up to them and slapped handcuffs on Maliver's wrists. A third man frisked him quickly and signaled to the others that he was unarmed.

Jake and Spicer ran across the street.

"Good going," Spicer said.

"No big deal," replied the first man. "Easy as anything." He was a good six-five and must have weighed three hundred pounds.

Alan Maliver looked totally confused. "What do you want from me? What's going on?" He looked at Jake without recognition.

"You're under arrest," said the second policeman. He pulled a card from his pocket and began to read. "You have the right to remain silent . . ."

Police cars silently converged, their lights all flashing.

"I don't understand," Maliver said. "I didn't do anything wrong. What's this about?"

Claire appeared in the doorway and then ran into Jake's arms. Maliver looked up at her helplessly. "Dr. Baxter, what's *happening*? Why can't you help me? Why are they doing this to me?"

She looked at him with pity. "To tell you the truth, I don't understand. I hope eventually I will. I hope sooner or later we all will."

"But you said you'd help me," he went on. "You said you'd take care of me. You made a promise."

CHAPTER 11

THE FANTASY THAT they were done with him was good for just a week.

It ended when a lawyer named Mary Buchanan made a call to Claire and introduced herself as Felix Kiehl's attorney. The woman said, politely but quite firmly, that they needed to meet as soon as possible to talk about Claire's findings. She had power of attorney over Kiehl's affairs and was in a position to pay generously for Claire's time. She didn't have to add that Claire had no choice in the matter.

Mary Buchanan was a redhead in her mid-forties with creamy skin that looked as if it had never seen harsh sun. She was much more attractive than Claire expected. She wore no jewelry, not even a ring, though she was dressed in the most expensive clothing Claire had ever seen anyone actually wear—all black and navy, precisely tailored, with graceful lines that showed her solid body to perfection. Once she began to speak, Buchanan was precise and focused in her questions and disarmingly direct. "Doctor, I don't think you'll be surprised to hear that this situation is going to require a great deal of psychiatric input."

Claire and Jake had decided it was best for her to say as little as she could and get rid of the lawyer as fast as possible.

Buchanan continued. "I assume you're well aware there's something unusual about him. The man is painfully confused. As far as I can tell, he doesn't understand what's going on. I do my damnedest, over and over again, to lay things out for him, but my explanations don't penetrate. The evidence is rather powerful, but he continues to insist, even when I assure him that everything we talk about is in the strictest confidence, that he *isn't* Felix Kiehl, that he's never heard the name, that he has no idea why he was arrested."

"Can he be put on trial?"

"Not in this condition, but I assume—I'd like to hear what you think, of course—that things will change."

"And you're sure he is this 'Felix Kiehl'?" Claire asked.

Buchanan nodded. "The police have fingerprints and a photograph ID. There's no way to deny that he worked at Potter, Weeks. He was there two years, and at least a dozen people can identify him. Where his mind was at the time is still an open question."

"He told me he was an artist," Claire said softly. "He said his name was Alan Maliver."

"You saw no sign that he was lying?"

"I believe what people tell me," Claire said. "I began to doubt, of course, after my husband found that he was seeing both of us. Eventually I doubted everything, which is more or less where I am now."

Buchanan shook her head in shared frustration. "It's all so strange. You understand that he was arrested for *illegal trading?* He made a fortune! He had a dozen false identities, each with its own Social Security number and brokerage account. He paid taxes for twelve different people—and he paid plenty! That alone must mean he's crazy."

" 'Crazy' would make him benign," Claire said.

"There isn't proof," Buchanan said quickly. "I know about California, I have every one of the reports. There's no conclusive evidence. Those doctors each saw thousands of patients. You know—someone did a study once—if you picked ten people at random, from all around the country, there'd be a damn good chance, mathematically, that they'd know someone in common. The D.A. in Los Angeles is nowhere close to bringing charges on those things."

Claire shook her head as Buchanan's words just hung there. "Those *things*? Is that what you call murder?"

"I don't claim he's an innocent. I know what happened to your house. But even if he was responsible for that, it doesn't prove that he killed anyone."

"I want you to know, no matter if they prosecute or not, that I believe he killed those people."

"You *believe*? Do you believe in evidence?"

"I'm trying to say I can't be of any use to you."

"Could we just talk a while? Could you at least wait until you know why I'm here?" Buchanan looked more and more anxious. "I'm not looking to get him off. I don't even know the man—that's the biggest problem."

"I know all I want to know."

"At least you worked with him," Mary went on. "He talked to you. He remembered your name from one week to the next." She looked at Claire helplessly. "I visit him every day and he still doesn't know who I am. I don't know whether to keep the case or give the damn thing up."

"I can't help you," Claire said. "I'm not objective. That must be obvious."

But Buchanan kept pushing. "You can't tell me if he's faking this or if he's really crazy?"

"They don't preclude each other."

"Any jury will believe they do."

Claire shook her head again. "It's not my problem."

"Would you call his rage insane? Would you support a plea of diminished responsibility?"

"Please—ask someone else. I don't even believe in such a thing."

"You don't care what makes him tick? You don't think, as his doctor, that it's your job to know?"

"I was never his doctor," Claire said bitterly. "He was not my patient in any *true* sense. We didn't work together in good faith. He lied to me all the time."

Mary looked at Claire and waited, toying with an expensive fountain pen. "You mean patients never lie?"

"I didn't say that."

"So why call it bad faith? Doesn't everyone lie, if not to others, then to themselves? Isn't that the nature of neurosis?"

"You're playing lawyer's games."

"I am a lawyer. I don't apologize for it. But I came for help, and you're treating me like the enemy."

"You're treating me like a hostile witness."

"I didn't start that way." Buchanan looked weary now. "Don't you want to know the truth? It amazes me that you don't care."

Claire shook her head. "Look, let me be clear. I'm a psychoanalyst, an anachronism—a psychiatrist who'd rather listen to people than pump them full of drugs. I don't do forensic work. I haven't done a single competency evaluation in my entire career. I'd be useless to you. If you need a report, I'll write a summary of my contacts with him, but I won't go to court."

They sat in silence; two striking women, not far apart in age and intellect, at opposite ends of the world. It might have ended there, but the expressions on their faces left room for more.

"You wouldn't have a choice," Mary said softly. "I would never press the issue, but you ought to know the truth. If I don't take this case, and if some creep does, he could *force* you to appear." She got out of her chair and walked slowly around Claire's office, examining the books. She found a classic by Freud—*The Interpretation of Dreams* —and flipped through pages. Standing in the center of the room, she started speaking: "Psychoanalysis was the great experience of my life —the most profound, the most deeply liberating. Was it anything like that for you?"

Claire kept staring at her.

"I felt you people were the great explorers, brave souls who ventured into worlds that terrified the rest of us. Was that a mistake? A leftover transference? A fantasy I should have overcome? I always thought the search for truth was what analysis was all about."

"In my experience, the truth I'm after is very different from the one that lawyers want." Claire knew instantly it was the worst thing she could have said.

"You've judged me prematurely. I came for help." Mary's voice turned shrill. Her green eyes blazed, and a red flush crept up her neck. Her hands clenched and unclenched as if she was about to throw a punch. "Maybe you're experiencing a little transference yourself. Don't you know that Freud's first ambition was to be a *lawyer*? I have no interest in anything you could *write* for me. I can buy all the psychiatrists I need to write reports. They're lined up outside my office, forensic experts with better credentials than you'll ever have, and yes, they're a bunch of whores. If and when I need them, I'll have my pick." Mary took a breath and smiled faintly. It seemed the worst had passed. "I know a thing or two about you. I respect your work, more than you do mine. It happens that you're exactly what I do need—a real analyst, not a hack, not a pill-pusher with a shock box or some 'doctor death.' This isn't about a trial. I don't even know if there can be a trial. What I know is that I have to *reach* the man, that's all. I know there's more to him, a lot more, but I can't get to it myself. I have to understand. You have to help me understand."

Claire was stunned. "I've already failed," she said weakly.

"Don't be so sure. He *asks* for you. It's the one coherent thing he says. Maybe you didn't fail."

Mary took a seat on the couch and leaned over next to Claire. It was much closer than patients ever came, and for the first time in their conversation, Claire didn't feel defensive. "I know what you went through. I know that you feel raped. I want you to know that I have scars of my own . . ."

"I still have nightmares," Claire said.

"If you saw him on that ward, you wouldn't be afraid. He's a helpless child. You'd want to hug him and protect him . . ."

"Maybe *you* would."

Claire was off balance. She was under the kind of spell that Mary was so brilliant at invoking in a courtroom. All she could think was that Mary Buchanan was an extraordinary woman—powerful, intelligent, vulnerable. And as hard as Claire had been resisting, she knew she wanted to work with her. Her clearest feeling was that she was in love. It didn't frighten her. There was no alarm, no risk. She'd been analyzed well enough to understand those buried corners of herself. It was just a feeling, a lovely, passing feeling. It left her happy and a little sad, and it put her stereotypes of lawyers on hold.

CHAPTER 12

B Y THE END of the day, Claire decided she would attempt what the lawyer had asked. She called Mary and told her that she was willing to make a visit to the hospital. She said she needed some perspective—to see for herself what Kiehl was really like.

At breakfast on the following morning, she announced the plan to Jake, sweet coffee and sour words. They sat at their kitchen table as morning sun brightened the room.

"I don't believe this. We've been naive enough already. Shouldn't we consider what the woman's up to?"

"We? Does he have two therapists again?"

"He's yours alone," Jake said. "You can have him for yourself, with all the little goodies that he brings along."

"I think you're full of envy . . ."

He shook his head helplessly. "Okay, I do have some. If you work with him, and if it does go well, you'll make a splash. You'll get action—reporters, interviews, all kinds of media. But you never wanted that."

"You aren't bitter that she picked me?"

"Of course I'm bitter. You said she's gorgeous . . ."

"Very funny. You really don't mind that I'm in the center? That the attention is on me?"

"I wanted to protect you."

"From what?" she asked.

"She wants you to *treat* the guy? Isn't it too late? Isn't the setting wrong? Isn't it more likely that she's groping for a way to get him off? I don't trust her strategy. I didn't think you'd want to get him off."

"It's not about a trial. She promised me."

He studied Claire over the rim of his coffee cup. "Sweetheart, life ain't that simple. You're not in some academic lab. This thing has major consequences."

"Don't condescend."

"I talked with Spicer," he went on. "He's very down on Mary Buchanan. Among the words he used are 'dishonest' and 'amoral.' He said she's one real tricky lady."

"I'm sure he's got his own tricks."

"He said that Mary Buchanan could make Richard Nixon look like an angel."

"And what does that make Spicer?"

"You're not dealing with him," Jake said. "He's not manipulating you."

"No one's manipulating me but *you.* I don't need you moving in on me."

"I live with you, remember?"

She looked at him sadly. Why did things always take this bitter turn? "If you want the truth, she got me thinking. I'm still afraid of him, but she got me wondering what's really going on. I want to do my job as an analyst. I want to find out what made him what he is. I also happened to like Mary Buchanan—I don't care what your buddy thinks. It's as simple as that."

"I don't find that simple."

.   .   .

Max Dorfmann was as skeptical as Jake had been. He hated lawyers for reasons all his own. He told Claire she was being used. They were in his apartment, in his bed together, as they talked about it.

On the Tuesday nights when Jake was playing poker, Claire was never out to dinner or at the movies with the friend who covered for her. She'd been involved with Max for almost ten years—from the final year of her residency, through the start of her practice and analytic training, through the intense beginning and then the slow decline of her relationship with Jake. Jake never guessed that what she felt for Max was anything more than neurotic idealization. Max lived his life, saw his patients, and wrote his cryptic articles in a sprawling, dark apartment that reeked of stale cigars and still housed his long-dead wife's clothing.

Claire was well aware that what she felt from Max was something she wished for from her father. Her training analyst, Dr. John Kliner, had made the interpretation at least a hundred times, and every time he said it she agreed. But it didn't change one thing. There were moments when Max would brush her hair and talk to her in his gruff, Germanic way, and she would feel safe and more content than ever before in her life. Claire knew Max loved the life in her, the passion she concealed so well. He didn't lecture her, the way her father always had, the way Jake did. He loved to listen. When she told him a story from her day or described an emotion she was feeling, a smile would light his face and his eyes would fill. When he held her in his arms, she would feel that all she wanted was to stay right there forever. It was no secret to either of them that she was the daughter he never had. It was no secret that he made up for the neglect of her alcoholic father. The secret was how well it worked. Relationships like this are supposed to be disasters.

The sex was nothing special. More often than not, Max had his problems. Technically, Jake was superior. She knew Jake would appreciate that detail; it might even make it possible for him to forgive her, though to Claire it meant very little. The emotions she felt with Max made the orgasms she never had with him seem trivial.

During her training analysis, Dr. Kliner had seen all this as pathological. He said *he* was supposed to be the object of her transference. She was supposed to work her problems out with him, not gratify them with Max. John Kliner was a benevolent, decent, ineffectual man, and the problem of the analysis was that Claire knew it. His words never touched her. She was fulfilling something at her core, something more important than career or marriage. She agreed with everything he said; people get what she was looking for when they are very young or they don't get it at all; the search for a better parent leads inevitably to painful disappointment. She had said the same thing to any number of patients with exactly the same effect it had on her—none.

Even Claire's biology lacked the power to change her. At a time when the major interests of her friends were their pregnancies, the availability of decent help, the difficulty of finding the right nursery school, and for more than a few, the impossibility of finding a suitable man with whom to begin the enterprise at all, she lived in another world. Call it a sicker world, a course of disaster—she often did. Most of the time, except when Max was unavailable, she had no wish to change.

"I don't want you hurt," Max said.

"Hurt in what way?"

"In every way. These people are capable of causing damage. Lawyers are not sublimated. They are invariably infantile. The ones who conduct trials have excessive narcissism. They cannot restrain their aggression." His accent gave him an air of profundity—deserved or not—that no American analyst could possibly achieve. "They will use you. They promise to treat you with respect, but once they have you in their clutches they show no scruples . . ."

"I don't mind being used." She stroked him gently. "There's part of me that likes it."

"I am not addressing your sexual proclivities."

"You did before." Actually, he'd tried and failed.

"I can still give you good advice. Let me be potent, at least, in that regard."

"I didn't complain."

93

"Then *listen* to me. Don't be a child."

She held him tight.

"Remember, these are *lawyers*." He said it like a curse, much more bitterly than Jake. "They don't think the way that we do. They want to win, that's all. Any trauma they subject you to will be irrelevant to them."

"I liked her," Claire said. "I think she's got integrity."

Max sadly shook his head. "People have hated lawyers for the last five hundred years. There are *reasons* for it."

"They hate us too," she said.

"For different reasons. We show them things that they wish not to see. We work with nightmares and are tainted by them."

"I had a nightmare," Claire said. "About this patient."

Max peered expectantly into her eyes, but she wouldn't tell him. "Fine. Interpret it yourself if that's what you prefer. Just don't put yourself into a real nightmare."

"I have to do this. It's very clear to me. I need to go through it and come out the other side."

Max shook his head again. "What kind of fantasy is that? Why do you assume there is another side?"

"There is for me."

He looked directly into Claire's eyes, with an intensity that shook her. "I hope you're right, my lovely one. I hope it is possible to grow from this. I must remind you of something you know quite well: A nightmare may be a warning. Your unconscious may have good reason to signal danger. There are times in life when it is wise to pay our nightmares heed."

"I *am* afraid. That part is true. I want to see him again, but I am afraid."

"You don't want to see him again," Max said. "Let's at least be honest—the one you want to see is her."

CHAPTER 13

SHE WAS NERVOUS in the cab downtown to Bellevue, but nerves were soon replaced by anger at the system.

In typical bureaucratic fashion, the hospital lost the notice from the court. The officer in charge had to make half a dozen calls to get Claire admitted to the prison ward, and he told her in no uncertain terms that the next time she appeared, if they hadn't received the proper documents, she wouldn't get in at all. Then she had to meet Dr. Charles Smythe, the ward psychiatrist. He was an aging relic of the seventies, benign and vague, with greasy hair that reached his shoulders and a blissful smile that wouldn't go away. He told her cheerfully that he was convinced Kiehl was malingering.

"Then I don't have to worry," Claire said. "He won't freak out on me."

"On the contrary. He could to make a point."

"You're a big help."

The bland smile broadened. "No need to sweat it. We don't do much psychiatry in here, but we have great security."

She stood in the center of Felix Kiehl's room after a muscular black aide shut the door and waited right outside. Kiehl sat motionless in a peeling vinyl armchair. His eyes were heavy lidded, and his face looked dead. It took him endless time to focus, and even after he managed it he could barely speak. He looked much worse than she had ever seen him—much more confused, much less a threat. She thought they must have pumped him full of Thorazine or Haldol.

"Your lawyer said you asked for me," Claire said.

He blinked and struggled hard to focus. "Who?"

"Mary Buchanan. Your lawyer. Do you remember?"

Claire watched and waited. His words came slowly, but at least they were words. "I'm . . . very . . . sorry."

"Sorry for what?" The pounding in her chest began to slow. She knew this man. It would be all right.

He looked bewildered, a poor lost soul, much sicker than she ever realized. He blinked again and shook his head. His tone was plaintive. "I don't know," he said.

"Is there some reason to feel sorry?"

He sat up straighter and seemed to pull himself together. "Doctor, what happened to me? How did I get here?"

"Hasn't anyone explained?"

"The lady tries." He nodded as he spoke. "Sometimes she shows me papers. I think I understand, and then it's gone. My brain is full of holes." He put his hands over his face and sagged down in his chair. "I can't keep anything inside. It doesn't stay one minute to the next."

She took a seat across from him in a metal chair that was bolted to the floor. "Maybe you should tell me what you do remember."

"Your office . . ."

"And?"

He tried to concentrate. "It's the only thing."

"Do you remember your name?"

"Alan Maliver."

She took a quick breath. She had decided she would not hold back: "Do you know the name Felix Kiehl?"

He looked more confused. He held his head with both his hands like a broken toy.

"Arthur Moss?"

He shook his head again. "Who are they?"

"You called yourself Arthur Moss when you visited my husband."

He shook his head helplessly. "I remember your office." The thought seemed to cheer him. "There were yellow lamps and a soft blue chair. I wish we were there instead of here."

"And outside my office?"

He looked puzzled as he mulled it over. "I don't know."

"The place you lived in? The way you spent your time? The things you did?"

He shook his head in response to every question.

"Do you remember your address? Your telephone number?"

He sat in silence. There was no anger. His words came slowly and the look on his face was of confusion and disbelief. "There was no phone. I'm sure of that."

"How can you be sure?"

His eyes were wide. "There was no place I lived in. Doctor, does this make sense?" He looked desperately into her eyes. "Outside your office there wasn't *anything*. Outside your office, there wasn't any *me* . . ."

"I don't know what you mean."

"I don't either." His hands began to shake. He looked around the room as if there was something that he feared. He focused on Claire with escalating terror. "Doctor, what's happening? I'm really afraid. What's gone wrong? I feel like I'm falling in a hole. What's wrong with me? Doctor, please help me, please tell me what I *am*!"

Finally, a glimpse of something she understood. There were risks, she didn't doubt it, but she was capable of dealing with them. On the way back to the office, Claire tried to imagine what it would be like to live inside Alan Maliver's head. She had a memory of a boy she treated once at a children's clinic in the Bronx. No one understood why he was so confused until, by accident, she had stumbled on the cause. He wasn't stupid, as his teacher thought, and he wasn't lazy, as his mother was convinced. He just had seizures—petit mal—one after the other throughout the day. They didn't glaze his eyes or cause him to fall, but they lasted long enough to keep him living in a world of blanks. His life was full of empty spaces that no one—especially himself—had ever recognized. He was only a sad little kid, not dumb at all, not bad, whose mother drank too much and took God knows what when she was pregnant.

CHAPTER 14

W<small>HEN CLAIRE RETURNED</small> to the hospital, the papers were in order, and she was ushered into the ward like a long-lost member of the staff. She liked the feeling.

First she stopped at the nurses' station and read the chart. She noted, to her surprise, that Felix Kiehl had been given no medication in his two weeks of custody.

His eyes were bright. He looked much better. There was no trace of the drugged look she had seen three days ago. He was more or less the man—or fragment of a man—she used to know.

"I wish you were my doctor again and we could work together just like we used to. I know how much I need you. I know I can pay. I have money, a lot of it."

"How do you know *that?*"

"My lawyer told me. She wrote it down. I have a bank account. The government has frozen most of it, but there's some money I can use."

"What would we talk about?" she asked.

He smiled shyly. He looked very happy. "I had a dream . . ."

"You really want things the way they were."

"You were in it," he went on.

She took a seat. "Do you want to tell me?"

He described his dream in the detailed way he used to describe them in her office: "There was a big white house. It was on top of a hill or a mountain somewhere. We were looking at it together, standing side by side. The scene was very beautiful, with trees all around and birds and fields full of sheep and cows. It was like a manor, a manor house, and we were lords of the manor . . ."

Claire's mind churned. What house? Could it be East Hampton? Could it be Nevada?

". . . I was taking you on a tour. I knew the house better than you did, though I didn't know it very well. We went walking through halls and looking into rooms that were filled with all kinds of ordinary things—beds and bureaus and lamps and television sets and washing machines and dishwashers. Then we came to a door that wouldn't open. It didn't bother me. I was willing to walk away from it, but when I told you it was locked you became upset—*extremely* upset—and you insisted that we break it down. I never saw you like that. You were furious. I pleaded with you not to, but you went ahead and kicked holes in the door and I couldn't stop thinking about how strong you were and how I'd better do everything you want . . ."

Her thoughts kept racing. Was it this place, this so-called hospital, this prison? Was it symbolic of him, his personality, his brittle defenses?

The patient's voice was hushed. He seemed reluctant to say more, but eventually he did: "Then the door opened and there was a dead man on the floor. I felt embarrassed—ashamed—but to my relief, you didn't get upset. We closed the door. You didn't mind. We were going to forget about him. We went back into the fields, but everything had changed. It was worse than winter. The trees were dead and the animals were dead and even the grass was dead . . ."

Claire interjected, "It's like the old days."

"Which old days?"

"When you came to my office and told me your dreams."

"I hope I can again."

She studied him carefully. "I have something to ask. Is there something upsetting you?" There was a long silence in which their eyes stayed locked. "What are you feeling?"

"This makes me sad."

"Do you know why?"

"I want to come back to you, to be your patient again. I want to show you. That's what the dream means."

"You don't want to show me everything," she said.

He was shocked. "Doctor, I would never keep things from you. You mean too much to me."

"Think about the door," she said.

"Do you think I'm holding back?"

"Sometimes . . . when someone means a lot . . . it's when we do hold back."

CHAPTER 15

"I SHOULD HAVE let him associate," Claire said. "I should have given him more room. If this were an ordinary treatment, I'd never ask so many pushy questions."

"You kick holes in the door," Max said. "On the surface he pleads for rescue, but the unconscious is saying you are too aggressive."

He was seated at their dining-room table for a rare midweek dinner. It was Jake's idea. He suggested that Claire get input to her work with Kiehl. If she wouldn't hear Jake's reservations, which she clearly wouldn't, she might as well hear Max's. The trouble was, all their ancient disagreements bubbled right up to the surface.

Jake was instantly annoyed. "She has to push. For God's sake, the man is in a prison! You can't ask someone to free-associate when he isn't free!"

"The setting does not control the process," Max responded firmly.

"I'm not as talented as you," Jake replied. "Or as self-absorbed. The world affects me."

"His mind is free," Max went on. "We don't work with settings, with superficial circumstances. We work with the patient's inner world. The only useful thing that we can give this man is the correct interpretation."

"Of what?"

"Of his dream, his unconscious fantasy. Isn't it what put him where he is?"

"I thought it was the police."

Max just shook his head.

"Interpretations are the last thing I would give this bastard," Jake went on. "I'd much prefer a prison cell or a bullet in the brain."

"In that we do agree," Max said. "I too believe this enterprise is a terrible mistake."

Then it was Claire's turn to be annoyed. "Do me a favor—both of you. If you want to pontificate, do it about the dream. If I find it helpful, I'll give you dinner . . ."

"And if you don't?" Jake asked.

"Dog food."

"We don't have a dog."

"I'll order out."

Max hardly seemed to hear. The only thing on his mind was alcohol. He gulped his second glass of wine and reached out to pour a third. The bottle was empty, and the look of pain that crossed his face was so intense that Jake took pity and went into the kitchen for another.

The place smelled of stale cigarettes. For an instant, Claire thought the room was wrong. The vinyl armchair had been turned to face the window and the view across the litter-covered courtyard. The man who faced her had a mean expression in his eyes and a cigarette between his lips. Where was Alan? Then she saw that there was no mistake. The body was the one she knew—it just didn't belong to Alan Maliver.

"Are you all right?" she asked.

"The question is, sweetheart, are *you* all right?" The voice was harsh and an octave lower than the one she knew.

"You sound different."

"Not to me."

It was obvious that he had changed. Another personality appeared to have control. She didn't know whether to run away or to feel pleased. Could this be Kiehl? At least he stayed seated. "I'm a little confused. Will you tell me who you are?"

He blew smoke in her direction. "Sweetheart, relax. Nothing bad is gonna happen. Lay back, enjoy the ride. Just close your eyes."

"Have we met?"

"What a boring question. Can't you think of a better one?"

"Such as?"

He shook his head. "You gotta do some work, sweetheart. You're being paid a ton of money. I can't do it for you."

"If you mean treatment, it's something we're supposed to do together."

"Any time—we can do it together."

She looked at him coldly. He was starting to irritate her. "This doesn't do much for me."

"Is there something that would?"

"Your name might be a start."

"The name is Victor."

"Have we met before?"

He shook his head.

"Do you know where you are?"

"Of course."

"Do you know how you got here? Do you know *why* you're here? Do you know what happened to Alan?"

"Fuck this. Too many questions. You're a pain."

His face was suddenly transformed. The harsh lines melted and the anger faded and a minute later—as if he'd peeled a mask away or put one on—he had become the man she knew. Alan Maliver took the cigarette out of his mouth and stubbed it out in the loaded ash-tray. "Doctor, how did I get *that*? I hate the smell . . ."

"Something very important happened," she said cautiously. "Do you know what I mean?"

He shook his head.

"You sounded very different. You looked very different. *You* smoked the cigarettes."

"I don't understand."

"Remember when you told me that you didn't know where you lived?"

"I still don't."

"I think I met the one who knows."

He shook his head again. He was more confused. She understood at last how incomplete he was, how much a fragment of a man. He was meant to be a little boy, and that was all he ever could be. He would have stayed that way forever, her good little boy forever. Then a new idea occurred to Claire. It was crazy, but no more crazy than her being there at all. "Have you ever been hypnotized?" she asked.

Alan shook his head.

"I think it would be useful," she went on. "Very often, when people lose their memory, it's the most effective way to get it back."

It went against the grain of every psychoanalyst. It was some-thing she would never have imagined she would try. But she stood beside his chair and held her right hand out and told him to focus on her ring. It was a birthday gift from Jake—a lovely opal that had flecks of gold and aqua and always reminded her of summer at the beach. She told Alan his eyes would soon grow heavy. She said no matter how he tried he could not keep them open. She said that he would fall into a restful sleep.

To Claire's great amazement, it worked exactly the way it was supposed to. She thought that she would stop at any hint that he was hypnotizable, but within a minute his eyes began to droop and a minute later they were fully closed. He started breathing deeply. He followed her commands as soon as she uttered them:

105

"Your eyes are getting heavy.

"You cannot open them.

"Your arms and legs feel heavy.

"You're feeling more and more relaxed.

"You're going into a deeper and deeper sleep.

"This is the most pleasant and restful sleep that you have ever known."

The entire process was infinitely easy. It was obvious that he was a perfect subject from his reactions to her commands. She spoke softly and repetitively and wondered as she spoke if she was going under, too. She was falling into a trance herself, but not so deeply that she had lost control. She told herself that maybe this wasn't such an outrageous idea.

She let him sleep. She made no attempt to probe his memory or contact other personalities. After ten minutes of silence she slowly brought him out of it. She told him he would remember everything. She told him that the next time she showed him her ring he would go into a trance at once.

The first thing Claire did when she reached her office was make a call to Mary, who turned out to be in court and unavailable.

In the evening, she told Jake.

"I think you're losing it," he said.

"It was an experiment. It's an approach that people have used with multiples for many years."

"I think you're off the wall."

"You think I'm off the wall for seeing him. You think I'm being conned."

"What else is there to think?" Jake asked. "First, he pulls some kind of brilliant computer scam that only about three people in the world can understand. After the deed is done and the money all salted away—along with a couple of bodies—he destroys your house. Then, conveniently, he turns into this harmless wreck who can't remember how to use the toilet. He gets a slimy lawyer to represent him, in between the crack dealers she prefers, and the two of them figure out a way to plead insanity." He rolled his eyes. "All they needed was a gullible shrink. You've been set up—it's fucking obvious —and now you're getting in deeper. If you want advice from me, it's to get as far away from these creeps as possible."

"We all dissociate," Claire said bitterly. "People wall off lots of things. It's not so rare. It's only a question of degree."

"Right," he said. "Like it could happen to you. You could be a multiple."

"You'd be surprised." Her voice was icy.

"Good old Dr. Baxter. Solid as a wall. A pillar of the analytic community. All of a sudden she dances in her leather bra."

"I'm not so solid."

"I know your weak points."

"You think you do, like you think that this is all so obvious, but it isn't really. You think you know it all, but you don't."

CHAPTER 16

O<small>N MONDAY MORNING</small>, Claire made another call to Mary, who had not responded to the calls she'd made on Friday and was still unavailable. "I gave her all your messages, Doctor," the secretary said. "She may have misplaced them. Things get a little crazy here when she's on trial. She's defending a very important man. Her picture was in the *Post*."

"Give her my sympathy," Claire said.

"But she looked beautiful . . ."

At the hospital that afternoon, Claire was greeted by Alan Maliver.

As soon as she showed him her opal ring, he fell into a trance. It was like an old movie in which the hypnotist snaps his fingers and the subject falls instantly asleep—but this was no movie. She told herself that if he was faking, he would have made it look more difficult.

She had been at the books all weekend. She felt reasonably

confident and got down to business quickly: "Please tell me your name."

"Alan . . ."

"And your age?"

"Twenty-five."

He was missing fifteen years. "Do you know where you are?"

"They say it's a hospital."

"Do you understand why you're here?"

"Because something's the matter with my mind."

"Do you know what's wrong with it?"

"I can't remember things." He sat there calmly, the perfect subject. His eyes were open. He seemed relaxed, responsive, willing to comply.

"I would like you to tell me where you lived before you came to this hospital."

He looked confused. "I don't know," he answered softly.

It made no sense. "Are you under hypnosis?"

"Yes."

"Is there a reason you can't tell me?"

"I don't know the answer," he said.

"You don't have to be afraid. I need to know about your life in order to help you."

"I'm not afraid."

"You used to tell me things. You told me about your sculpture and your loft . . ."

"He made it up and made me tell you."

"*What? Who* made you tell me?" she asked, trying to keep calm.

"The one who tells me what to say."

"Is someone else in there?"

His eyes closed for several seconds and then opened again. The voice that answered was one she had never heard. "You know perfectly well there is."

Her heart thumped wildly. "Are you Felix Kiehl?"

He was silent.

"Please tell me who you are."

"Which one are you addressing?"

Claire was stunned. No wonder people who worked with multiples used hypnosis. The door was open. There were others. She'd broken through! Her head was spinning and her heart was pounding, but the strongest feeling was one of pride. "I want to talk with the one who tells you what to do."

His eyes began to flutter, and his breathing became irregular. The calm expression faded, and lines of tension appeared where there were none before. "You're the broad with all the questions," he growled with the harsh voice she had heard the other day.

"Victor, is it you? Do you tell them what to do?"

"I tell them when I can—most of 'em."

"I'm glad to see you again. I assume you remember that my name is Dr. Baxter."

"You call me Victor and I call you 'Doctor'?"

"Would you prefer it if I called you Mr. Kiehl?"

"That's not my name."

"Well, mine *is* Dr. Baxter. If you tell me your last name, I'll be glad to use it."

He began to grin. "Not Claire Silver? You don't answer to that?"

"How much do you know about me?"

"Not as much as I'd like. I'd like to really know you. Like in the Bible."

"Did I understand correctly? Do you tell Alan what to say?"

"When I'm not drunk or stoned . . ."

"What about Felix Kiehl?"

"Never met the man."

"But you know things that Alan doesn't know?"

"You got that right."

"You know what got you into trouble?"

"*Which* trouble?"

She felt a chill, but she fought it off. "We can start with the trouble that got you here . . ."

"They claim I made illegal trades."

110

"And Alan had nothing to do with this?"

"Do you think he's capable?"

"And Arthur Moss—did he play a role?"

"All that one knows is how to get me laid."

"But you know them?"

"What little there is. They're not important." He looked around the room. "How about a cigarette?"

She found a pack of Marlboros in his dresser drawer, along with a disposable lighter. "Who did the planning?" she went on. "Was it you? Are you really a computer expert? Where did you learn it? Did Felix Kiehl know what was happening?"

He puffed his cigarette and shook his head and then his eyes closed suddenly.

In hindsight, it was obvious that she went much too far too fast.

"Is something wrong?"

Victor sat motionless and silent, his face unchanged, his eyes shut tight, his hands now resting on his thighs.

"What's happening? Where are you?" She felt more and more panic as she got no response. "Did I upset you? Where did you go? Are you still hypnotized?" The questions spun out uselessly until the smell of something burning brought her back—he was burning! His cigarette had slipped from between his fingers and rested on his thigh. A ribbon of smoke curled upward, and the room was filled with the ugly stink of melting polyester. She reached out for the lighted butt and saw a brown burn on his trouser leg and a line of ash.

"Victor—are you all right?"

Nothing.

"Are you there? What happened? Why did you let this happen?"

Still no response.

"Alan? Are you there? I want to talk with Alan."

At last, to her relief, his eyes began to flutter and his expression softened. He was Alan again. It was possible to bring him back. She asked if he wanted to forget or to remember what just happened. He mumbled the word "forget," and she told him that he would forget

_____

and that he'd wake relaxed and comfortable. She said his leg would heal and he would feel no pain. She told him he would be eager to be hypnotized again.

She told herself, later, that if he really were eager, it would prove he was insane.

CHAPTER 17

C LAIRE SKIPPED HER aerobics class and took a cab downtown to Mary Buchanan's Park Avenue office. She was puzzled and irritated that Mary was always so hard to reach, but relieved that at long last they had scheduled a meeting.

Claire stepped out of the elevator and walked down a hallway and into Mary's waiting room. The room was unusually dark, with small, dim pools of light that fell on alternating cushions of the black leather couches. It would not have been possible to read the newspaper or get a good look at someone seated across the room. It seemed like a cave, a place for creatures that only came out at night.

The receptionist was in bright light, walled off behind a pane of glass.

"I'm Dr. Claire Baxter. I think I'm expected."

"You most certainly are." She opened an inner door and led Claire down another hallway to a conference room. They heard muffled argument, which ended abruptly when the woman knocked. Mary Buchanan's two associates were seated at a teak table the size of a cabin cruiser. They rose together and shook Claire's hand in turn: a slender, bearded, prissy man named Wallace Hilson and a freckled, light-skinned black woman named Maya Jones.

"Mary had to leave," said Hilson apologetically. "She asked me to tell you she was very sorry. She had to catch a helicopter."

"Ah, what an exciting life you lawyers lead," Claire said, annoyed.

"Her client is in federal prison in Pennsylvania. He's there for life, supposedly, but he's got the money to pay for anything he needs." Hilson looked quite proud. "She had no choice about the visit. He's convinced that she can help him. This is a man who makes offers you don't refuse."

"*Can* she help him?"

He shrugged. "How do you respond when patients ask you that?"

"I tell them the truth," Claire said.

"And you *always* tell the truth."

"I didn't say that."

The receptionist brought coffee on a silver tray. They sat at one end of the huge table, and Claire wondered whether to go ahead and tell them where she was with Kiehl.

The woman named Maya Jones spoke first: "Wallace and I have been researching the requirements for the NGI defense. You probably know that the criteria vary quite a lot depending on the jurisdiction." She saw Claire's puzzled look and knew instantly what caused it: "*NGI*. Not guilty by reason of insanity. I assume Mary told you we would go that route."

"She didn't tell me *anything*. She doesn't bother to return my calls."

Glances passed between the lawyers and Hilson spoke. "Doctor, we've been on trial. This is our first free week in months. I can assure you, Mary cares very much about this case. It's a new departure for the office, and we're all excited by it. It would help if you briefed us on Mr. Kiehl's condition. I know she wants to hear. I assume you've been keeping careful records . . ." He tugged at his well-trimmed beard as Claire sat staring at him with her mouth open.

114

"Records?"

"When you get on the stand you'll be asked to document your conclusions."

"On the stand?"

"You'll have to do a little more than give your opinion."

"Should I make a video? Maybe we could show them that."

He missed the sarcasm. "I'd *love* one. The trouble is, if you did use tape, we might have to let them see it all. You know what happened to Richard Nixon . . ."

"I'm not Nixon," Claire said coldly. "And I'm not here to prove that anyone's insane. You had better talk to Mary. This job you're handing me is not the one I signed on for."

To her surprise, Claire's words had no effect. "Doctor, whether you like it or not, that's the job we all have. Our goal is to prove that Felix Kiehl is insane. It's his only hope. If it isn't what you're doing, what's the point of seeing him at all?"

"Mary and I had a clear agreement . . ."

"Which was?"

"That I function as a therapist. That I try to understand this man. I'm not here to gather evidence. We never even talked about an insanity defense."

Hilson studied her thoughtfully and then began again: "Doctor, I've done some reading on this subject—it's kind of a pet interest of mine. Therapy is an attempt to bring repressed material into awareness, isn't that correct? This is not really a change of anything. All we're asking is that you tell us, and the jury, what you find in Felix Kiehl's head—in particular, the stuff that proves he's off the wall. I don't have to tell you that this is in his interest. You do want to help him, don't you? We thought we were all together . . ."

Claire fought to control her fury. But Hilson was so wrong in so much of what he said that she couldn't let it pass. "Your description of therapy is fifty years out of date. Even if I accepted it, which I don't, it wouldn't justify my doing what you ask."

"Doctor, in therapy you try to understand what controls a person, which means you try to understand what happened in his life.

115

Isn't that correct?" Hilson plucked his beard and studied a hair between his fingers. "If it's unconscious, you make it conscious. Doesn't it all have to do with information? Doesn't the information you come up with tell you something about his state of mind—and therefore his criminal responsibility or lack thereof? Doctor, you can call it anything you want, but everything you do with him, every question you ask, every answer he gives, can help us prove that he's insane."

It was only the beginning. Hilson's questions came more and more rapidly. He ignored her answers. It was infuriating—until, finally, it dawned on Claire that their content was beside the point. He was trying to find out how she would handle herself in court. She was being tested. And whether or not she planned on appearing in court, she saw no choice but to take the bastard on: "Freud knew that generalities don't help. In decent treatment, you address what a person is able to address. It isn't information or some diagnostic label that matters anyway, it's always process . . ."

"I beg your pardon. It's always *what?*"

"What's important in treatment has very little to do with the facts of someone's life."

Hilson looked confused, which pleased her greatly, but it didn't slow his barrage of questions. "Doctor, doesn't everything in a person's unconscious reduce to certain facts? Even with dreams—don't you start with what Freud called the 'day residue'? Doesn't that refer to a specific event, something that really happened? Isn't it true that therapists who focus on fantasy are now in the minority?"

"The important question in treatment is what things mean to people."

He shook his head slowly. "That sounds profound, but what are you saying?"

"*Wallace* . . ." Maya Jones interrupted with a look of irritation. Claire noticed an intricate doodle on her yellow pad.

But the only effect on Hilson was to shift his questioning slightly: "Doctor, Mary was planning to show you this. We would like your thoughts about it." He passed a sheet of paper with a list of names. There was Alan Maliver and Arthur Moss followed by ten others with the same initials. "Can you tell us which of these you know?" There was no Victor, nor was there a Felix Kiehl.

"We really need this," Jones said.

"Just the first two," Claire replied.

Hilson went on: "Every one of these so-called people had a telephone account with a different broker. We have Merrill, Lynch; and Morgan, Stanley; and Kidder; and Salomon, and so on down the line."

"Maybe you should make another list . . ."

He grinned. "Each of these people had a different Social Security number and a different date of birth. They even claim, on questionnaires they filled out for their brokers—each of them in a different handwriting—to have different investment goals. The government claims that every one is an alias of our lost friend Felix. They say the accounts were run right out of his cubby hole at Potter, Weeks."

"I read about it," Claire said.

"What you didn't read, what they're too embarrassed to tell reporters, is that no one knows how he managed it."

"So how do they know it's illegal?" she asked.

"It's at issue, believe me. We thought for a while that we might go that route. Our experts say that sooner or later they'll work it out. It's in his computer—it was done by his programs, they know that much. They just have to decipher the damn thing. It's illegal to trade on inside information."

"How do they know that's what he did?"

"He never missed. They have computers of their own to track these things. He'd buy options for one of his accounts just a couple of minutes—sometimes a couple of *seconds*—before the stock shot up. The moves were perfect, unbelievable. He would look less crazy if he took some losses."

"Perfection is insane . . . or if not insane, illegal."

Hilson grinned again. "You could put it that way, unless the man has ESP—or his computer does. On the assumption that they don't, then he was trading on information he was not supposed to have."

117

"Most of the trades were done automatically," Jones added. "His computer talked to his broker's computer."

"Maybe the computer should go on trial."

"We proposed it, but they weren't buying . . ."

Claire looked down the list without really focusing. She wondered if it was a preview of who she would meet.

"You will notice that Felix Kiehl isn't on this list. He has no account—or none that anyone has been able to locate."

"I'd like to locate him myself," Claire said. She wondered why he had been so indifferent to the risk of getting caught. Was he grandiose? Self-destructive? "I can't tell you if he's insane. What I can say is that he has big problems. Most multiples were sexually abused . . ."

Hilson opened his eyes wide.

"Not the kind *you* have in mind," Claire said.

He blew her a kiss. "I wish my shrink had been so perceptive."

"You must have been a handful."

"Sweetheart, I'm still a handful. Didn't you notice?"

"You did extremely well," Jones said as she walked Claire to the elevator. "We all know that Wallace is impossible. He's a bulldog—it's what makes him so good at cross-examination."

"Actually, I kind of liked him," Claire said. "I felt a presence, an effort to communicate. At least there was someone in the room." She might have said more, but she could tell that her message got through. She was sure it would make it to Mary.

CHAPTER 18

ALAN MALIVER, WHATEVER his limitations, was sincere and un-complicated and happy to see her. There was no residue of trauma. He settled in his chair, a relaxed expression on his face, eager to go back into a trance. As soon as he did, Claire made a formal statement: "Mr. Maliver, Victor, Mr. Moss, Mr. Kiehl. You have shown me now that you are more than a single individual. But there is something very important that I still don't know. I believe I can best help you if the one in control introduces himself. If we want to understand, you'll have to be more open." She waited nervously, but there was no storm. He stayed calm as she went on: "I will do everything in my power not to cause any of you pain. But I know I can't prevent it. I expect you know that too. We may have to talk about some of the painful things you lived through . . ."

The silence that followed and the tiny twitches she saw around his eyes made it obvious that a change was under way.

And the voice was one she had never heard before: "Doctor, we're fully aware of your good intentions. If we did not already know of them, we would never have come this far. You are, however, making a basic error. What makes you think there is anything to understand?" The tone was conversational, the voice gentle and articulate and a little stuffy, and she knew instantly that it was someone new.

"I'm pleased to meet you. I assume you're Felix Kiehl."

But he smiled benevolently and shook his head. "They call me 'The Professor.'"

"Professor?"

"It was a name first given me by other children. We use it now among ourselves."

"You *remember?*" It was progress even if he wasn't Kiehl.

"A substantial amount. I have been excluded from some events. As you well know, our psychopathology leads to certain gaps . . ."

"Your *psychopathology?*"

"I have multiple personality," he said calmly. "I've known my diagnosis for many years."

"But you never sought help," she said.

"I seek it constantly. I am not always capable of the steps that would procure it."

She asked about the past.

"I remember the events," he answered calmly. "I recall when I first went to school and when my mother went to the hospital for a concussion, and when we had a year without any rain, and when we had a year of floods. I remember when I ran away."

"Do you know the reason?"

"That is the question, isn't it?"

He shut his eyes. She waited, but he stayed silent. After a little while he put his hands on his temples and held them there. "I have a headache."

"Like Arthur Moss," she said.

"Infinitely worse." The Professor's pain was evident in the tortured expression that soon spread across his face.

"It hurts a lot?"

"It feels like someone is jabbing an icepick in my eye . . ."

"I can make it better," she said. "Hypnosis can be used that way." She let her words sink in. "Close your eyes. Listen to me. The pain will leave as you listen to my voice. Soon it will be completely gone. You'll feel much better. You'll be able to talk without any pain at all."

She could see his expression change as her suggestions took effect.

She waited until he spoke again.

"I was a good student. My ability went way beyond my peers. I was beyond my teachers."

"In what subjects?"

"In every subject."

"And where did it lead you? Did you want to become a real professor?"

"It led me here," he said.

Seated in the cab during the ride uptown, Claire had the fantasy that "The Professor" was born in a concentration camp. He was much too young, but she knew that her fantasy had meaning. He had lived through horrors, that much was clear. Somewhere underneath the masks, the reason they all existed, were events too horrible to think about.

Victor was standing at the window and puffing on a cigarette the next time Claire arrived. The heavy odor of stale smoke told her he'd been dominant for hours.

"How goes it, Doc?" he asked.

"Fine. How does it go with you?"

"It doesn't, Doc. No one here to make it go." He grinned lewdly. "I'll have to settle for hypnosis."

"Is it what you want?" she asked.

"You got other options?"

She might have questioned the sexual innuendoes. She might have asked why he preferred hypnosis to an ordinary conversation.

121

She might have wondered if he was trying to avoid some other subject. She told herself—not for the first or for the last time—that this
was no ordinary treatment, not like anything she'd ever tried before.

She held her hand out. He looked at her ring and went under.
And then his face changed.

"I hope you're feeling better," she said. She knew it was The
Professor.

In quiet tones, he told her that he had been thinking about her.
He was grateful for the way she cured his headache. He wanted to tell
her everything he knew. He hoped that she might be the means by
which he could change. He said he had knowledge of Alan and Arthur and Victor. He said that he knew others who had not yet shown
themselves. Beyond those personalities, he said there were still *others*
—stranger ones—that he knew only dimly.

He had a special bond with Victor. "You wouldn't think so. He
doesn't want to be thought of in this way, but in fact he's rather a
sensitive person."

"I can't picture that . . ."

"But he takes care of me. He protected me from the children
who taunted me. He was born to keep them from doing any harm."

"Born? Who gave birth?"

He smiled at her. "No labor pains—just a kind of shift. One
minute you're in one place, a puzzled child, a shy boy with answers to
all the questions but the important ones. A minute later you can beat
up everyone in sight."

"Does Victor come when you ask for him?"

He shook his head. "It's in someone else's hands."

"Someone else?"

"I don't know everything."

"Could you mean Kiehl?"

"There are things that I don't know."

Then she recognized that something was troubling him. His
brows were knotted. He said his head hurt. It was a clear warning, and
she took it seriously. She said it was time for them to stop. She told

him to close his eyes and let himself relax. She told him that the headache would soon fade.

He woke as Alan, with no recollection of anything that they had talked about. Along with his memory, the headache was completely gone.

He was Victor the next time Claire arrived. She asked how his head felt.

"Nothing helps. All that money they pissed away on doctors was a waste."

A minute later, he was in a trance.

She knew the changes. He had become The Professor once again.

"I wondered how you felt . . ."

"I should keep you always. I could hold you close whenever I was in pain."

The phrase was meaningful, not at all his style. It was Oedipal again. The theme kept coming back with each of them. She decided not to comment. There was no point interfering with his fantasy. She wanted the transference to grow in all its glory.

Then he surprised her again: "I know all about psychogenic headaches. Every doctor I visited had a different theory. I include in that collection one Dr. Jacob Silver. His theory was of repression— repressed emotions; repressed tears; repressed rage . . ."

"You met my husband? You have a memory of that?"

"I observed him."

"That day, when he was in my office, were you conscious?"

"I apologize for what they did."

"Who did?"

He didn't answer.

"Why did you choose us?" she asked then.

There was no response.

"Where are you? What just happened?"

"I feel nothing."

"Did you go somewhere?"

"Not me. Only my feelings," he said calmly.

It still seemed safe to push. "Where are they?"

"There is a place where feelings go."

"They *go?*"

"They are contained."

"Do you mean inside someone? Another person?"

"You could put it that way."

"Is it someone I could meet?"

"She doesn't speak," he went on softly. "She mostly cries . . ."

The face of The Professor softened, and Claire saw yet another change. Huge tears began to trickle down his cheeks. She had never seen anyone cry so intensely without making a sound. Was this the one who didn't speak? Was he now a woman? Claire watched his face for several agonizing minutes before she spoke again: "You feel the pain for all of them."

He reached for Claire's hand, and she let him hold it. His grip was gentle. It was the first time in her career that she allowed herself —other than a brisk handshake at the start of an analysis and another at termination—to be touched by an adult patient. It seemed the right thing. She knew she had been cast in a maternal role. She knew his real mother had failed him. She thought he might feel emotions with her that would help to heal those wounds. It was far from classical analysis, very different from the way she practiced, but she remained confident that her approach made sense.

CHAPTER 19

"EVERY TIME I see him I meet someone new," Claire said. "Everyone I meet takes me deeper."

"Keep at it," Jake said. "Maybe you'll hit oil or shit or something."

"Will you get *serious!*" Claire said.

"Why?"

"Because I care about this."

It was a Wednesday afternoon, and they both had unexpected cancellations. There was snow in the air and ice on the road, but they were on their way to the tennis bubble on Randall's Island. The place was dirty and patrolled by vicious Dobermans. It shared the littered park beneath the Triborough Bridge with a crumbling athletic stadium and a half-empty mental hospital—the former inhabitants now wandered the streets—and some burnt-out buildings where firemen were trained. But the price was the lowest in the city, and they always had an open court.

They paid the fee and were sniffed by the terrifying dogs and walked through the frigid passageway onto their court. They piled their coats on a chair beside the net and unzipped their racket covers and opened a can of balls. Claire took the time to stretch.

"Have you met the famous Kiehl?" Jake asked.

"I've more or less stopped looking."

"It's that bad?"

"It's that good," she said. "You have no idea. I wish it would go as well with all my patients."

"Maybe you should hypnotize them."

"It's more than that. The hypnosis part is almost irrelevant. It's who he is. It's what he went through. He really interests me. He can be scary, but I like him."

"You don't want me to interpret this, do you?" Jake asked.

"Frankly, my dear, no."

The girl without a name was a ghost out of the nightmare past. She lived in hiding. She did have a voice, but she spoke so softly Claire could barely hear her. She said she was called "Maura," a secret name no man was ever allowed to know. She was more a child than a woman. And she was filled with questions.

"Do all men have those *things*?"

"I'm not sure what you mean," Claire said.

"Those things they poke with."

"Do you mean penises?"

"Do all men hurt children with them?"

"No. Did someone hurt you?"

There were hints, fragments, incidents that were never clear. She struggled to tell. It seemed as though there had been repeated rapes. And her father had been the rapist. Maura was helpless and fragile and incredibly naive. And she seemed completely real—a young girl whose body had been abused.

Claire had to remind herself throughout the session that seated in front of her was a man of forty.

·   ·   ·

Maura never came again.

In some ways, things got even stranger.

The next time Claire arrived, Alan Maliver greeted her. After she showed him her ring she asked for The Professor, but she got no response. She asked for Victor and then for Maura and then for anyone else who wanted to talk, but nothing changed. He was still Alan.

At first Claire worried that something was seriously wrong. Had she pushed too hard again? Was it meeting Maura? Was it the talk of rape? She wondered if hypnosis had begun to fail. Could it, like certain medications, lose effectiveness?

She sat with him in silence. It began to feel like someone else was in the room—some silent, ghostly presence that gave her chills. She didn't know him. He never showed himself. There were no words. He wasn't Alan but an alien creature that tried to imitate him. There was only a faint indication of his presence—a clammy breeze that blew across Claire's skin. When she asked his name he shook his head, which he did to each of her questions: "Are you Felix Kiehl? Are you Maura? Do you have a name that I don't know? Is there something I should do? Is there anything you want to tell me?"

Claire realized in the next session that there were others who never spoke—a silent audience of hidden selves who hovered nearby. Who were they? What were they? What did they want? Could she contact them? They gave her no names, described no experiences, showed no emotions. But they were always close—listening, waiting for something she didn't understand. She came to think of them as frightened creatures—wide-eyed little animals who watched from the edges of a forest clearing. It could have been a Disney movie . . . with a very dark twist.

When she left the hospital, Claire was too dazed to put notes on paper. She leaned back in the cab, her head still spinning, as they zipped up First Avenue and then across town through Central Park. She kept her eyes closed and made no response when the driver spoke. It was all she could do to prepare for her next patient, who was waiting in the street when the cab arrived. The patient, a social worker who'd been in treatment with an assortment of therapists for almost twenty years, stretched out on the couch and shared her fantasies of where Claire had been: a workout; her own analyst; a visit to her child in the hospital; a lover; a gay affair; a visit to a cosmetic surgeon. No matter how bizarre the fantasies became, they were never close to the reality of what Claire had experienced at Bellevue.

After Thanksgiving, Claire spent a long, exhausting day in Boston attending a conference on multiple personality, where she listened to presentations by an assortment of well-known experts. The concepts were familiar, but the clinical descriptions and discussions of hypnotic technique took on new significance. She waited behind to question the final speaker, Dr. David Karlin, a heavyset bald man with a confident manner and a national reputation.

"Doctor, I'd like your opinion on how important it is, in relating to various 'alters,' to establish a relationship with one that can be clearly identified as the 'core' personality. Have you ever been in a position where you couldn't find a 'core'?"

She saw his eyes flit to her identification badge and then her breasts. She knew instantly that she had made a mistake.

His smile was much too warm. "Doctor, I've seen patients with whom it took a year or more to find a core. I've worked with others where an apparent core changed five times before things stabilized."

"Is there a way to tell if the one you're dealing with is the correct one?"

"Doctor, don't be obsessional. There's no *correct* one." He moved in close and breathed on her. "Is this your first multiple?"

She said, self-consciously, that it was.

"You know, it's more or less like sex—after you've done it a couple times, you relax. They're all parts of one person. The major thing is to bring the trauma into the open so she can deal with it . . ."

"It's a he."

128

Karlin was surprised. Fewer than ten percent of multiples are men. "Same rules apply."

"There's pressure on me," Claire went on. "He's scheduled for a trial."

Karlin shook his head and frowned. "That's a different ball game. Once you get caught up in the legal system, everything changes. You get all kinds of manipulative garbage superimposed on issues that are hard enough to understand."

"I wonder constantly if he could be faking."

"Pretty hard for a guy to do . . ."

She ignored the way he touched her arm. She hadn't dealt with this kind of creep in years, and she felt a certain fascination with watching the wheels turn. His eyes darted quickly around the room before he spoke again. "Look, I'll tell you what. I have people I have to see right now, part of my appearance, sundry strokes for sundry egos. Why don't you meet me when I'm done? We could have a drink or even dinner. I'd be more than happy to give you a little supervision . . ."

"That's very kind." She looked at her watch. She wanted to say something really nasty. Jake would have had the words. "I have a flight to catch."

"I'll tell you what, Dr. Claire Baxter from New York: I'll look you up. I get to your city fairly often. If you're still treating this man without a core, we could talk about him. If you're not, there might be other things . . ."

"I don't think so." She would have liked to kick him in the groin, but she just walked away.

With or without a core, there were more signs of progress.

Victor announced that hypnosis was no longer necessary: "We talked it over. A decision was made. We don't need the mumbo jumbo anymore. All you have to do is *ask*. If the one you want can talk, and wants to talk, he'll come to the center of the stage."

"I'm very touched," she said.

"Just remember you have me to thank."

"Would you tell me what you mean by *stage?*"

"It's like I'm standing in front and there are others in the wings . . ."

"Is Felix Kiehl in the wings?"

"I can't answer that."

"Does that mean you don't know?"

"I think you should forget about him."

"Mr. Kiehl," Claire said, "if you can hear me, if you're in the wings, it really is time we met. Please introduce yourself."

She got, instead, The Professor.

He was glum and serious: "You need to keep in mind that there are risks. You must not forget that all progress is double-edged. We go forward and we go back . . ."

"I don't know what you mean."

"A day may come when some of us will not exist."

"You're afraid of *integration?*" She knew the theories. Some said that in order for him to get better, certain personalities would have to "fuse" into a single individual. She could understand how some of them might think of it as death.

"Wouldn't you fear it?" he asked.

She thought of Jake and her marriage, her own struggle against fusing into anything. "I just hope, if someone is afraid, that we can talk about it."

"We decided to tell you why we were arrested. We decided to let you meet the one who did the work."

"I take it you don't mean Felix Kiehl."

There was a pause, a cough, and then another change. This personality sounded adolescent, a pimple-faced compulsive masturbator who was still in high school. His voice was grating—an ugly bray with a raspy, irritating edge. When he laughed, which happened unpredictably, it was much too loud. His name was "The Nerd."

He was eager to tell Claire all about himself.

The trouble was, he was less a self than Alan Maliver, less a person than a machine.

He followed orders. All he did was work. He was talking to her because Victor told him to. He said Victor chose his name. He said Victor would beat him if he didn't do what he was told.

Claire wasn't dumb about computers, but she soon found The Nerd incomprehensible. He went on and on about RAMs and chips and operating systems and programming languages and memories that were hidden inside of other memories. He didn't notice when she tried to change the subject back to familiar territory. It never seemed to cross his mind that she couldn't follow. It didn't dawn on him that she had no interest in the details of what he'd accomplished.

The Nerd was waiting eagerly the next time Claire arrived. He made no mention of the fact that the Christmas holiday had come and gone. It was as if the world outside—and time itself—did not exist. He had never heard of Felix Kiehl or, with the exception of Victor, any of the others. Much of what he talked about remained incomprehensible—a lecture on the intricacies of assorted programming languages that she could not divert. He went from BASIC to Pascal to COBOL to Assembly to Machine to UNIX and to C.

It was obvious to Claire that The Nerd knew nothing about ordinary human interaction. It was as if he'd lived his entire life in a basement or a closet or a cage. He had no imagination and no initiative and appeared only to function as a tool. He lacked the ability to manipulate anything but a string of numbers. He had worked for endless hours, hunched over his keyboard and monitor, writing whatever programs Victor wanted him to write, unaware of the passage of time.

Despite all she learned, Claire still couldn't determine who was in control. It wasn't Victor. She did know that there was someone hidden behind the "stage," and he was playing with her, teasing her, seducing her into a place called deeper.

The patient was now the center of Claire's life. Everything that once engaged her was upstaged by their work. She was drunk on reading.

She careened haphazardly from dusty books on Anton Mesmer and Pierre Janet, on vital fluids and hypnoid states, to up-to-the-minute articles on the way hypnosis changed the chemistry and conductivity of the brain. The books and journals multiplied in teetering piles on every flat surface in her office and her home. She spent each night curled up with something new. She would have been the first to say that what she was doing was closer to an eating binge than a research project.

Something shifted in her work with other patients. It was satis-factory, technically correct, but it was no longer everything. Certain patients—especially the most disturbed—soon recognized that a change had taken place in Claire. She returned their phone calls as promptly as always, but without her old intensity. No one was ne-glected. No one was harmed. On the contrary, the shift brought cer-tain benefits. Some patients complained, but no one fell apart. Some actually grew up a little.

Claire was reading.

Jake came out of the steamy bathroom with a towel wrapped loosely around his waist. He had scrubbed his body and brushed his teeth and even tried a touch of the cologne she used to like. Claire looked tempting in her panties, her breasts exposed as she sprawled in bed. He thought it was an invitation, but the apartment just hap-pened to be too warm. She never glanced in his direction. Books were scattered everywhere, and it was obvious they were the only thing on her mind.

He slid in next to her and tossed the towel onto the floor. He touched her naked back and ran his hand up to her neck. She shiv-ered slightly but made no response. He tried to work his way around to the front, but her arm was in the way. She was writing quickly, making notes on a yellow pad.

"So what's so interesting?"

She finished before responding. "All of it."

He looked over her shoulder. On the bed in front of her was a new book on the sexual abuse of children.

"Any good ideas in there?"

"I don't find that funny."

"I don't either. I'm just getting a little desperate."

She put the book aside and looked in his eyes. "I'm just not into it."

"That part is obvious."

"It's not about you."

"I understand."

"Hey, I'll come around."

"I blame your friend Felix."

"I'm sure you're right."

"And?"

"It won't go on forever. I'll be done with him . . ."

"It sounds like an affair."

"I suppose it does." She leaned to kiss him, but he pulled away. "No guilt. No pity. I'll wait until you're in the mood."

She kissed his arm. "I promise I will be. It'll all catch up with me one day. I won't be able to get enough. I'll be too much for you."

"Seeing is believing."

CHAPTER 20

THEY WERE WORKING out on adjacent stationary bicycles in Mary's health club. It was six in the morning, the only time she had available. The secretary who called told Claire that it was this or nothing. A new trial was under way, and she was swamped again.

"So what do you do with all the money?" Claire asked.

"I have expensive habits."

"Don't tell me you went back into analysis . . ."

In response, seated on her bicycle and pumping away as if her life depended on it, Mary shook her head.

"If this is what your life is like," Claire went on, "maybe you ought to think about it."

"Doctor," Mary said, "I think your countertransference is showing."

The club was plush and well equipped and exclusively for women. The equipment was more elaborate than any Claire had seen, and instead of rock they played Mozart. Every woman working out was sleek and dedicated. If their efforts flagged, there were trainers with perfect smiles and perfect bodies who made the rounds. They even went after Claire. But she kept to a pace she could manage comfortably. She wasn't there for exercise. "He kept talking about this *virus*," she went on. "At first I thought he meant some new disease . . ."

"Maybe he does."

"It isn't a disease and it isn't new."

"That makes it harder."

"I knew vaguely about the things, but it took a while before it dawned on me that he was talking about a computer virus he had made himself."

"It's not some fantasy? Are you telling me that he's intact?"

"He's intact and not intact. The one who's called 'The Nerd' does everything the others ask. He writes programs. It doesn't matter how long it takes or how much effort is required. It's as if they have their own pet robot."

"I could go for one of those." Mary was sweating heavily. Despite Claire's presence, her workout was no compromise.

"They come at quite a price."

She smiled in Claire's direction. "All I need is another trial . . ."

"It's more than that. It's dissociation. It's splitting yourself in pieces. It's turning yourself into a machine."

Mary breathed deeply. "Who runs the machine?"

"That's still the question, isn't it?"

"You don't know?"

"No."

"Are you close to knowing?"

"Not really. I push when possible, but I don't get the answer. It's as if there is no Felix Kiehl. I spoke to someone who's seen a lot of multiples, and he said it could go on like this for quite a while."

"This Nerd—is *he* responsible? Could we make the case that Kiehl is not responsible?"

"You really want to ask me that?"

"Of course I do."

135

"What happened to *understanding?*" Claire asked.

"This is part of it."

She had been seduced. It was obvious to Claire that all Mary cared about were the grounds for an insanity plea. "Understanding" was a joke. The woman was much too busy with her parade of trials and triumphs to care about her client's inner world—she didn't even care about her own.

Mary slowed her pace. "If he's split into these different people, if they don't know what the other parts are doing, doesn't it mean that he can't appreciate the consequences of his acts? It still sounds like we could win on the M'Naghten Rule."

"You want to know what I really think?"

"Of course I do. That's the point of this."

"Aren't you split in fragments of your own? Do you know the consequences of your own acts? Are *you* responsible?"

Mary looked at her with surprise. "Are you playing devil's advocate?"

"As far as I'm concerned, all you *advocates* work for the devil." Claire pushed buttons on the panel of her cycle to increase the intensity of her workout.

"You're that pissed off?"

"You said I wouldn't have to deal with legal garbage. We had quite a talk, if you recall. Of course I learned, from my meeting with your staff, what your goals really are."

"Are you with us?"

Claire pedaled faster. It was the only answer she was prepared to give. Side by side, stroke by stroke, they pumped their stationary cycles. The flywheels hummed and the calories burned and the muscles firmed and the sweat dripped down onto the pristine carpet. They fought it out in a race that got them nowhere.

In the dressing room, after showers, Mary was uninhibited about showing her striking body. An attendant had brought a tray with coffee, which Claire sipped eagerly. She was already half-dressed as Mary stood naked in the center of the room, slow and languid in the way she dried herself with her towel. Her breasts were large and firm, those of a much younger woman, exceptional enough for Claire to wonder if they had been surgically enhanced. Maybe *that* was how she spent her money. What struck Claire most was what she saw when Mary turned—a small tattoo on her left buttock. It was a faded heart wrapped in a thorny rose, with initials Claire was not close enough to read. A sixties relic? A vestige of another life? It was the only thing about the woman that still appealed to her.

"So what does this virus do?" Mary asked. "I guess I need to know."

"I can only answer in generalities," Claire said. "He would have been happy to tell me the details, as much as I wanted, but most of it was way beyond me. I know he wrote a secret program when he worked for Potter, Weeks in California. He buried it somewhere inside their system. It didn't call attention to itself. It didn't do any damage. It just sat waiting until he needed it. There's some code he used to get it going. It had the capacity to read through all their records and find references to certain stocks. As far as I know, it's still buried there . . ."

"He did this *years* ago? In California?"

"That's what he told me. He said the computers are all linked, so it doesn't matter where he is. He said he can turn it on and off whenever he chooses."

"He had a long-term goal? You're sure of that?" The more she learned, the more unhappy Mary looked.

"I'm just telling you what he told me."

Another woman entered the room, and Mary began to dress.

Claire went on in a softer voice: "It didn't just deal with records. It reacted to current information—to *everything* that went through the mainframe. I have no idea how it did this, but I know it sent data to New York. I know it all got funneled into a computer of his own."

"You're sure? This is not some fantasy he made up? This is possible?"

The new arrival opened the locker next to Claire and changed into her stylish workout clothing. Claire said nothing more until the woman left the room.

Mary spoke again: "You really did get through to him. I may not like everything you found, but I can't tell you how impressed I am."

"So what'll that get me?" Claire asked coldly. She saw surprise in Mary's face as she went on: "Am I learning? Isn't that the way you think?"

Mary was dressed by then in a handsome silk suit. She put her hand on Claire's shoulder. "You're a good shrink, I know that. I really am impressed with you, but I have to tell you that you don't understand me at all."

CHAPTER 21

THE AIDE WHO greeted Claire at the entrance to the prison ward was much more talkative than he had ever been before. "We got action, Doc. Those folks all checkin' out your boy."

"*What* folks?"

"Those other doctors."

"*What* other doctors?"

"Don't know their names."

The aide walked beside her. "Your boy's going to be on the street real soon. Man's gotta do something with all that cash."

"You think he'll get a chance to spend it?"

"I got twenty dollars sayin' so . . ."

"You don't think he should be in a hospital—or jail?"

"Don't matter what should be. My money says he walks . . ."

She went directly to the nurses' station and read the chart and saw, in the record of his previously uneventful days, that Felix Kiehl had been visited yesterday by a Dr. Winston Palmer. There was a second note, made early that very morning, that he'd been seen by a

Dr. Maurice Kahn. She wrote both names on a piece of paper so she could look them up later.

When she saw her patient, Claire would have bet against the aide. He was flat on his back in bed, staring straight up at the ceiling. His face was blank, his body rigid. He didn't look capable of walking anywhere.

"Are you all right?"

He did not respond.

"I understand that you had visitors."

He looked at her and blinked.

"Was it very hard for you?"

He just kept blinking.

"Did they push you to talk?"

It was Alan who finally sat up. He dangled his feet off the edge of the bed, not touching the floor, and he kept looking at her blankly. It was obvious that he was more confused than he had been in months.

"We need to talk. Is there someone else around?" she asked.

He made no response.

"*Victor*, will you please come out and tell me what's going on?"

The blank expression didn't change.

"Do you remember who I am?"

"You're . . . Dr. Baxter . . ." Alan said haltingly.

"*Professor*, would you please come out and talk to me."

Alan flinched when Claire reached out to show him her ring. His eyes went from her face to her hand to her face again. "It's a nice ring," he finally said.

"I just heard, a few minutes ago, that you were seen by some new doctors."

He did not respond.

"I want you to understand—*all of you*—that I had nothing to do with this. I don't know these people; I didn't ask them to come. If I had known, I would have told you."

She waited, but he didn't say a word. There was no trance, and it occurred to her that there might not be another.

"I assume that they were brought in by the prosecution. Do you understand what I'm saying here?"

There was silence again, but finally he did speak. It was a whisper: "They weren't nice."

"What wasn't nice?"

"Everything."

"Can you say more? What did they do?" She tried to think. Was this still Alan?

"They hurt me. They hurt a lot."

"How?"

He looked at her accusingly. "They made me bleed. Where *were* you? Why didn't you help? Why did you sleep?"

Could this be real? Was he delusional? "Bleed? Did they take blood? I had no idea . . ."

"You should take care of me."

"I didn't know . . ."

"You should not drink."

"*What?* Drink what?"

"You should help the child. You should not let him bleed. You should not let him suffer."

It was like Alan Maliver's dream—a reenactment of something in his distant past. Whoever these people were, no matter how aggressive or incompetent, they couldn't have made him bleed.

"It must have been very upsetting when those doctors came. Will you tell me what they asked?"

His eyes stayed blank and he stared straight ahead. Claire showed him the ring again, but he didn't respond. She sat with him for the remainder of the time. He would not speak. He would not look at her. She noticed that his hands were fists.

CHAPTER 22

WHEN CLAIRE ENTERED the room, her patient was seated in the armchair beside an overflowing ashtray, staring at the door as if he had been waiting for her. He reached into his breast pocket, found a cigarette, then lit it as Claire watched.

She was relieved. She much preferred to deal with Victor. "You've had a busy week," she said with forced good cheer.

"What do you want?"

"Nothing different than before. To try to understand."

"That's finished," he said bluntly. "We're history."

"I'm not connected with those people. They were brought in by the prosecution."

"I know all about it. You're *my* doctor, right? You're on *my* side."

"That's true, I am."

"But it's not worth a damn," he said.

"Why not?"

"Because I'm bleeding." He looked at her with rage. "You can't help me. I used to think you could. I was that dumb, but you're not capable. I don't need help anyway."

She saw his fists clench tightly, and for the first time in all her visits, Claire was afraid. "You need all the help you can get, even help that isn't perfect."

"You're useless," he went on. "You make promises, but you don't keep them . . ."

"Are you sure that you mean me?"

"Who else?"

"I think the past is haunting you." It was a last resort, but she had to try: "*Listen* to yourself! Can *any* of you hear it? Face the truth. This pain is from the past."

His face turned red, then almost purple. The veins on his neck swelled. "You were there. You were happy! The bastard *fucked* me and you didn't do one thing! You're a useless drunk. They're all *fucking* me!!" he screamed.

The aide yanked the door wide open.

"It's all right." Claire's ears were ringing, but she stood her ground.

"Doc, are you sure? This man don't look good."

"I said it was all right."

The aide looked Victor in the eye and shook his head in warning and then closed the door.

"It's not all right," Victor warned.

"I spoke to your lawyers. I'm not neglecting you. I want you to be clear. There's nothing anyone can do. The prosecution has every right to bring in experts."

"You said you'd take care of me . . ."

"Bad things were done to you. You buried your feelings—you split them off—and now they're coming out. I want you to understand as clearly as possible that your reaction now is left over from the past."

Suddenly, Claire saw some kind of change. He looked younger and more fragile. His eyes were wild and darting; his voice was high-pitched, agonized. "He pushes so hard. It hurts." He looked at Claire. "Please . . . Ma . . . please . . . Mama . . ."

"Did you hear what you said?"

"Please . . . Mama. He hurts me bad, real bad. Wake up! Please wake up!" The patient grabbed Claire's arm and held tight with both hands.

She kept on talking. "It's not happening again. All that is in the past. This is your way of remembering the past . . ." She let him hold her, she thought it could help. She thought contact could make a difference. It was instinct.

Her patient relaxed—utterly exhausted, on the verge of collapse. His personality had changed again. "Despite everything you know, my dear, you still miss the essence . . ." The voice was that of The Professor.

She could only wait.

"He had a present for you."

"Who?"

"I'm sorry to say you don't deserve it."

His eyelids fluttered and his head dropped forward. He was either asleep or in a deep trance that had nothing to do with hypnosis. She had lost him. That much was obvious.

Mary Buchanan's secretary left a message on Claire's machine that a package was on the way by messenger. She asked Claire to call the office to confirm its arrival and then again as soon as possible after she read its contents. The secretary's tone was clipped, unfriendly. An hour later, in the middle of a session, the doorbell rang, and Claire had to leave her patient to answer it. When the patient left, she opened the manila envelope and found a Xerox copy of a collection of handwritten notes. It appeared to be a diary, most of it written in neat script, some paragraphs written in different styles. She didn't have time to read the notes, but she knew instantly who wrote them.

Later in the afternoon, Claire called Mary's office. The receptionist connected her to Maya Jones, who said that Kiehl had given the notes to Dr. Winston Palmer. According to the prosecution, Kiehl told the doctor that they were a gift. The notes then went from Palmer to the prosecution lawyers and finally to the defense. The law required that they share their evidence, and they were scrupulous.

Claire read the notes in the car that afternoon on the way out to the beach. After one time through in silence, she read them aloud to Jake, despite the fact that reading in a car always made her nauseous.

There were plenty of other reasons why she felt nauseous.

The short sections sounded like Victor and The Professor, but most of it was the work of someone new. It amounted to an autobiography, telling the story of the patient's past and confirming the insights she had so painstakingly acquired. It described an isolated life in the hills outside the town of Stirrup. It described a sadistic father. It described the failure of an alcoholic mother to protect her child. It confirmed Claire's belief that the patient's current crisis was a reenactment of the past. The author of the diary knew suffering and pain as facts of daily life. But he hadn't been destroyed. He wrote with pride. Somehow, he had risen above the nightmare of his life. The notes were clear and precise and completely rational. Their author was highly intelligent and fully aware of his intelligence. He identified himself as Felix Kiehl.

CHAPTER 23

FOR THE FIRST time in all her months of visiting the hospital, Claire was late. First she got tied up on the telephone, then she had trouble getting a cab, and then she got stuck in traffic. When she reached Kiehl's room, it was ten minutes past the time of their usual appointment. She knew better than to believe her own excuses. They might sound good, but the bottom line was a mix of terror and anger and failure. Her punishment had been the ride itself, where she was subjected to the ramblings of a West Indian driver who, knowing her destination, provided a discourse on the curative powers of herbs that grew on his native island.

When Claire finally arrived, she found Kiehl on his back in bed.

He was fully dressed, but the sheet was pulled up over him, covering his face like a shroud, and her first impression was that he was dead. It was just wishful thinking.

"Last two days like that," the aide said. "We prop him up for meals. He drinks a little, but he don't eat nothing. We pull the sheet off every hour but when we don't come around, he pulls it up again. Dr. Smythe is worried. He asked to see you later."

"Looks like you lose your bet," she said.

The aide shrugged. "Already paid on that one. Got another workin'."

"Which is?"

"We're trying to pick the time he eats."

"And if he doesn't eat?"

"Then we take the time they stick the tubes in him."

She stood beside Kiehl's bed and slowly pulled the sheet back to expose his face. His eyes were closed, and his skin was pale white. He really did look dead. "Are you awake?"

He made no response.

"Can you hear me? Is anyone there?"

Nothing.

"I know you feel hurt. I read a copy of what you wrote. I want to say, again, that I'm not who you think I am. I hoped you'd see that. I hoped the work we did together would count for something."

Still no response at all.

"Maybe you're not the only one who feels let down."

What Claire did next was half an insight and half a sadistic joke —her payback for what he had put her through and a clear act of countertransference. She knew it was inappropriate, but she did it anyway. She took his hand and lifted his arm twelve inches above his body. When she let go, the arm remained extended. She waited for several minutes and saw no change, no indication of fatigue, no tendency to move. It looked like something the textbooks called "waxy flexibility," a symptom of catatonia. She raised his other arm. With both outstretched he looked like a monster rising from a swamp.

"I'm not your mother. It isn't my fault that you were abused when you were young. I thought it might help if we talked about it. I really do want to help."

He still was silent.

She pushed his arms back down onto the bed. Now she felt the

147

urge to mold his body into some grotesque position. She was reminded of anatomy class in medical school and the bizarre jokes some people played with their cadavers—amputated penises poking in or out of dead vaginas.

Still not one word.

She could do anything she wanted except get through to him. It occurred to Claire that her fantasy was one of rape.

She walked aimlessly around the room as Kiehl lay motionless. Whatever they had done together—good work or not, a huge mistake or not—it was clearly over. It was obvious that she could never work with him again. Now she wanted a cigarette. She opened his dresser drawer. There wasn't much: gray underwear, socks, a few packs of Marlboros. She fished a cigarette out of an open pack. He owed her that much. She didn't see his lighter. Had they taken it away? She moved a stack of T-shirts. Beneath them, suddenly exposed, she saw a knife.

At first it hardly registered. *A knife?* Stainless steel, institutional, stolen from the cafeteria or the wagon that transported food, the kind that's too dull to cut a piece of steak—except that this one wasn't dull. She held it in her hand and touched its blade. The scratches down its length and its sharp, unnatural point made it clear that someone had worked long and hard to get it this way.

The thought crossed her mind: The Nerd.

She glanced across the room.

He was seated upright, looking at her intently. "Did you find what you were looking for?"

She held her hand against her side. "Are you awake? I wanted a cigarette. I hope you don't mind. Can you speak now?"

"Of course I can speak. But, Doctor, there are no cigarettes. You know that I don't smoke."

"Do you know what's happened?"

He lowered his feet to the floor and got off the bed. "I know you're late."

"It's more than that."

His eyes were focused on her hand. "I've been asleep . . . I got tired of waiting for you."

When he moved in her direction, she darted for the door and banged on it. The aide jumped, fiddled with his keys and pulled the door open. When he saw what she had in her hand, he put his fingers in his mouth and whistled loudly. Three more aides appeared. They surrounded Kiehl and pressed him facedown on the bed. He struggled briefly and then went limp. He spoke in a whisper: "Mother . . . don't you see what he's doing? I need you now. Why don't you help?"

Dr. Charles Smythe focused on the fact that the patient had slipped in and out of apparent catatonia. It was the most interesting development he had seen in years. What did Claire make of it? Had she ever heard of such a case? Did it have implications for her diagnosis of multiple personality? One thing was sure—it got him thinking. There were paradoxes that he found intriguing. Was it possible for one personality to have its own pathology that was separate from the others? Could there be a catatonic alter? Could others have other diagnosable disorders? Did Claire think it was possible that beneath the layers of dissociation there could be an underlying schizophrenic process? Didn't it raise all kinds of fascinating questions about the nature of the mind?

She was numb. "I have no idea."

"What should we put him on?" Smythe wondered. "Should we treat him for catatonia or for depression or for something else entirely? Can we medicate one of the personalities and not affect the others? Should we treat each personality in a different way entirely?"

Claire was still shaken. "I'm not the one to ask. I think, if you left it up to me, I'd put him on cyanide . . ."

PART III

Brian Pederson hit an arching lob that was meant to force his opponent to the back wall of the court. It was a decent shot, but it wasn't good enough. Anthony Middleton leaped to meet the ball and slammed it low and hard and unreturnable—another point for him.

"So what do I have to do to get out of here alive?"

Middleton grinned happily. "Say uncle."

"Uncle what?"

"Uncle Anthony . . ."

They were the two best racquetball players in the Beverly Hills branch of Potter, Weeks and among the best in all the branches in Southern California. They were also on their way to becoming friends, though it was evident to Brian that with Tony Middleton, the rising star of data processing, friendship would be a long, slow process.

The guy was strange. Uncommunicative. A recluse who suffered from constant headaches. Brian sent him to his wife, Dr. Sheila McGarty-Pederson, to get himself checked out, but she found nothing wrong. She knew enough psychiatry to know he needed another kind of help. For one thing,

Middleton was completely isolated. If Brian hadn't coaxed him from underneath his rock, he'd still be working out at the Y and going home to eat canned spaghetti and play with his computer.

"You're joining us for dinner," Brian said in the locker room. "I want you to know it's all arranged. Sheila would be insulted if you didn't show."

"If she wants me, then I'll come."

She was different from any doctor he ever visited before, and different from any woman he knew. He fell in love with Sheila on the day she examined him. There was something about her hands, about the way she touched his body, about the way she looked into his eyes. It was like she'd always known him.

Brian drove his Lamborghini to the house in Malibu, and Anthony followed in his Olds. He had bought the car six months ago, before Brian became his friend. Now it no longer seemed so grand.

Brian was showing him a whole new world.

The chicken was marinating and the wine was on ice and the Rolling Stones were blasting on the stereo as Dr. Sheila McGarty-Pederson swam laps in the pool. Her stroke was strong and steady, and her kick was powerful. At Brian's instigation, he and Anthony snuck up on her. She didn't notice them until Brian, still wearing his suit, jumped right in. She tried to swim away but he grabbed an ankle. She rolled onto her back and splashed water in his face as Anthony stood beside the pool and watched them struggle. It was more than a game. He knew it was no accident that she was naked.

Sheila got out of the pool and wrapped a towel loosely around herself. She stretched out on a lounge chair as Brian opened the wine. She lit a joint, inhaled deeply, inhaled a second time, then offered it to Anthony. Her nipples were exposed, wrinkled little flowers that he couldn't stop staring at. She grinned at him wickedly. "So now you know your doctor's little indulgence."

He refused the marijuana. "Is this another test?"

She reached across the space between them to pat his leg. "You already passed."

They ate on a patio that looked out over the ocean. The mist was gone, and there were no clouds to obscure the view of the huge orange sun *sinking into the sea. He had never seen anything like it: not the sunset; not the house; most especially, not Sheila. He knew he would never forget this day. But something felt wrong.*

Sheila looked at him and saw his discomfort. "Anthony, are you in pain?"

"You can tell?"

"When did it begin?"

"A little while ago."

"Not tonight, my dear," said Brian. "I have a headache."

Sheila put her hand on Anthony's brow, which felt cold. "You don't look right. Can I give you something?"

They went to her study, where she had a drawer full of samples from the drug companies. "No more alcohol. Take two of these—"

"—And call me in the morning," Brian said.

Anthony looked at him angrily. "Why do you talk that way?"

"What way?"

"She's trying to be nice. She wants to be kind to me. Do you have to be so mean?"

"Hey, I'm sorry . . . no offense . . ." Brian said, raising his eyebrows at Sheila. He figured it was the headache.

But the pills she gave Anthony were no help at all, and the pain got worse. He sprawled helplessly on the couch in her study. "Maybe you should call a cab," he said weakly.

Brian shook his head. "Not a chance. You have people here who care about you—even if you don't like my jokes. You have a place to stay and you have a doctor."

Later, from the couch they made up for him, Anthony could hear them making love. He tried to block it out and pretend it wasn't happening, but there was no escape. He heard their bed creak and felt the floor above him tremble. It made him sick. It made his head hurt worse. Were those sounds of pleasure? Could she feel pleasure with that man? How could she be so kind and loving and then betray him?

In the middle of the night, long after the noise upstairs had faded, the young man who called himself Anthony Middleton got off the couch and made his way through the silent house. His headache was gone and his mind was very clear. She had failed. He had given her the benefit of the doubt, but there was no longer any doubt. She had betrayed him. She was a coldhearted woman. It might have hurt him once, but he had no feelings now. He went down into the basement and found the shut-off switch for the alarms.

The orange sun had long since set. There was no moon. There was darkness everywhere, and the air from the ocean was cold. He took newspaper from the kitchen and squeezed the pages tightly into balls, setting each ball aflame with his lighter. He walked through the living room and dining room and scattered balls of fire. He rolled them underneath the couch, behind the draperies, against the walls. He spread his own bright stars across the sky, his own bright orange sun. He went out onto the patio for the plastic bottle of fluid Brian used to start the barbecue. He squirted a stream across the room and ran a flaming track straight up the stairs.

He stood in the driveway beside Brian's fancy car and looked up at the bedroom on the second floor. He could see flames flickering inside the house. He could see wisps of dense black smoke seep from tightly sealed windows. Then he saw the woman. She staggered across the bedroom and up against the window. She was blinded by the smoke, confused by lack of air. She was suffocating. In some recess of her mind she must have known. He watched as she tried to pull the window up. She couldn't work the latch. It never occurred to her to break the glass. She clawed at the drapes, and then he saw her fall.

He told himself it was what she deserved.

He went back into the house and switched on the alarms. He could feel the heat he had created down in the dark cool cellar. He could feel his power. They would not torture him again. She would not fail again. When he heard sirens in the distance, when the flickering inside the house burst through the roof into his brilliant golden star, he drove away.

CHAPTER 24

MARY AND HER assistants left the restaurant with full bellies and warm good-byes. The happy man who had been their host led them out into the freezing night with only his silk shirt on to keep him warm. His bodyguard draped a coat across his shoulders after he embraced them each in turn. A limousine was waiting, at their disposal, and they settled back for the ride uptown. "God, we stink of garlic," Hilson whispered. For the first time in five years together, he and Maya were actually on their way to Mary's apartment. The reason was obvious: It was their biggest victory since they had come—right out of law school—to work for her.

Mary's co-op was in a postwar building on Fifth Avenue in the Seventies. They rode the paneled elevator to her penthouse and then stepped directly into her starkly furnished living room. The U-shaped couch was buttery black leather; the walls were white; the only color in the room came from one small antique Persian rug and a purple Rothko on the wall that faced the couch. There was a view that, for

Maya and Wallace, outdid the art: floor-to-ceiling windows over-looked Central Park and the buildings to the west and south.

She led them onto a huge terrace that circled the apartment on all four sides. "When the weather's good I live out here," she said. Right then the wind was wicked. It tore at the burlap wrapped around her potted trees and made their eyes tear. It woke them from the lethargy that the heavy food and alcohol induced, but it fed their high.

Hilson stepped up on a wrought-iron bench and spread his arms. *"Look, Ma, I made it—the top of the world . . ."*

"After he says that he gets blown up," said Mary calmly.

"I'm not Cagney. This isn't a gas tank—"

"I'm glad to hear it."

"I think you're wonderful! I think your place is wonderful! I think the jury was wonderful! I even think our client was—well, I won't go *that* far." He moved to put an arm around her, but Mary stepped away.

They followed her back into the living room. She took a bottle out of the refrigerator, uncorked it carefully, and filled a glass for each of them. She poured a small amount of the greenish dessert wine, hardly more than a tiny mouthful, into her own glass.

"I can't deal with more alcohol," Maya said.

"This, you deal with," Mary said firmly. She led them to the couch. "This is our antidote. We drink our own good wine to counteract that swill we had to swallow."

They raised their glasses. As they sat sipping the sweet, delicious wine, Mary took a thick manila envelope out of her briefcase. "For the victors," she announced. The envelope was crammed with hundred-dollar bills. She counted out two fat piles and slid the cash across the coffee table. Each pile came to twenty thousand dollars. The money that remained, much more than she dispersed, went back into her briefcase. "Just be discreet about the way you spend this."

By the time they finished the first glass of wine, they had covered subjects that ranged from how much cocaine their client had actually brought into the country to whether the prosecution lawyers were as stupid as they seemed. Could they have been paid off? Were they scared of what might happen if they got too aggressive? Wallace and Maya were half drunk and half asleep, but the woman who employed them was far from ready to end the evening. Mary was wired—high on her win that afternoon and unable to end the day until she made progress on her next one. "So tell me—what are we supposed to do with our good doctor?"

"Good?" Hilson was still too drunk to censor anything.

"You don't think she's good?"

"I think 'good psychiatrist' is an oxymoron."

"You're going to see your share of them . . ."

"We deal with all kinds of sleazeballs," he replied. "Drug dealers . . . hookers . . . rapists. What's a shrink or two?" He patted the wad of bills that rested now in his breast pocket. "You don't hear me complaining, do you? We do what we have to do, and when it's done, we drink good wine and wash the taste away." He raised his glass. "I can see why you serve this stuff—it's wonderful."

"You make it sound like we give them blow jobs." She ignored his happy grin. "I'll be specific. I want to know if we have problems."

Hilson went on: "We have lots of problems. In my opinion, she was conned."

"You know better than the shrinks?"

"You really think he has this *illness*? You think it is an illness? You think the shrinks would call it one if they didn't make a living out of it?"

"I think *she* would. It's why I picked her. She has integrity."

Maya Jones had done her homework, and she relished her chance to show it: "According to the psychiatrists I interviewed, Dr. Baxter's approach was questionable in certain ways—but none of them said her diagnosis was wrong."

"It doesn't matter. No jury will believe this garbage," Hilson said. "They'll laugh the shrinks right out of there."

Jones went on: "Our real problem with Baxter is that she used hypnosis. All three of them questioned her expertise. She wasn't trained in it."

"What *are* these assholes trained for?" Hilson continued. "No one monitors the bastards. She could do a bypass if a hospital would let her."

Mary touched her wine with the tip of her tongue. "Was it malpractice?"

Jones shook her head. "It just wouldn't take too much to portray her as naive."

"She *is* naive," Hilson said.

Mary ignored him. "This whole thing cuts two ways. The jury knows that they'll go after her. They know that we'll attack the prosecutor's people. They expect all that. The thing I'm betting on is her sincerity. She comes across as honest. I think, even if she has made some mistakes, that if she's handled right a jury will believe her."

"Fifty-fifty—a battle of the so-called experts. We show them ours and they show us theirs, and the bigger one wins . . ."

"If we depend on you, I guess we lose."

Mary's jibe didn't faze him. "The problem is, *we're* the ones who have to prove insanity. The law requires clear and convincing evidence."

To Mary's surprise, Jones agreed with him: "It *is* their experts versus ours, and we *do* need more than what we have. Kiehl made an awful lot of money. We'd have problems with this case if we got Sigmund Freud to testify. I'm beginning to think we might do better if we tried to make a deal."

The look on Mary's face was chilling, and Maya Jones knew instantly that she had made a bad mistake. "My friend, you disappoint me. I don't work that way, and my reputation depends on my not working that way, and I think by now you ought to know it. I need strength from you, not weakness. So what if our experts suck? It won't be the first time or the last. Does that mean we just lie down? Do we give up all the things this case can do for us—the money we would control, the incredible publicity, the chance to get visibility in a brand-new area? Did you like the little bonus you got tonight? Do you want more of them? Find me a way to get clear, convincing evidence. Don't give me this bullshit about making deals."

Tears came to Maya's eyes, but she managed to blink them back. They wouldn't help with Mary. If anything, they would sink her in a deeper hole.

When they were in the elevator, away from Mary, Hilson wrapped his arm around Maya and kissed her forehead. "She really is a bitch," he said. "She knows how much you want to please her, but she couldn't let you go home happy. The woman's goal in life is to poison everything."

CHAPTER 25

People who went to parties at the Institute for Classical Psychoanalysis fell into three broad categories: the ambitious, who came with the hope of getting an inside track on the latest political developments; the lonely, who came with the wish for simple companionship; and the pathetic, who couldn't fill their open hours and came—smiling, their hands outstretched—with the hope that someone would think them talented or charming or just convenient, and refer a patient.

Claire had come to hear a tribute to John Kliner. He had recently retired and was about to leave for Arizona. He wasn't brilliant or profound, but more important, he had been kind and she still felt affection for him. Now he hugged her warmly, something he would have never ventured if he were still in practice. She had brought Jake along, to introduce them finally, but he was off debating with some old buddy from his residency. He had no idea how much she needed him. She knew exactly what was coming as Max made his approach, a large Scotch in one hand, not his first, a large cigar in the other. There was nothing left to do but face him on her own.

"Ach," he said. "Dr. Baxter, just the lady I've been looking for. I was hoping you might deign . . ."

"Hi, Max. How are you?"

"Would it be possible . . . is there a moment you might set aside for a weary colleague?" As he spoke he steered her, cigar as cattle prod, toward the least-populated corner.

"I see you've had a few."

"Do you think so?"

"I'm sure it's obvious to everyone."

"My dear, I am utterly indifferent to the way that anyone in this room perceives me." He made a sweeping motion of his arm and splashed Scotch across the carpet. Stray spots appeared on the jacket of a man with his back to them.

She took his arm. "We'd better sit."

"I've made my mark," he went on. "My articles are classics. My hours are booked. My house and my apartment and my cars are paid for. I own a cemetery plot . . ."

She led him to a couch that two men vacated when they saw them coming. He sat down heavily, spilling more of his drink, and she took the place beside him. "Max, what's going on with you?"

"Why don't you guess?" he growled. "Let's consider it a test of your analytic talent."

She shook her head. "I've been *working*. For God's sake, I've had to do all kinds of research. So you haven't seen me for a while. Grow up . . ."

"I've been abandoned. The bond is torn asunder."

"Max, please," she said between her teeth. "Get a grip. Jake's here."

"Your own true love," he went on. "Or is there someone new?"

"You're out of control. You're going to hurt us both. I swear I won't forgive you."

Whether it was Claire's warning or whether the alcohol had finally overwhelmed him, Max stopped talking. He sat in silence, his mouth opening and closing rhythmically. "I need to go home," he said suddenly. "Before I get sick. I'm sick already. My dear, please help me."

She found their coats and told Jake where she was going. When she returned to him, Max was standing, swaying, listening vacantly to a story an animated colleague was telling him about a power struggle at a local hospital.

She handed Max his coat, which he draped around his shoulders. It made him look more drunk. "You'll have to excuse us," he said to the other man. "This charming lady's been pursuing me for months. Tonight, to her good fortune, I have room in bed."

He made a clumsy effort to help Claire with her own coat, but she managed without him. By then, the other man understood the situation. He walked beside them to the outer door and held it open as Max put an arm around her. "Good luck with him," the man said, winking.

Unexpectedly, it was bitter cold outside, a frigid slap in both their faces. The early rain had stopped, and the temperature had fallen twenty degrees in the hour they'd been indoors. The puddles had turned to glistening ice, and Max clung to her as she guided him around them. He seemed much older than John Kliner.

Max lived in a building on Fifth Avenue only a few blocks from the Institute. The doorman took Max's other arm and helped them to the elevator. Claire took his keys, opened his door, and then held his coat while he ran off in the direction of the toilet. She waited for over ten minutes, first in the hallway that doubled as a waiting room, then in his living room and kitchen. The place was filthy. There was dirty clothing draped over the furniture. Half-eaten cartons of Chinese food, beer cans, and empty whiskey bottles lay everywhere, creating a sour smell despite the fact that the kitchen window was open wide and a freezing wind was gusting into the room. It was obvious that Max was in real trouble.

"Better." His face and hair were dripping wet. He stood before her in a gray T-shirt, but at least his color had come back.

"Are you sure?"

"A little projection," he said. "Melanie Klein would be proud. It worked the way she says. The poison was inside, and it made me sick, so I took the paranoid position. Vomiting is indeed the best defense."

"That isn't even true in infancy," Claire said.

"I am an infant."

"You've made that clear."

She pushed the window halfway shut and put the teapot on and started dumping the most disgusting things into a plastic bag. "I don't like the look of this." She found a usable mug and a jar of instant coffee. "I'm not talking about your decorating style."

"I told you once I was a closet alcoholic."

"This place is a toilet, not a closet."

He made an expression of helplessness.

"I had *work* to do. I explained it. And you *didn't* tell me—I never pictured you like this." She piled dirty plates into the sink and dumped containers of rotted food to make space at the table.

"I didn't expect to fall apart. It just crept up on me."

Claire poured and stirred his coffee. She felt sad for Max, concerned about him, but the strongest feeling was that she had to leave.

She patted his shoulder and he reached for her hand, unaware at first that she was going. His hands were freezing. "Get the place cleaned up," she said. "If your cleaning lady abandoned you, then call a service. I won't come back if you don't get it done."

"You're a hard woman . . ."

"Not anywhere as hard as I would like to be."

He didn't have the strength to see her to the door.

Jake was still caught up in conversation, but he ended it when Claire returned.

"He's a wreck," she said. "You wouldn't believe what his apartment looks like. How could a patient go there?"

"They don't," Jake said. "You haven't heard? He's got a few students who come for supervision, but I have it on good authority that he's really lost it. At least he stopped seeing patients. There are any number of people in this museum who've been dead and stuffed for years. It doesn't stop *them* from practicing—they even claim to have the best technique."

She was speechless.

"Surprised? Where have you been? There was even a rumor that he had Alzheimer's . . ."

"You know exactly where I've been," she said.

"Thank God you're done with Felix Kiehl," Jake replied. "You're back in the world. Maybe you'll even come back to me." He put his arm around her and squeezed her shoulder, and the pleasure that she felt was a nice surprise.

"Take me home," Claire whispered. "Make love to me. It's been too long. It feels like it's been a million years."

CHAPTER 26

DURING THE PERIOD in which Claire was consumed with Felix Kiehl, Jake took solace—or tried to take it—in a new poker game and a tennis league. He found himself over his head in both. Maybe in lesser company he would have been better off, but he wasn't interested in lesser company, and in the company he'd chosen he kept getting beaten. He went one for five in the league, stuck hopelessly at the bottom of the pile, his one win coming on a night his opponent had the flu. At the poker table it was even worse.

Jake and John Spicer stood together on a shabby street in SoHo, outside the loft where the new game was held—three thousand square feet of Italian marble and pickled oak. The painter who once lived and struggled there had moved to a garage in Jersey, and the mortgage broker who renovated it only used it midweek—when he wasn't in Southampton or skiing in Vail. The men played on an antique poker table with chips made of ivory, and the remarks about dead elephants didn't trouble the owner at all. They smoked Cuban cigars, and when they weren't studying their cards, they could rest their eyes on paintings by Haring and Miró. Jake would have been better off just looking at the paintings.

It was five in the morning and snow was falling heavily and there were no cabs. Jake had lost eight hundred and twenty dollars while John Spicer had won at least two thousand.

"You think we should take the subway?" Jake asked.

"You *crazy*, man? I got all this cash. It's fuckin' dangerous down there."

"Even for prosecutors?"

"*Especially* for prosecutors!"

A minute later came another sign that Spicer was truly blessed. A gypsy cab responded to his wave, and they hustled in for the ride uptown. As they settled back in the overheated car, they smelled the scent of marijuana. The seat was shredded and the transmission clunked, but the man behind the wheel drove skillfully around the cars and trucks in trouble with the snow. The radio was loud, but the jazz was perfect.

"Tough night," Spicer said.

"You *could* say that."

"You don't fold enough."

"I keep telling myself . . ."

"Telling ain't good enough, my man. You can't go chasing dreams."

"I make a living at it," Jake said.

Spicer slowly shook his head. "Not poker dreams. You won't make any living that way."

The driver turned to look at them. Like most people, he had trouble reconciling Spicer's speech with his conservative attire.

Spicer lit a cigarette and cranked the window open. "Listen, there's something I got to talk to you about."

"Isn't the rule not to give up secrets?"

"This ain't poker."

For a moment, Jake thought it was something personal.

"That dude you worked with, the famous Felix Kiehl . . ."

"The brilliant financier."

"You could call the fucker that."

"I could call him all kinds of things."

Spicer dragged deeply. He was the only person Jake knew who still smoked cigarettes. "I won't complicate your head with the bullshit leading up to this: Assorted fuckin' agencies all scuffling for power; numbers being pulled by the FBI; two states looking to nail the bastard on a murder rap; some dude in the SEC looking to make a name. It gets pretty fucking Byzantine. Suffice it to say that as of two days ago, the case got dumped into my lap."

Jake reached for his hand. It had to be a major plum. "No kidding! Congratulations! You're really on a roll."

"I *told* you, let's not be dreamers here. The truth is, I got it by default. The dude who was supposedly in charge—his wife having just run off with her personal trainer—couldn't keep his act together. So the head man comes up with the brilliant theory that a humble nigger would look real good against a Wall Street rip-off artist."

"It does make sense."

"It's racist bullshit. On top of that, it's stupid. Juries aren't that dumb."

"I think you could win," Jake said. "From what my wife—"

Spicer stopped him quickly. "I'm not *asking*. I don't want to know about her or fucking Mary Buchanan. This is just you and me, my man—I want to keep it that way." He dragged on his cigarette as flecks of snow blew into the car. It was really coming down.

"Hey, brother," the driver said, "would you close that thing?"

Spicer flipped his cigarette away, then shut the window. They skidded side to side as they made their way up Broadway. The music of Charlie Parker filled the car. "This ain't exactly subtle. She's pleading him NGI. We know she's lining up consultants. She's got access to the fucker's money—enough to buy all the hired guns she needs. The way this thing is going down, it's obvious you shrinks hold all the cards."

"It's about time," Jake said. "I was beginning to think that lawyers ruled the world."

"My man, I *told* you to stop dreaming. Holding cards don't mean you rule this world."

"If you hold the right ones . . ."

"You still don't get it, do you? The most you win is one fucking hand."

Jake's misery had been compounded by his being dealt four aces during a hand of draw. He had played them cautiously, but somehow everyone got wind and folded, and he'd made next to nothing on the hand.

"Look, man, this isn't poker," Spicer went on. "Poker isn't life. I have something serious to put to you."

Jake kept his mouth shut.

"I need your help. I never had to deal with psychiatric garbage—I always stayed away from it before. I used to specialize in tax law. Now I'm up to my neck in shrinks. It's a joke, my worst fucking nightmare—I need a shrink to help me figure out what the other shrinks are doing."

"I assume you don't mean terminology," Jake said cautiously.

"I read some books. The theories aren't exactly complicated. What I don't know is the way it works in practice. I need to know if a shrink who has his head screwed on, who wasn't getting paid to say it, could really call this mother insane. I need to know where to push the fuckers when I get them on the stand. There are big stakes here—huge."

"For your career?"

"In addition. I don't have to tell you what went down out west. If he gets off on NGI, it's gonna be damn tough—even if they get a solid case together—for someone to prosecute on that."

Jake thought about it as the car went up Eighth Avenue. They passed Forty-second Street. The sordid strip looked pretty in the snow. "I don't get it. You sound like you need better shrinks."

"My predecessor got a list from someone who's supposed to know. On paper they are the best." He lit another cigarette and opened the window again. They were stopped at a light, and a hooker stood on the curb in a miniskirt as the flakes fell heavily on her bare shoulders. She peered into the car, but Spicer quickly cranked the window closed. "No offense, but I don't trust these shrinks. The first one makes some kind of sense, and then the next one says the opposite, and he makes sense too."

"Sounds like psychiatry all right." Jake fought his urge to grub a cigarette.

"Everyone has an axe to grind. I don't know what to believe."

"I have the same experience myself sometimes."

"I keep feeling like I'm *missing* something," Spicer went on. "Like I don't know enough, like I need someone who can tell me what's underneath the bullshit."

"That's what a decent shrink is supposed to do—look underneath the bullshit. You know," Jake went on, "shrinks do have different theories. Sometimes they all work and sometimes they all fail. The work we do is not exactly science . . ."

Spicer faced him. "If you're not too sick of Kiehl, if you still have interest in the case, I would ask you to consult with us. We've got some money, though nothing near what they have."

Jake was stunned. He didn't care about their budget—he would have paid to work with Spicer. But there was, regrettably, another problem: "Wouldn't it be weird to have my wife and me on different sides? Doesn't it represent a conflict of some kind?"

Spicer shook his head. "If there is a conflict, it's not a legal one. I wouldn't put you on the stand. I'm not asking you to go against your lady. I'm not asking you to talk about the case with her—I would prefer it if you didn't, frankly. The question is, would it be too weird for you?"

"I can tell you I'm tempted. But I'll have to talk with her. The question is whether the marriage could survive."

"I'm not looking to put you in any kind of trouble."

"Don't worry about that part. We do it on our own . . ."

The cab skidded to a stop in front of Jake's apartment building. The sky had brightened, but the snow was coming down even more heavily than before. He reached for his wallet, but Spicer waved him off.

The cab moved uptown into the storm. Jake stood in the street and looked around. The dawn was windless, completely calm, so quiet that if he listened hard he could hear the new flakes settle. The city was white and clean and still. There were no plows, no pedestrians, no one out early with a restless dog. He felt full of hope. He felt like the first skier off the lift as the sun came up after a night of powder.

Instead of going to the apartment, Jake went to his office. There was no point getting into bed and waking Claire. There was also no point trying to sleep—he was due to work in a couple of hours, and he had things to think about. If he got lucky, some patients would cancel and he'd have time to take a nap after he calmed down. Right then, his mind was racing. This was just what he had been praying for —a chance, at last, to get out of his analytic cage and out into the world.

CHAPTER 27

"YOU DO WHAT you have to do," Claire said coldly. "You're a big boy. Make your own decision."

"That's all you have to say?"

"I knew a long time ago that you were jealous."

"I told you what I felt . . ." He had fought fatigue all day, and now, seated across the living room from her, it was really getting to him. His eyes kept closing, and he had to force them open and drive the yawns away. His work had gone decently, but there was one more crisis to solve.

"Would it make a difference if I did say more?" she asked.

"Of course it would."

"And then I'd suffer for it."

He shook his weary head. "You're being paranoid. I don't understand what's upsetting you so much. I won't interfere. I mean it. I accept the fact that you have priority. If you don't want me involved, just say so and I'll stay away."

"Why should you give up anything?" she asked. "I don't own the man—God forbid! Priority is not the issue. He was once your patient, just as much as mine. This isn't a mining claim. You have the right to do whatever you please."

"I told you what I please."

"John Spicer's your buddy, isn't he? You have this *bonding* thing. Why should I get in the way?"

Jake knew from long experience that the best thing he could do when Claire felt invaded was make sure everything stayed as clear as possible. "You have the right, as my wife, as the woman I love, to tell me what you need. If you feel it's intrusive, I'll back off. I have no desire to screw it up for you."

To his surprise, she suddenly began to cry. "It's screwed up as it is. Don't you *know* that? It's been screwed up for God knows how long . . ."

He crossed the room and pulled her close.

"I look like an idiot. I'm a sitting duck. My patient writes this story of his life and never tells me anything about it! I'm supposed to be treating him! I claim to understand him! I'm supposed to testify in court as an *expert*. Can you imagine what they'll do to me? To use your favorite word, it's just pathetic." She was still crying hard, but she didn't pull away.

"You accomplished something that few people could ever have accomplished," he said gently. "You got through the facade. You met parts of him that have been buried for thirty years. You never claimed that he was cured. He would have given that stuff to you if he didn't get freaked by those other interviews."

"Bullshit," she said bitterly. "Don't pretend you believe that garbage. I made it up to protect myself."

Jake sat on the couch, still holding her, not sure what he really did believe. "If I work for Spicer, it would probably protect you," he said. "I don't mean from cross-examination—I assume you'll take your lumps like any other witness. But there's no way he'd be vicious."

Claire looked sadly into Jake's eyes. He thought the tears might stop, but instead they flowed more freely. They trickled down her cheeks and formed large splotches on her blouse. "I don't know what to think, I really don't. I don't know who to trust, and that includes him and you and me . . ."

"Am I being thick? This is not a disaster. I still have no idea why you're so upset. I don't have to do it. If you don't want me to, just say so and I won't."

She had to turn away. "If you knew the truth, you'd never help me."

"What are you saying? What truth?"

She took a breath. It wasn't enough. She took the deepest breath she could. "There's something you should know." With her face pale white and a look of terror in her eyes, Claire faced Jake again: "You're going to be upset, you're going to think it's crazy and awful and sick and disgusting, but I have to tell you, finally, about me and Max."

He stared at her. He withdrew his arm from around her shoulder. *"Max?"*

"We were involved. We had an affair."

"Max?"

"I said it was crazy."

"How long?"

"Too long."

He shook his head in disbelief. "I can't picture it."

"You don't have to."

"Don't tell me he's well hung."

"Don't be an idiot."

"You could do better."

She shook her head. "It wasn't about sex. There was something I felt with him, some kind of warmth, some kind of safety."

"Oh God, not Oedipus," Jake said.

"I tried to analyze it. We worked real hard. It didn't change."

"It's been that long . . ."

"I tried to keep it separate. I tried to stop it from hurting us."

"That's a crock. We know life doesn't work like that."

"I don't know what I know."

"I know this sucks." He got off the couch and paced the room. "It really sucks."

173

Claire looked frightened. "I can't let you help me. I would understand if you want to leave."

"Are you saying you want me to?"

"No."

"You're sure of that?"

"I really am." She was sure in a way she never had been before.

"Is it over now?"

"Yes."

He faced her finally. She appealed to him as much as ever—maybe more so. "I should have known."

"How can you say that? I was incredibly discreet. How could you have known?"

"There were signs . . ."

Most of Jake's anger stayed fixed on Max. He said that Max had taken advantage of her, exploited a transference. He said that Max was as bad as any therapist who has sex with his patient. What Jake didn't say, but what he finally understood, was why Claire had never been ready to have a child.

"I don't want to go anywhere," Jake said, after the conversation had trailed on into the early-morning hours. "I want to see what things are like when it's just the two of us."

CHAPTER 28

INSTEAD OF ATTENDING the Tuesday morning conference at the Institute, Jake stood on a long slow line for tokens and the chance to push his way into a crowded subway car. The wheels of justice were beginning to turn. He was on his way to John Spicer's office and filled with a feeling of intense excitement. He'd escaped his cage. He could stay in the real world until after lunch and experience its joys and horrors and especially its action.

He arrived at the Federal Courthouse twenty minutes early. He wandered through marble halls where small clumps of men whispered softly outside the padded doors to courtrooms. They huddled close together, their eyes darting in all directions; the entire atmosphere was charged with tension and anticipation. At ten-twenty-five, he took the elevator to the seventh floor, where he found Spicer's office, a small, cramped room strewn with legal books and papers and filled with the smell of stale tobacco and strong coffee. It didn't matter that the space was unimpressive—the atmosphere, including the signed photograph of Justice Thurgood Marshall, was better than Jake had expected.

"So the little woman got in line," said Spicer as he poured coffee into a heavy mug.

"I wouldn't exactly put it that way. The little woman has mixed feelings."

"Don't they always." Spicer rolled his eyes. "My man, I got some things to teach you . . ."

"I thought I was here to teach *you* things." Jake took a sip from his mug and felt the rush of caffeine instantly. "You could get busted for this stuff."

"It gets me going. I got in late last night."

"Is there ever a night when you don't play cards?"

"In order to *what?*"

The question shocked Jake. "I don't know . . . make love . . . go to a movie . . . see a ball game . . ."

Spicer smiled cheerfully as he shook his head in response to every option.

There was a knock on the door, and a young man in his late twenties stepped into the room. Spicer introduced Peter Millar, the first of his two assistants, who precisely fit Jake's image of a prosecutor: He was trim, clean-shaven, with close-cropped blond hair and a drab blue suit. He would have bet that Millar's law school was Fordham or St. John's, but he was wrong—it was Yale. "We're ready to begin. Shuster just arrived. We put him in the library."

"Let's do it then. We pay this asshole by the hour . . ."

"Wait a minute—you pay *me* by the hour," Jake said.

Spicer wrapped an arm around him. "Don't sweat it, my man. This sucker's a leftover. You're *my* asshole."

They carried their mugs across the hall to a tiny conference room and library. Filled to the ceiling with shelves of legal books, with a dirty window that opened on an air shaft, it was the kind of place that sends the message that the people who use it are serious and capable and underpaid. In the center of the room was an oak table, scarred with cigarette burns and the ancient rings of countless coffee cups. Two men were waiting. The older one—grubby and obese—held a cardboard cup of tea. Two thickly buttered bagels sat in front of him on the bare wood. Beside the bagels were two packs of un-filtered cigarettes.

"I'm glad you made yourself at home," said Spicer, "but you didn't have to bring that piss. We're hospitable here; I'd have given you a cup."

"I heard all about your coffee. The last thing I need is one more hole in my gut, or any more palpitations."

"I imagine the cigarettes do that anyway," Jake said.

The fat man looked him over. "I take it this is the famous doc-tor?"

"I'm not famous, yet," Jake said.

"You never will be, if the best you can do is tell people to give up smoking."

Spicer took the chair at the head of the table and motioned Jake to the empty one at his right. Then he made the introductions: The fat man, who had bushy eyebrows and a thick gray beard, was Dr. Ira Shuster, formerly of Columbia University, a sociologist who had been forced out of academia and now made his living as a free-lance consultant in the field of jury selection. He wore jeans and a stained denim work shirt, and he had crumbs in his beard. The younger man, seated behind a neat pile of carefully labeled folders, was Spicer's second assistant, Avi Roth, who was in his mid-twenties and wore a yarmulke. Roth smiled constantly—with anxiety. He wore thick glasses and had tiny, dead-white, useless-looking hands. In another era, he would doubtless have been a rabbi.

Spicer spoke with a sardonic grin. "As you can see, my man, money is no object in this case. The decision was made, at the highest level of the office, to *nail* this fucker. Felix Kiehl goes to *prison*, hard time, no country club, no hospital where they let him out in six months. We're the first jurisdiction with a crack at the bastard, and the one thing we *don't* do is fuck it up. You understand? They're still collecting evidence out west. We don't know what he's up against after we get our shot. Under no circumstances whatsoever can we live with NGI."

"What if he's really crazy?" Jake asked.

"We don't have to deal with that," said Spicer flatly, "because even if he is, even if he's a fucking fruitcake, it don't make the bastard *legally* insane."

"The law is on our side," Roth explained. "There have been important changes in the last few years. The burden of proof is all on them."

"When the system is under fire," Ira Shuster said, "the artillery is brought to bear." His voice was deep and self-assured, as if he was lecturing a classroom full of eager students.

"What you talking about? What system? Where the fuck you at?" Spicer's dialect was more exaggerated than Jake had ever heard it.

"The system that pays you."

"It don't pay you?"

Shuster lit a cigarette. His brand was one that was favored by the gay men in Jake's practice. "As you know, my consultations are usually on the side of the defendant . . ."

Spicer waited silently.

"But I've been itching for a chance to nail one of these creeps."

"Which creeps?"

"Milken . . . Boesky," Shuster replied. "The Wall Street parasites."

Spicer shook his head. "Let's take the man for what he is—it's bad enough."

Shuster studied him. "Did he really kill those people?"

"They can't prove it—yet. My bet is that he did, but they may never prove it."

"This is not a ploy to set him up?"

"For *what?*" Spicer was irritated. "If that's the way you think, you won't be any use to us."

Shuster dragged deeply on his cigarette and sipped his tea. First he swallowed, then he exhaled. "Maybe I went too far. I just want you to be clear about my politics. I know you don't expect to hear this kind of thinking within these hallowed precincts of the state." They could have been back in college, stuck in a course on Marxist politics. In some peculiar way, he reminded Jake of Max.

"That isn't thinking, it's sentiment," said Avi Roth. His tone was harsh and his look surprisingly combative. "We don't hear it because the sixties ended twenty-five years ago."

Spicer shook his head as if to get rid of cobwebs. "Everyone's got some fuckin' axe to grind. The Soviet Union packs it in, and this man's still touting the revolution. Where do you live, in a fucking time warp? This case has nothing to do with politics."

"My goal is to address what jurors care about," Shuster said stiffly.

"I don't need this crap. I don't care if Kiehl's a capitalist pig—so is everyone else in this greedy country, including you, including any jury."

Shuster's tone was solemn. He was beginning to wilt. "Maybe it's time to tell me what you do need."

"Let me be real direct. I need a jury that won't be conned by shrinks. If you can find me people who can see through psychiatric horseshit, who won't be in awe of these medical assholes, who won't turn into Jell-O when they hear some sad tale of how the bastard got his butt kicked by his nasty father, then you're my man. If you can't do that—if there's some bullshit revolution you'd rather lead—then we should end this now."

There was a long pause as Shuster studied his cigarette. Insulted or not, it was obvious that he wasn't going anywhere. "I get the message. There's research I'd like to read. I'll do it on my own time. I won't bill you for it."

"Psychiatric *horseshit*?" Jake asked after the meeting ended.

"I don't mean you," Spicer replied.

"How can I be sure?"

"You can't."

Ira Shuster called out from behind them, "You take your fucking chances, just like the rest of us."

179

CHAPTER 29

Assorted arcane motions were filed and in their turn rebutted. Two more psychiatrists conducted interviews with Kiehl. There were no surprises. The investigations in California and Nevada proceeded inconclusively. The strategy of both sides now converged: The sooner they got Felix Kiehl to court, the better.

At five minutes before eleven on the first Monday morning in March, the lawyers assembled in the polished conference room adjacent to the chambers of Judge Marion Parrish: Spicer, Roth, Millar; Buchanan, Jones, Hilson. They had convened for a hearing on Felix Kiehl's competency for trial. It was supposed to be informal—a ritual, the outcome preordained. Spicer had brought Jake along with strict instructions to keep his mouth shut—no matter what.

"At long last," Mary said. She held Jake's hand with her cool fingers and looked into his eyes. "I'm so glad to meet you. My only regret is that it has to be in the present circumstances."

"You mean we can't keep meeting like this?" he asked. She really was a knockout. If anything, Claire had understated it.

Mary pouted. "Is there some other way? Could I still get you?"

"Depends on what you want me for . . ."

She paused just long enough. "Advice. Insight. What else?"

He had to grin. "We could talk about anything you want—except, of course, this case."

To Jake's surprise, Spicer had lost all sense of play. "Mary, you're well aware that Dr. Silver is our consultant. What you're doing is not appropriate. Do you have to come on to everyone?"

"I won't steal him, John. You don't have to worry." She turned back to Jake. "You should be careful with this man. He plays games. I don't mean cards." It was obvious that they had a history. Spicer might have warned him.

The door opened at eleven o'clock exactly, and Judge Marion Parrish stepped into the room. A young woman walked behind him carrying a sheaf of papers. A man followed her with a portable steno-type machine. The lawyers began to rise, but Judge Parrish motioned that it wasn't necessary. Instead of a robe, he wore a beautifully tailored suit. Instead of a briefcase, he carried a canvas bag out of which protruded the well-worn handles of three squash rackets. He was tall and evenly tanned, with an athletic body and a thick head of dyed brown hair. He had pale blue eyes and chiseled features. His face was deeply lined, the only sign that he was close to seventy. Except for the distracted air that suggested he would rather be on the squash court (he was fifth in the world in the over sixty-fives), Judge Marion Parrish looked the essence of a perfect judge.

"I see we've got the troops today," he said in a deep and mellow voice. He placed his bag beside the door and took his seat at the head of the table. "I'm glad to see it. I would like this matter settled as expeditiously as possible. I want you folks to know that I've got some serious summer plans."

Spicer had explained to Jake that a defendant's competence was decided before he got to trial. Most of the time it was self-evident, but in insanity trials it became more complicated. The question was whether the defendant was rational enough to know what was happening and to assist in his own defense—to know at least that he was going through a trial and not a religious ritual or a Hollywood audition. This was separate from the larger question of insanity, which would be argued later in front of a jury. It was entirely possible for someone to be competent for trial and still legally insane.

Judge Parrish took his Rolex off his wrist and placed it beside a pile of papers. He turned to Mary. "My understanding is that you folks agree. Young lady, is that correct?"

Maya spoke: "Your Honor, the defense is eager to begin . . ."

"Please give us a summary of your man's condition."

"We wouldn't call it wonderful, Your Honor. He's still a sick man, but he's improved considerably. We feel, and our doctors feel, that he's ready. He knows where he is, and what he's done, and why he's going to trial."

Judge Parrish wrote slowly on the page in front of him. Without looking at Spicer, he spoke. "I assume our prosecutor is also eager?"

There was a pause. The judge kept writing. After a little while, he looked up.

"We have some problems, Judge." Spicer's voice was soft, but the effect of his words was powerful.

Judge Parrish looked confused. "Mr. Spicer, these documents indicate that you had the man extensively evaluated by four doctors of your own choosing, and that you intend to oppose a defense of NGI. They further state that you regard his hospitalization to be unnecessary. I have here your old petition requesting that he be removed from the hospital and placed in jail . . ."

"Your Honor, as you recall, we've had some changes in our office. Our position as stated in those documents has gone through a reevaluation. Our view now is that the issues of competence and insanity are unique in this case, and need to be regarded as inextricable. Mr. Kiehl's lawyers assert that key parts of his personality are simply not present, not conscious, and that this will be the basis for their claim under M'Naghten. If this is so, we believe it raises basic questions about the man's ability to understand and participate in *any* legal process. We think it may be necessary to keep Mr. Kiehl in a hospital and refrain from trial until there is evidence that he has actually been cured."

"What? *Cured!*" The look on Mary's face was of amazement. "That's ridiculous! Where do you come off? There's no basis . . ." She stopped in midsentence, took a single deep breath, and became instantly composed: "Your Honor, the prosecution has already committed itself to going ahead. Now they see that their case is weak, and they're trying to delay. The way I read this, their goal is to keep our client incarcerated so as to put us under pressure to make a deal."

Spicer looked cheerful. "Your Honor, according to these documents, Ms. Buchanan believes that Bellevue is helping him . . ."

"We did *not* say that. We said his condition was improved."

Spicer went on calmly, not looking at Mary. It was evident that Judge Parrish was willing to let them fight it out. "Your Honor, Ms. Buchanan knows as well as I do that competency is a *variable* state. The issue can be raised at any time. There are thousands of cases in which it was raised in the middle of a trial . . ."

"Mr. Spicer," Judge Parrish interrupted. "Frankly, I expect delays from defense attorneys. I always believed that prosecutors prefer to prosecute."

"We do, Your Honor . . . I do . . . I would." Spicer sounded utterly sincere. "Let me take a moment to spell this out: When I prosecute a case, I expect the defendant to be both physically and mentally present in the courtroom. I know you expect the same thing, Your Honor—it's the reason we have a competency evaluation in the first place. But given what the defense states in these documents, it's entirely possible that the defendant—who committed these crimes as Felix Kiehl, who was arrested and indicted as Felix Kiehl—will not be conscious during the trial of Felix Kiehl. They claim he has an illness that makes him shift between different personalities. According to their documents, the condition is so severe that he qualifies as insane under the M'Naghten Rule. But if that's true, how can we try him? We have no guarantee that the rational part of him will be present at the trial. If Kiehl isn't present, how can he assist in his own defense? We therefore have no choice but to consider him incompetent . . ."

Mary was visibly seething as Spicer rolled on smoothly: "If we can't try Felix Kiehl, who can we try? If Felix Kiehl is not conscious,

183

who will be? If we convict a personality who is not Felix Kiehl, which personality goes to prison? Because of these serious complications, I respectfully submit that a trial is impossible at the present time. The defendant should be declared incompetent and confined to a psychiatric hospital; and he should remain in a hospital until we can be assured that the personality known as Felix Kiehl will himself appear."

Spicer's words just sat there. Judge Parrish peered at one attorney and then the other. Now he looked every bit his age. "I don't understand. There isn't any doubt about the man's *identity* . . ."

Spicer continued more slowly. "Not his physical identity. But there is considerable doubt about which portion of his mind will be in court. Your Honor, the claim of insanity is based on the assertion that the criminal acts occurred during a dissociated state of awareness in which Felix Kiehl was not in rational control. All I'm saying is that if such a state exists, it behooves us to ask what certainty we have that it will *not* exist throughout the trial. If he isn't conscious during his trial, what kind of trial would that be?"

"Ah," Judge Parrish said, his brows deeply furrowed, "I think I see . . ."

Mary shook her head vigorously. "I want to state for the record that my client is entirely capable of assisting in his defense. I've been dealing with this man on a regular basis, and I think I'm a better judge of his state of mind than a manipulative prosecutor . . ." She took another deep breath and then continued: "Your Honor, this is sophistry. Mr. Spicer is creating a false and misleading paradox. Felix Kiehl has a psychiatric disease known as *multiple personality disorder*. The essence of the condition is that his consciousness is fragmented. During periods when one personality is dissociated, another personality takes control. But they're not really separate. All of them are parts of a single person. We're trying a single person."

"Which personality are you talking about? Can you name the one that will be present? Do you even know their names?" Spicer suppressed a grin.

"It doesn't matter—he's one person." Mary spoke directly to

Judge Parrish. "I've reviewed the data, all of it, including all the re-ports submitted by all the psychiatrists, and I assert again that my client is competent for trial."

"Can you guarantee that Felix Kiehl himself, not some alter ego named Alan or Arthur or Victor or God-knows-who-else, will be pres-ent at this trial?"

"I don't control his mind. No one does. I can't say what part will be there. What I can say, no matter who appears, is that the man is competent . . ."

"He was dissociated when he did these things, but he's not disso-ciated now?" Spicer smiled openly.

Judge Parrish sat helplessly. It was a hint—and not a promising one—of how he would function when the trial itself began. Maybe he looked the part of judge, but no one was there to read him his lines.

Mary's voice was tight and her expression grim. "Your Honor, I believe these recommendations of the prosecution would create a sub-stantial hardship for my client. If Mr. Spicer persists in his ridiculous opposition to a trial, I will submit motions to have all charges va-cated."

"It won't be necessary," Judge Parrish said. The sudden decisive-ness surprised them all. "I've made up my mind. Mr. Spicer, *you* may be willing to dismiss the doctors, but I am not. We have depositions from six eminent physicians, both prosecution and defense. That hap-pens to be good enough for me. If you think it's warranted—and if you have evidence to support it—you have the right to make your claim again at any point during the trial."

Spicer made one last stab: "Your Honor, my job is to prosecute Felix Kiehl, not some fragment of his personality . . ."

"He *will* be present," Mary said for the judge's benefit. "Felix Kiehl. In the flesh. It doesn't matter what he calls himself, he'll still be Felix Kiehl."

No one knew what game John Spicer had been playing, but they felt he had won. "If you put it that way, we're prepared to go ahead. My only stipulation is that I need time for additional research. I can be ready two months from today."

185

Mary shook her head. "One month."

"Six weeks," Judge Parrish said. If there had been a gavel he would have pounded it. Instead, he left the room without another word, his bag slung over his shoulder, his assistant trailing frantically. Everyone else stayed seated.

"What the fuck was *that* about?" Mary asked. "If you need a delay, why not just ask for one like a normal person?"

All Spicer did was grin. It reminded Jake of a book he once read on poker strategy. The author bragged about the way he faked psychosis to intimidate opponents. By the end of the book, it didn't seem like faking.

Mary shoved her papers into her briefcase and headed for the door. "We need another competency hearing," she said as her assistants followed. "We have a turkey for a judge and a lunatic prosecutor."

Spicer just kept grinning. He turned to Jake when Mary was gone. "Next time she won't come on so confident."

"Next time, she'll bring a machine gun," Jake said.

CHAPTER 30

THEIR APPOINTMENT WAS for eleven in the morning and she was early, but as of eleven-thirty Claire was still waiting in Mary Buchanan's outer office. By now, she was thinking of just walking out—and in the process, walking out of the whole sorry enterprise. Then the door opened and Mary finally appeared. She stood locked in a protracted handshake with an elderly man who seemed unable to let her go. He gazed mournfully into her eyes while he pumped her hand with both his own. Eventually, with a gesture meant to get rid of him as much as to give him comfort, Mary pulled him up against herself and hugged him quickly and whispered in a voice that Claire could hear: "Stop worrying. Just leave it in our hands. You know how bad this is for your blood pressure." Looking over his shoulder, directly at Claire, she rolled her eyes.

"Disgusting," Mary said when they were in her office. "You wouldn't believe the kind of trouble a man of seventy-five can get himself into." She sat next to Claire on the couch and poured coffee from a carafe on a low marble table. "I'm really sorry. I couldn't get the bastard *out*."

"You do a lot of work for these sleazy gentlemen . . ."

"This one's no gentleman." Mary wrinkled her nose as if a bad smell lingered. "It's so good to *see* you. It's been too long."

"Not my doing," Claire said coldly. "There was a time when I had other hopes."

Mary spread her hands. "Here I am."

"We have forty-five minutes. I have to be back uptown at a quarter of one."

"You're annoyed."

"I have a patient in the middle of a major crisis."

Mary pressed a button on her telephone and asked Maya Jones to join them. She turned back to Claire. "Wallace is in California—a couple of interviews."

"Is there something new?"

"Not exactly . . ."

"What about inexactly?"

Jones entered the room and greeted Claire warmly.

"I need to know," Claire went on. "I'll look like an idiot if they ask about California. I look bad enough already."

"It won't come up. They're not allowed to bring it up. I think it's better that we not discuss it."

"Kiehl killed those people, didn't he?" Claire said. "Are there more bodies? Is that why you've been avoiding me?"

"No more bodies."

"Just the ones already dead . . ."

"Whether anyone can prove a thing is a different story."

"I didn't ask you that. I never imagined this . . ." Claire went on.

"Then don't imagine," said Mary firmly. "Do what you're paid to do and let it be enough."

"It's not so simple. You should have seen my house. You're asking me to block out something that I know, to forget that someone *kills*."

"You may be wrong. There's room for doubt. And furthermore, it has nothing to do with what we're doing here. I can tell you honestly that I have no idea if Kiehl will ever be indicted for any other crime. What I know for sure—the same as you—is that he's got major psychiatric problems. Whatever he did or didn't do, the simple truth is that he's not responsible."

"We're all responsible," Claire said flatly.

"What are we now? Philosophers? What kind of dream world do you live in?"

There was silence until Maya opened her folder and spoke to Claire: "I was going to bring you up to date on my meetings with the other doctors . . ."

"You might as well."

"You know the names. They're both big guns. We had him interviewed by Dr. David Karlin and Dr. Peter Brim. Karlin remembered you from a conference in Boston and sent regards. They're both prepared to testify that your diagnosis is correct and that Kiehl's condition is severe enough to qualify him as insane under M'Naghten . . ."

"Isn't that good enough?" Claire asked. "Maybe you don't need me after all."

Another silence filled the room. In a voice that was drained of all emotion, Mary finally spoke: "You don't really want to help us, do you? You're not really on our side." She turned to Maya. "I need to be alone with the doctor now."

Maya closed her folder and left the room without looking back at Claire. Mary leaned close. "I didn't think that things would go this way. I honestly had no idea . . ."

"You sucked me in. At least admit it. You never gave a damn about what I had to offer. You don't really care about understanding. You don't care about treatment. Everything they said about the way I would be used turns out to be true."

"Everything *who* said? Do you mean John Spicer?"

"Of course not. Why would I believe a lawyer? I don't have boxes in my head the way you people do. I don't keep everything in separate *categories*. I never want to live that way."

"You already live that way," said Mary calmly. "You want us to stop pretending? Okay, let's stop. You're not so pure. I know a thing or two. You have your own little categories . . ."

Now Claire was silent.

"We ran a check. Standard procedure, except the people I use are not so standard."

Claire was on her feet. She looked for things to gather up, but she had none. "My husband knows everything."

"A modern marriage," Mary said, but she looked surprised.

Claire started for the door.

"Dr. Baxter, before you leave, I want you to know it's much too late to think of backing out." Claire stopped and turned. "I want this very clear. You understand our client better than anyone, and he needs you to convey that understanding to a jury. You've been paid, quite handsomely. I promise to keep life simple for you. Describe the work you did and what you observed. Explain your diagnosis and your belief that he is not criminally responsible. You'll be finished with us then. You won't be embarrassed or in any way discomfited. If you force me to subpoena you and treat you as a hostile witness, it won't be nearly as simple. It will be very unpleasant, and it might have unhappy consequences." Mary finally stood. "Very unhappy."

"What are you?" Claire asked, with unconcealed disgust.

"You're the shrink—figure it out yourself."

"I heard all kinds of horror stories. I didn't believe them."

"And now you have your own."

"It makes you happy?"

"I would have preferred it otherwise, but I can live with it." Mary glanced at her watch. "We do have to stop now, Doctor. Your time is up. This session is at an end."

"Do you hate psychiatrists?" The question came to Claire without warning. "Is that the story? I take it the story of your wonderful analysis was all a crock."

"I told you what I needed," Mary said. "Not what I got."

"And it left you bitter?"

"I might have told you more. I felt, when we first met, that you could understand."

"Is that supposed to give me hope?"

"I don't believe in hope."

"Outside of money, do you believe in anything?"

"I'll tell you this—I believe that a young woman, attractive, bright, naive, with serious problems, with a nightmare at home and nowhere else to turn, could be manipulated by a psychiatrist and used by him for anything he chose . . ."

Claire stood staring at her. "You were sexually exploited by your therapist?"

"Yes . . . for years."

"I think that is horrible."

"That makes the two of us."

"And now you want revenge? On the entire profession? That's outrageous. Aren't you smart enough to know better?"

Mary's eyes narrowed. "What do you think, Doctor? Would analysis help me work it out?"

191

CHAPTER 31

THE MESSAGE ON Jake's answering machine came from John Spicer. "Doctor, get your pink and puffy ass in gear! We're on our way! Your chance for fame and fortune has at last arrived. We are about to pick a jury."

On the day the voir dire began, he met Spicer's team for lunch at a packed restaurant in Chinatown, a few blocks from Federal Court. All five of them sat wedged around a tiny table: Spicer, Roth, Millar across the wet Formica, and Ira Shuster, wearing a suit and tie, reeking of tobacco, even fatter than Jake remembered, jammed tightly up against him. They had left the courtroom just ten minutes ago, and Spicer, high on what was happening, began to fill Jake in: "This is federal. The voir dire is conducted by Judge Parrish. The lawyers don't get a chance to say too much."

"Sounds great already," Jake said cheerfully.

Shuster slapped his back.

Peter Millar shook his head. "You won't say that once you've listened to Parrish. The man is from Neptune or Pluto . . ."

But Spicer looked blissful. "We challenge the ones our fat friend thinks will go against us—for cause if we can manage it, peremptory if not. This jury will be good! Even sleepy old Judge Parrish is lookin' good to me."

"You're in big trouble," Roth said.

"I still disagree about the young one," Shuster said to Spicer. "I thought at first we saw it similarly . . ."

"We did, and then we didn't."

"You're supposed to be cool and rational."

"I am."

"She's the wrong age. She's the wrong ethnicity. She's got the wrong job. She might even get turned on by him."

"She's attracted to me," Spicer said.

"You're off the wall. She grew up on Staten Island."

"I saw it in her eyes."

Shuster grinned as he shook his head. "This man is on drugs."

"Not for this case. There's no need. This is a winner if ever I dreamed of one."

"You told me not to dream," Jake said.

Though they never ordered, they were interrupted by platters of steaming, delicious-looking food. It was the kind of restaurant where you took what they dished out and were grateful for it. They shoveled the stuff onto their plates and ate as they kept up the banter. Avi Roth took only rice.

"These ladies won't be conned," Spicer went on. "Not either of them. Have confidence. We can show them everything about the dude . . ."

"Assuming they listen," Shuster added.

"Of course they'll listen. They told the judge that they have open minds." He winked at Jake.

"You think you'll have the black one on your side?"

"Let me tell you somethin'," Spicer explained to Shuster. "That lady is their big mistake. She ain't as kind as she looks. She's hard as nails. She don't forgive. She ain't on any side but the side of righteousness. I know the type. My mother's one, and I was married to another. The lady may grin like Aunt Jemima, but if she puts pancakes on your plate, you damn well better eat 'em, and if you do wrong, you're damn well gonna pay the price."

"*You* were married to an Aunt Jemima?" Jake asked.

"That was another life . . ."

"And Mary Buchanan? Are you gonna tell us why *she* hates you?"

"I gave her cause."

"We need to know," Jake went on. "I need to know so I can give you good advice."

"She made mistakes today, that's what you need to know. She lacked the balls to dump an old black lady."

"She's got the balls," Roth said. "She has a collection in her bedroom."

"She ain't got mine," said Spicer. "She tried her damnedest, but the lady ain't got mine."

It was college again, a collection of undergraduates. They were roommates, fraternity brothers, high on events instead of beer. He knew it was infantile, but Jake loved every minute.

It was Peter Millar who changed the mood: "You know, there's one thing I can't get out of my head. I could be wrong, I don't know the woman, but if I had to say one thing about Mary Buchanan, I'd say she doesn't care. She's supposed to be so good. She wins cases no one else will touch. She's supposed to be a scrapper. But I didn't see one sign of it. She was weak at the competency hearing and even worse today. She looked like someone going through the motions. It's as if she knows her case is lost. She was like an automaton."

"She also fucked that way," said Spicer.

They looked him over carefully. Jake couldn't believe it—Spicer in bed with Mary Buchanan?

"She's a lawyer—what can you expect?" said Shuster. He spooned huge prawns—the largest Jake had ever seen—onto his plate. "The only things that get them going are money and power."

It finally dawned on Jake that if he didn't quickly grab his share of food, he'd be shortchanged. He reached for a platter as he spoke to Shuster: "I think you're wrong. Lawyers know how to fuck. I've treated plenty. They can really get into it. The only thing is that it has to be up someone's ass."

PART IV

Dr. Sanford Schwartz seemed old and tired and in poor health. His hands shook, he had black circles under his eyes, and he needed a haircut. His bedraggled appearance might have bothered some new patients, but after an endless string of useless doctors, Victor knew that fancy suits and fancy diplomas were no guarantee of anything. Victor got the doctor's name from a man at work who said that Schwartz had cured a friend who lived all his life with agonizing headaches. Victor knew better than to hope, but when the pains came on, he had to grab whatever was at hand . . .

The examination was more old-fashioned than any he had experienced. Dr. Schwartz smelled of cigars and Scotch, but he was thorough. He poked and prodded and pinched and tapped. His tools were pins and little rubber hammers and his own thick fingers. He pressed a tuning fork against assorted parts of Victor's anatomy. Schwartz told him to close his eyes and place his index finger on his nose, his ear, his chin, his other elbow. He tickled him with a moth-eaten feather. He put small objects into his hands and asked their names. He said the names of other objects and asked Victor to find them in a picture.

According to the doctor, the news was good: "Mr. Moss, if I had your body, I could think of more pleasant things to do with it than visit neurologists."

"Same old story? There's nothing wrong?"

"Tension, maybe. Young man—listen to me. You've had tests enough to last anyone a lifetime. Stop pissing away your time and money. Migraines don't mean there's something wrong. We don't know why some people get these pains, and we may not know in a hundred years from now. I bet I'm not the first to say that what you need is a good psychiatrist."

"You're not the first."

Victor liked the old man anyway. He was direct and honest and down-to-earth. Victor liked the doctor's well-preserved old Caddy in the driveway and his rough New York accent. Most of all, he liked the doctor's office—so different from the sterile cubicles the others had. There were photographs of grown children and little ones who looked like grandchildren, and there were pictures of pleasant tourist spots in Europe and Hawaii.

Then he saw the woman. She looked out of a picture and straight into his eyes. She was not young, but she was full of warmth. He could tell instantly that she was a good wife and mother. She didn't drink too much or sleep too much or tell lies to children. He could tell by looking at her that she would never let him down.

He came back after dark. The lights were out and the car was gone. The house looked empty, cold, deserted—like another house he used to know. But between the slats of the closed Venetian blinds, he saw flickering colors. At first he thought it was a fire. Then he looked in the window and saw the shape of someone stretched out on a couch in front of a television set. He rang the buzzer, but there was no answer. He kept looking in the window, but the person didn't move.

Without warning, brilliant headlights flashed on him, pinning him like a bug against the glass. He stood in the glare, covering his eyes, and heard a woman's angry voice: "What the hell are you doing there?" It was her, in the Cadillac.

"What the fuck are you doing?"

He smiled and blinked. "I came to see Dr. Schwartz. I'm his patient."

198

"You have no right . . ." She shook her head with disgust. "If you need a doctor now, go to the hospital. If you can wait, come back in the morning."

"I'm his new patient."

"You already said that." She got out of the car and looked in his eyes. "Are you all right?"

"I don't think so."

"What's the matter with you?" Her tone was rough. She was not as kind as he had hoped, nowhere near as nice.

"I don't know . . ."

"Are you on drugs? Were you in an accident?"

"I don't know . . ."

She looked out toward the empty street. "Where's your car?"

He spread his arms helplessly. "I don't remember."

"Wait right here." She opened the door to the doctor's office and slammed it hard as soon as she got inside. He saw the lights go on. He saw her talking on the telephone. He could tell she would not help him. From the look of irritation on her face, from the way she sucked her cigarette and puffed white smoke into the room, he knew that she was not—and never would be—the gentle woman he once hoped she was.

Ten minutes later, when the police arrived, Victor was hidden on the floor of Bette Schwartz's Cadillac beneath the lambswool blanket he found on the back seat. He heard her talk with the men who came, and after a little while he heard them drive away. He heard her call out to her husband. Her voice was loud and harsh and angry, but she got no reply.

Victor waited a long time before he left the car. All the lights inside the house were out. He used the screwdriver that he found in the glove compartment to pry open the office door. He walked down the long hallway that led into the rooms where people lived. He held the tool in front of him as if it was a weapon. But there was no need. The doctor was sleeping on the couch and snoring peacefully. The television set was no longer flickering. He opened the bedroom door and saw the woman. She slept beneath a pile of blankets in the middle of a giant bed. The air conditioner was turned up high, and the room was freezing.

She sat upright in the bed.

At first she was confused, still groggy. She didn't recognize him. Then she tried to scream, but he clamped his hand over her mouth and pinned her down with his knees. He jabbed her hard. He plunged the tool deep into her chest. He drove it home, again and again, spraying blood all over both of them.

She stopped moving.

The blood was warm but the room was icy cold. He had to get away. He stripped his clothing off and left it on her bed. He stood there naked, freezing. He opened the closet and found a shirt and trousers that belonged to the doctor. He put them on, but they didn't stop the chill. He found paper in the doctor's office, the notes that Dr. Schwartz had made that day. He took his lighter out of the pocket of his bloody trousers. As quickly as he could, he scattered balls of burning paper. He spread them across the floor, against the walls, beneath the furniture. The flames spread quickly. Before he left, the house was warm.

CHAPTER 32

A PANELED COURTROOM: waxed wood, fresh ceiling paint, huge dirty windows that faced the glass slabs and ornate old buildings of the financial district. The spacious room was jammed with reporters and curiosity seekers and groupies: the ones in love with Mary Buchanan, who followed her from trial to trial as if she were a rock star, and the ones—they existed already, drawn by scattered photographs and stories in the newspapers—in love with Felix Kiehl. Some sent him letters that he didn't read—though Maya Jones read each one carefully and even saved a few.

Jake sat at the prosecution table beside John Spicer. The atmosphere was his first surprise—the eagerness, the joy, the excitement, the lust for blood. It felt obscene—like the crowd at a boxing match he once attended. The lawyers buzzed, each side studying the other from the corners of their eyes, no one troubled in the least at the show that was unfolding. It was meant to be a show. It was the best thing possible for everyone's career.

Felix Kiehl looked lost in his own world, completely disconnected from the scene around him. He sat beside Maya Jones, who had been assigned by Mary to be his caretaker. He was slouched in his chair, with his head tilted forward and his chin resting on his chest. His suit was creased and much too large. His hair was cut too short, and the collar of his shirt was crumpled by an ugly tie. He looked like a reject from a mental hospital who had been sleeping for a week in Penn Station—which was exactly the way Mary wanted him to look.

The jurors looked at Kiehl for only the briefest moment. They were supposed to know better, but they were still afraid. At his slightest motion—as if looking were an act of provocation, as if he were crazy enough to come right after them if they looked too long—their heads jerked away. From across the room, where Jake was seated, they looked exactly like a colony of skittish birds.

Jake wrote notes, observations, assorted questions that occurred to him in a cryptic scrawl on a little pad he had bought for the occasion. Why did Mary sit so near the jury, so far from Kiehl? Was she afraid? Was it a hint of how she intended to proceed? Did she want them to feel afraid? He made a note of every thought, no matter how absurd. He planned to tell Spicer anything that could conceivably be helpful.

Ira Shuster had done his job with surprising effectiveness. The ten men and two women who made up the jury, along with the two male alternates, contrasted sharply with the spectators and lawyers. They looked tense, businesslike, lacking imagination, eager to get the whole case settled, amply capable of ignoring anything a starry-eyed psychiatrist might claim.

Whenever Alan opened his eyes, he felt confused. He wished that he could think things over, sort them out, make sense of what was going on. It was much too much for him—all the people, the movement, the constant noise. He wished that he could shake his head or pound his head or do something with his head to get it right. He wished he could be back in Dr. Baxter's office. He knew it was impossible. He knew that there were lawyers and police and people judging him. The lawyer said he needed to do everything they asked. He didn't like it, but he went along. It was a phrase he remembered from long ago. All kinds of people would be looking at him and making decisions that would affect him. He sat there like a statue and let them think he was a statue, but he heard every word.

They rose on cue as Judge Marion Parrish strode briskly into the room. It was like a dance, an old ballet that began too early in the morning but still had the power to get the juices flowing. The judge seemed taller than Jake recalled, stronger-looking, much more imposing. Had he changed the color of his hair? Alan missed the bailiff's call and had to be pulled up to his feet by Jones.

At the bailiff's signal, they took their seats. They heard the words they knew by heart, the ancient incantations to the gods of justice. Whether they learned their roles from life or books or movies made not the slightest difference: Everyone knew his part and played it to perfection, proud to be a member of the show.

CHAPTER 33

THE BURDEN OF proof was on Mary and her associates. It was not just a matter of rebutting the prosecution—they had to prove their claim that Felix Kiehl was insane. In contrast with an ordinary trial, the defense presented first.

From looking at Mary one would not have known that it was any kind of burden. She came to life like a movie star in front of a camera or a great conductor in front of an orchestra. She had charisma, a glow that came from somewhere deep inside. It was intense enough to light the courtroom.

"Acts have meaning." Mary repeated the phrase again and again: "Acts have meaning. Acts have meaning. Every religion teaches it, every philosophy, every theory of the law. Our acts are not random, and they aren't always simple. The things we do in life have meaning. This is what makes us different from animals."

She looked at John Spicer with undisguised contempt and then turned back to face the jury. "As you know, Felix Kiehl has already conceded that he committed the acts of illegal trading with which he has been charged. We do not dispute that he engaged in this activity. We do not dispute that what he did was wrong. What we *do* dispute is his criminal responsibility. We intend to prove that Felix Kiehl's state of mind, while he performed these acts, was one in which he lacked substantial appreciation of the consequences of his behavior. We believe that for this reason, which we intend to prove in very considerable detail, you should find him not criminally responsible by virtue of insanity." She looked at Spicer with scorn.

"I believe that the prosecutor will suggest that you see this case as cut-and-dried. He will tell you, 'This is what Felix Kiehl did, it's very serious, and he ought to be responsible for his actions. Don't strain your mind too much by worrying about what any of it *means*.' "

She made eye contact with each and every juror. "We have a very different goal. I should tell you at the outset that it's a more complicated goal. It may go against the grain at first, against certain conclusions that seem simple and obvious. Our goal is to show you that what looks at first glance like one thing may in fact be very different. Our goal is to show you that people are complicated and the things they do are complicated. We're human beings. We aren't animals. We don't live in the jungle. We have culture and philosophy and religion. We have a legal system that doesn't blindly punish, but tries to understand the complexities of human behavior. We recognize that acts that look the same are not always in fact the same. We do our best to understand motives. This is, after all, America. We have compassion."

Peter Millar objected: "Your Honor, counsel is preaching . . ."

"Indeed you are . . ." Judge Parrish said.

Mary hardly paused. "It is a fact that illegal acts were perpetrated. It is not a fact that they are simple. If there is a single thing that can be said about this case, it is that it is not simple. Someone didn't take a gun and hold up a 7-Eleven. It was not a mugging or a burglary or a murder or a rape, no matter how hard the prosecutor works to make you think of it that way. Felix Kiehl is not responsible for any bank failure or for the financial collapse of any company. He did illegal things for reasons that are rooted in his tormented past.

205

"We intend to show you something of that past and the serious psychiatric disorder that resulted from it. We will show you that Felix Kiehl engaged in a series of complicated acts that had complicated causes rooted in a life history that was horrible enough to have destroyed many of us."

The jurors responded with apparent sympathy, and Mary grew more confident and even more appealing as she went on. "In a portion of his mind, Felix Kiehl was calm and rational. He appeared to be quite sane. Anyone who knew him superficially would think he *was* quite sane. No one could manage the things he did without great intelligence and clarity and focus." She paused dramatically. "But you will soon discover that there is more to this poor man than intelligence and clarity and focus. You will learn that these qualities may mask the most overwhelming problems. You will come to understand why I call Felix Kiehl 'poor' no matter how much money he acquired. I will show that the things he did to acquire this money were much closer to a fantasy or dream than to his daily life. He didn't live on it. He didn't spend it. I will show that the money was part of a fantasy life, not a real life. With regret for revelations that I know will cause him pain, I will present evidence to show the nightmare past of Felix Kiehl and the mental abnormalities he developed in order to survive it."

She came up close to the jury box and peered at each juror in turn. "You were accepted as jurors because we believe you have the capacity to understand a complicated human being with complicated problems. I believe that in the course of this trial you *will* understand, and that your understanding of Felix Kiehl's life and mind will lead you to compassion. Your understanding will lead you to the clear conclusion that the acts of Felix Kiehl were those of a man who was compelled by inner demons to act in ways he could not control and could not understand. We can only think of these acts as insane."

The suit John Spicer wore was only slightly better than the one on Felix Kiehl. He spoke in deferential tones, a black man they could love, both civil and a servant: "Ladies and gentlemen, Ms. Buchanan may disparage facts, but certain of them are not in dispute and should be considered by you with the utmost gravity. Felix Kiehl has admitted to a series of extremely profitable stock transactions that were made possible by information he illegally acquired. He used methods that required careful planning and highly technical computer programming over a period of at least four years. I want to repeat: four *years*. This was not a sudden impulse, not a moment of weakness. The man who committed these crimes was capable of exceedingly careful and thorough planning. He was aware of consequences. He had foresight. His illegal transactions enabled him to accumulate upwards of seven million dollars, which he secreted away so successfully—once again, over a period of years—that substantial amounts still have not been found.

"These are established facts. They have been acknowledged by the defense and spelled out in documents you will soon have an opportunity to examine. We can't ignore or explain away these facts as fantasy. If a verdict were to be based solely on these facts, this trial would be unnecessary.

"Obviously, that has not occurred. As Ms. Buchanan has pointed out, there is very serious dispute about the *meaning* of these facts. Ms. Buchanan has also pointed out that we regard them differently, though I would submit that the prosecution is not quite as ignorant of human complexity and as indifferent to human suffering as she suggests. We simply disagree. We think this man knew exactly what he was doing and that these acts would have been impossible for *anyone* who did not know exactly what he was doing. We believe the evidence will prove our position. We believe, and we intend to show, that the acts of Felix Kiehl—however unfortunate his past—were rational and considered behavior for which he bears criminal responsibility. We have as much compassion for human suffering as our kindhearted defense attorney, but we intend to show that Kiehl's acts were not the deranged behavior of someone who is insane. We believe you will agree. We want to remind you that in an insanity trial, the defense must *prove* what it contends."

Spicer spoke extremely slowly. He did his best not to rush the jurors or manipulate their emotions. He was there to make them think. ". . . In the course of this trial, you will be hearing a great deal of testimony from psychiatrists. Some of it, I'm sure, will be impressive and convincing, and some, I'm equally sure, will not be. You'll probably learn enough about psychiatry to set up an office of your own—or to stay away from them no matter what!"

After the snickers ended, he came up close to the jury. "You know, doctors like to sound like they know all the answers. As their patients, unfortunately, we know too often that they don't. It's important to remember that the final decision in this trial will not be made by doctors or lawyers or even the judge, but by you. The law, in its great wisdom, puts power in the hands of ordinary people—a jury of one's peers. It is up to *you* to sort out what the doctors say and test it in the crucible of your own wisdom and your good common sense." He ventured just the tiniest of smiles. "Common sense is the key. We didn't choose you because we thought you were deep thinkers or budding psychoanalysts who liked to read hidden meanings into things. We chose you because we think you have solid, old-fashioned, common sense. I would suggest you make use of it and trust in it and apply it in relation to everything you hear."

Alan Maliver listened carefully. His eyes stayed closed but he paid attention. He agreed with everything the black man said. He liked the man.

"What does your common sense tell you about the defendant's actions? We think the truth is self-evident. Could anyone on this earth do all the things that this man did—we'll do our best to explain them to you—while he was at the very same time insane? We don't think so. We intend to show you that it is not possible. We will show how Felix Kiehl, while an employee of the investment firm known as Potter, Weeks, illegally manipulated the computer system in order to gain access to private information. We will show that he buried certain programs in the computer memory while he worked for the firm in California, and that he activated these programs two years later, after he moved to New York. We will show how he used the information provided by these programs to purchase stocks and stock options that brought him enormous profits. We will show how his transactions precisely anticipated large stock purchases that were initiated at Potter, Weeks. We will show that this entire enterprise could have never been carried out by anyone whose mind was even the least bit impaired. I want to repeat: The responsibility is on the defense to show how someone who was seriously impaired by insanity could have managed this."

Spicer stood close to Kiehl, who kept his eyes shut. "It doesn't sound so bad, does it? Compared to what goes on out there on the streets, it sounds kind of harmless. You might even think that someone who managed all of this was rather clever—a kind of warrior against the system." Spicer slowly shook his head. "It's a trap. Don't fall into that way of thinking. Don't forget that someone pays for every crime. Our children and our grandchildren will be paying for those raped S and Ls for God knows how many years.

"Remember that when the system fails, the crimes that happen on the streets become inevitable. The man who did these things was no Robin Hood. Ms. Buchanan says he didn't mug anyone or rob a 7-Eleven, and maybe we should be grateful for that. But Felix Kiehl mugged the system—he mugged the people who invest in it, including those of us with pensions and bank accounts that are invested in the system. Like the bankers who sucked the money from their depositors, like the junk-bond dealers and market manipulators who took huge profits and left the interest payments to the shareholders, he was not in the least insane—except maybe in his greed. Felix Kiehl knew exactly what he was doing, and the time has come to hold him responsible."

Wallace Hilson stood. "Your Honor, Mr. Spicer seems to have forgotten that we're supposed to have a trial before we get to the summation."

Judge Parrish nodded. "Sustained."

Spicer stood in front of Kiehl. He was hoping for a glance, a look of any kind, but the man stayed unresponsive. With a tiny shrug that managed to convey contempt and skepticism, he went on: "Sometimes, under certain circumstances, people lack the capacity to distinguish right from wrong. They may not understand that they are doing wrong. They may understand, but be unable to stop themselves. The mind can be deranged. We don't deny that. We feel compassion for people who are the victims of their own sick minds. We hope we can continue to feel compassion and not have it eroded by individuals who manipulate the system for their own purposes.

"Over the years, our legal system has evolved certain standards to help determine whether an individual is criminally responsible. You will be learning a great deal about these standards as this trial proceeds. I can tell you in advance that it will be irritating, infuriating, and sometimes, hopefully, enlightening. Whether you want one or not, you are going to get a psychiatric education."

Spicer studied the jurors intently. "But you have to keep in mind, throughout this process, that the final decision is *yours*. No matter what the experts say, this trial will come to rest on your good judgment. You will hear the evidence. You will weigh the doctors' words and their opinions. You will try your best to imagine what it might be like to have a serious mental disorder. You will struggle to understand the legal concepts of insanity and criminal responsibility. You will hear about the things that Felix Kiehl accomplished—how complex and difficult his project was, how much self-discipline it took. You will ask yourselves if this could be possible for someone who was insane. Ladies and gentlemen, we will try to show you that there are many words that one might use to describe Felix Kiehl, but insane is not among them."

CHAPTER 34

M<small>ARY CALLED CLAIRE</small> Baxter.

She had to pick her way through a maze of tables to reach the witness chair. She walked slowly, her face tingling, her ankles wobbling, thinking that the first mistake was choosing heels, knowing it was not likely to be her last. By the time Mary led her through the preliminaries—education, experience, the manner in which she first met Alan Maliver, the manner in which she learned the truth about him, the manner in which their connection was reestablished, the contacts she had with him while he was on the prison ward—Claire's head was throbbing.

"Doctor, how much time did you spend with Felix Kiehl?"

"Putting the two phases of our work together, it comes to a total of fifty hours."

"Do you consider that to be an adequate amount of time?"

Claire spoke slowly and carefully. She was reconciled to going through with this, but she didn't have to like it or pretend she did.

"Adequate for what? It's a very long time for a typical diagnostic study. It's a long time for certain forms of brief psychotherapy. It's a short time for a psychoanalysis. It's a tiny time in the totality of a human life."

"Was it enough time for you to reach an understanding of Mr. Felix Kiehl?"

"I came to understand him to a limited degree."

The word hung there and Mary looked displeased. *"Limited?"*

"There's a great deal about Felix Kiehl I still don't understand."

The buzzing began. Spicer and his associates looked at each other with undisguised pleasure. Reporters scribbled and spectators whispered and even Judge Parrish looked surprised. It was obvious that Dr. Claire Baxter, the very first expert Mary Buchanan called, the cornerstone of her case, was not a friendly witness.

"Doctor, is it typical that after fifty hours of interviews there would still be gaps in a competent psychiatrist's understanding of a patient?" Her eyes drilled into Claire.

"It isn't typical at all."

"Could you explain for us?"

"I would explain it by stating Mr. Kiehl's diagnosis, which is multiple personality disorder. It's never easy to understand someone with that disorder—especially when the doctor doesn't know at first that the person has it. It frequently takes years for people with multiple personality disorder to get diagnosed correctly."

"Did you say *years?*"

"Yes."

"Frequently?"

"I'm referring to studies published in the scientific literature."

"Doctor, will you please explain why it would take so long?"

"It's a disorder characterized by a mechanism known as dissociation. A person walls off segments of his conscious mind. He forgets or blocks out huge portions of his life. He hides things from himself and from anyone else who tries to understand. He may have several distinct personalities that have no knowledge of each other."

"Do you mean that you didn't understand him because he kept things from you?"

"Not only me—the important part is that he kept them from himself. The nature of this illness is that things are hidden and walled off from a person's own awareness."

No one could say Claire was not professional. No one could say she did not cooperate. She was thorough and knowledgeable. She responded fully to every question Mary asked. There just happened to be a certain edge to her voice. She was very different from what anyone expected in an expert witness. She clearly disliked Mary. It was obvious that she was no pawn and that her views were very much her own.

"Doctor, did you see Mr. Kiehl go through these changes in personality?"

"I saw many changes, sometimes several in the course of a single visit."

"Please tell us what they were like."

"He seemed to become a different person . . ."

"Seemed? Do you mean he played a role?"

"He wasn't acting. I would say that he became a different person. He called himself a different name and had a different style of speech and different memories. Even his face would change—the result of changes in his muscle tone."

"It wasn't voluntary?"

"I don't think so. I became convinced that what I saw were separate, dissociated personalities."

"Doctor, is that your opinion with a reasonable degree of psychiatric certainty?"

"Yes. My diagnosis is multiple personality disorder."

"Doctor, could you now describe some of these different personalities . . ."

"There were four I came to know reasonably well. There was Alan Maliver, the personality who consulted me initially. There was an academic type known as 'The Professor' and a rather tough and aggressive one named Victor. There was a computer expert who said he was called 'The Nerd.' There were others I met only briefly or heard about indirectly. There was a woman. There were children . . ."

The room began to buzz, and Judge Parrish rapped for silence.

"Did these personalities have knowledge of each other?" Mary continued.

"That's a complicated question. Some had fairly complete knowledge. Some had partial knowledge. Some knew nothing whatsoever."

"Did you meet all the important personalities?"

"I don't think so. For one thing, I never met Felix Kiehl. I tried many times, but he never revealed himself."

Mary slowed her pace and increased the volume of her voice. "You never met the personality with his given name? Doctor, will you explain for us what that might mean."

"Maybe he never trusted me enough."

"Doctor, why wouldn't he trust you?"

"I didn't take it personally," Claire replied. "I knew the cause was in his past. Typically, people with multiple personality disorder were abused when they were children. They have difficulty trusting anyone, for quite good reasons."

As soon as the subject of his childhood came up, Kiehl began to fidget nervously. He shook his head. He rocked from side to side. He slid his hands up the front of his body and covered his face. The jurors kept watching him uneasily. Judge Parrish gave Maya Jones an irritated glance.

"Doctor, could you give us some idea of the kind of abuse people with multiple personality disorder have typically been subjected to?"

"It's always traumatic."

"Could you explain?"

"In psychiatry, the word refers to an experience or series of experiences in which a person feels overwhelmed and completely helpless."

"Do you mean like a death in the family or like losing a job?"

"No. Those may be very difficult, but they're more or less a normal part of life. We'd all be multiples if it was caused by that."

"Please tell us about the kind of trauma you do mean."

"Sexual abuse is by far the most common. A very high percentage of people with multiple personality have been sexually abused." Kiehl shuddered visibly as Claire went on. "Dissociation is a desperate measure. It typically occurs when a person is too young to escape abuse or deal with it in a more effective way. The mind falls back on building walls, on blocking experience, when it has no other option . . ."

"Doctor, I want to make sure I have this right. Are you saying, with a reasonable degree of psychiatric certainty, that Felix Kiehl suffered traumatic abuse when he was a little child? Are you saying, with a reasonable degree of psychiatric certainty, that, as a result of this traumatic abuse, he suffered major damage to his personality?"

"Yes—to all of that."

Kiehl shook his head and rocked back and forth. Jones whispered something and he was briefly still, but in a short while he began to rock again.

"Doctor, could you now be more specific about the nature of the abuse? I know it's not a pleasant subject, but the jury needs to know what the defendant actually lived through . . ."

It was Avi Roth who made a vain attempt to rescue Kiehl. His voice was low and his tone gentle. "Your Honor, we all know that the defendant had a difficult life. We don't dispute it. We have no desire to see him suffer more. But this line of testimony has no bearing on the issue of sanity."

"Your Honor, the torture Felix Kiehl experienced in the course of his life has a very great bearing on his mental state."

"Overruled." Nevertheless, Judge Parrish looked unhappy.

Alan looked straight ahead. His hands rested in his lap, and the expression on his face was now calm and untroubled. No one who saw him could possibly ignore the change.

"Doctor, can you tell the jury what led you to conclude that Felix Kiehl was sexually abused?"

215

"At first it was indirect. The dreams he reported were filled with images of abuse. I believe that anyone in my profession would have known that he suffered a great deal. As our work went on, after I made contact with the buried personalities, he became more open."

"Please." Kiehl sounded like he was in agony. Jones tried to calm him as he gripped the table, and the table itself began to shake. *"Please . . ."*

Judge Parrish looked alarmed. "Sir? Are you all right? Does he need a recess?"

Jones whispered something, but Kiehl made no response. The heavy table rattled.

Mary spoke: "Judge Parrish, I can assure you that my client has been carefully prepared for everything the doctor will discuss. We knew in advance that this was going to be extremely stressful."

Alan opened his eyes and studied her. He was relaxed and calm again.

The jurors looked confused as Mary went on. "Doctor, I have a general question. If one of these multiple personalities were to commit a criminal act, do you believe it would have the same meaning as if the act were committed by an ordinary person?"

Judge Parrish looked at Spicer, expecting an objection, but there was none.

"As far as I'm concerned, when it comes to criminal behavior, our pasts don't justify *anything*," Claire said firmly. "Some of us suffer more than others, some of us have bad luck. It's very sad, but it's no excuse."

The spectators buzzed again.

"Doctor, that isn't what I asked. The question is: Can the standards we apply to normal people be applied to people with MPD? Are they able to grasp reality in the way that you and I do?"

"I don't know how you grasp reality. I haven't had the pleasure of conducting a psychiatric interview."

There was laughter, and Mary smiled along. "I mean ordinary people."

"They know right and wrong," Claire went on. "Every personality that I met had a knowledge of right and wrong."

Once again, there was reason to wonder why Mary had called her. If anything, Claire seemed to support the other side. But Mary pushed on: "Doctor, are you sure? To a reasonable degree of psychiatric certainty, are you sure they understand the consequences of their actions?"

"Do you understand the consequences of yours?"

"Doctor, I'm not playing games." Now Mary looked stern.

Judge Parrish looked at Spicer, but once again he chose not to interrupt. Whatever the legal issues, this was hurting Mary.

"Doctor, with a reasonable degree of psychiatric certainty, do you believe that *all* these personalities understood the consequences of their actions?"

Claire did not look pleased. "I'm not sure. Some of them were children. Some had no language. I would say that some of the personalities understood, while others did not."

"Well then, what can you conclude about the person as a whole?"

Claire looked confused. "*What* person as a whole?"

"Felix Kiehl."

"I don't know that person—I thought I made that clear. I know fragments, bits and pieces. I don't know that there *is* a person in the ordinary sense. I don't know what there is."

Mary stood before the jurors as she spoke to Claire. "Doctor, this is extremely important, and I don't want to misunderstand. Did you just say that this man does not exist as a person in the way you and I and the jurors do, that he is so *fragmented* that you think of him as belonging in a different category entirely?"

Claire finally saw what Mary was after, but it was too late to do anything about it. "I did imply that."

"Are you saying that his mind works in a way that is profoundly different from that of an ordinary person?"

"It's different. I don't know whether it's profoundly different."

"Aren't you saying that he understands reality in a very different way?"

"You could put it that way."

"Thank you, Doctor," Mary said cheerfully. "That will be all for now."

Alan's eyes were open wide as he gazed at Claire. It made him sad to see her so unhappy.

CHAPTER 35

THE CROSS-EXAMINATION OF Dr. Claire Baxter was conducted by Avi Roth. It soon became clear that he intended to push as hard as possible. The fact that Jake was seated at the prosecution table did not inhibit him at all.

"Dr. Baxter, your specialization is psychoanalysis, is that correct?"

"Yes."

"Psychoanalysts don't treat every patient, is that also correct?"

"Nowadays, they treat who they can get." She smiled, but he did not respond.

"Isn't it a fact that a patient has to be quite *healthy* to be accepted for psychoanalysis?"

"It's not as true as it used to be."

Roth held up a journal. "You're familiar with this publication?"

She knew the blue cover and the ornate letters: *Classical Psychoanalysis.* "I subscribe to it. It's put out by the Institute where I was trained and with which I'm presently affiliated."

"It's a publication that's respected in your field?"

"I would say so."

He opened to a page with a paper clip attached. "According to this, the patient must have the *quote* ego strength to tolerate the profound deprivations and regressive pulls *unquote* of the analytic situation. This article was published two months ago, by a Dr. Raul Berger. Do you dispute it?"

"No."

"Are you familiar with Dr. Berger?"

"He's the president of our society."

"A society that honors the work of Sigmund Freud?"

"Hopefully."

"Didn't Freud believe that psychotics were not treatable?"

"Not at all. He said they weren't *analyzable*. It's not the same thing. They could certainly be treated by other methods."

"Doctor, do psychoanalysts often work with people who suffer from multiple personality disorder?"

"There aren't many such people."

"Do psychoanalysts study multiple personality disorder in the course of their training?"

"Psychoanalytic training is not directed toward specific diagnostic entities," she replied. "Analysts are trained to use an analytic *method*."

He looked innocent enough—a pudgy young man with pale white skin and pale white hands, but she was learning that he had venom in him. "Doctor, prior to your meeting Felix Kiehl, did you have any experience with any patient suffering from multiple personality disorder?"

"No. Of course I'd read—"

"Was the subject ever discussed in any of your classes?"

"Not formally. It may have come up in passing. It was never a major topic because it was thought to be so rare. I read the books and saw the movies . . ." She could tell from his cheerful expression that she'd made an error.

"Oh, are movies a part of the psychiatric curriculum? What about television?"

There were laughs, and a flush crept up her neck, but she struggled to defend herself. "Why shouldn't they be? *Anything* that teaches us about the human condition is relevant to psychiatry."

"Doctor, isn't it accurate to say that you are not trained and not qualified to treat a victim of multiple personality disorder?"

"It's not accurate at all. There's a very substantial literature that I carefully examined. I can assure you, I'm not the first, nor will I be the last, physician to deal with a difficult case through the writings of others. I attended a conference where I consulted with a recognized authority. The skills I mastered during my many years of training were the basis for my treatment of this man."

He shrugged. "We know you're a good student. You need to be to get through medical school . . ."

"And law school," she added.

She got a laugh, but that was as good as it got for Claire.

"Doctor, did your treatment of Felix Kiehl include hypnosis?"

"A portion of it did." She knew the issue would come up, but she felt like she had just been kicked.

"How often did you hypnotize him?"

"I'm not sure exactly."

"Doctor, please, make an estimate."

"Seven . . . eight . . . maybe ten times."

"*Ten times.* Could you tell us how much of your training was devoted to the study of hypnosis."

"We had a segment during my residency." She felt about to vomit.

"Would you kindly define 'a segment.' "

"Some lectures and a demonstration."

"Doctor, have you ever had actual clinical training in the technique of hypnosis, either for diagnostic purposes or for treatment?"

"The technique is simple. I read the books."

"You like to read."

221

"Is there a problem with that?"

"Other than Felix Kiehl, how many patients have you hypnotized?"

"You're missing the point."

"Please answer the question."

"None, but—"

"Do you hold any certification in hypnosis?"

"No."

"Are you a member of any professional organization of hypnotists?"

"No."

"Doctor, how much direct clinical supervision have you had in the use of hypnosis?"

"None, but—"

He paused and pretended to be deep in thought. "Doctor, yesterday I read a book about brain surgery. I studied hard, and I'm a good student. Do you think I could try out what I learned on you?"

She kept hoping that Mary would throw her a lifeline, but she kept sinking, and she knew she was alone.

"Doctor, do psychoanalysts often use hypnosis?"

"No."

"Do you know a single psychoanalyst who makes use of hypnosis in his or her professional work?"

"No."

"Not even one?"

"No."

"Could you tell the jury why that is?"

"Freud opposed hypnosis."

Roth feigned surprise. "He did? Is that so? Would you tell us why?"

"Because hypnosis involves suggestion. He didn't want to be accused of putting his ideas into people's heads."

"Brilliant man, wasn't he," Roth said. He waited for the jury to get his point, and then he hammered away at it: "Doctor, did it ever occur to you that the methods you used with Felix Kiehl—these

222

methods you were not trained to use and had no experience in using —might have produced the changes you observed? Did it ever occur to you that hypnosis itself created these so-called dissociated selves?"

"I thought a great deal about it," Claire said. "The possibility is discussed in the literature. I took every precaution . . ."

Roth spoke softly now. "Doctor, I don't doubt your integrity. The trouble is, Doctor, good intentions aren't always good enough." She thought he might be done, but then he came at her from another angle: "Doctor, Felix Kiehl has a powerful stake in being thought of as insane. It would mean a great deal to him, wouldn't it?"

"Of course."

"Most people would rather be in a hospital than in a prison."

"Those places aren't country clubs."

"If you had *your* choice, which would it be?"

"A hospital."

"Did it ever occur to you that Felix Kiehl might try to manipulate you?"

"Of course it did."

"What did you do to avoid it?"

Whenever Claire thought he was about to let her go, Roth opened another can of worms. His questions came so fast and so persistently that everything dissolved into a blur. She began to answer automatically, no longer thinking of implications or trying to frame her thoughts. It was just the two of them, locked together in a nightmare dance. She followed his rhythm and went where he led her and did everything he asked.

"Did you meet all of these so-called personalities?"

"I don't think so."

"Why didn't you meet them all?"

"There was no time. This was not an exhaustive treatment."

"Why didn't you meet the one named Felix Kiehl?"

"I can't tell you exactly. My guess is that he mistrusted me."

"Didn't he lie?"

"I wouldn't put it that way."

"Don't people often lie if they mistrust someone?"

223

"Some people . . ."

"Won't people lie if it can keep them from a stay in prison?"

"Most people . . ."

"Doctor, how can you possibly claim *good rapport* with a patient who wrote an autobiography that he never discussed with you?"

"You have to remember that this man is fragmented. I had good rapport with certain of his dissociated personalities. Clearly, I did not have good rapport with all of them."

"Doctor, what is your actual evidence that he was sexually abused?"

"What do you mean by actual evidence?"

"Medical records, objective proof of any sort, anything other than fantasies."

"I take what people tell me very seriously."

"Other than this 'little girl,' did any of the other personalities tell you they were raped?"

"Indirectly . . ."

"What does that mean?"

"In dreams."

"Do you have evidence of any real events that would confirm what you read into these dreams?"

"I discovered his place of birth through a reference in a dream."

"Doctor, did he ever tell you *anything*, one single thing, that could be confirmed by another person?"

"This thing he lived through was very painful and very humiliating, and therefore very private."

"Doctor, do you really think a jury should make an important decision about an admitted criminal because of the way you interpret his dreams?"

The worst experience of Claire's life—a good deal worse than the violence done to her house—finally came to an end. She felt that Roth had crushed her utterly. There was more he might have asked, but he had the sense to see that it would only lead to pity. It was enough to have destroyed her credibility and any claim the defense could rest on it.

She left the witness stand with a ringing in her ears. She left the courthouse and ran into the street where she was almost hit by a cab. She was lucky to find one.

To Claire's surprise, Jake was waiting in front of the building when she got home. "The subway's faster," he said, "but I guess, right now, speed is not the issue."

He took her in his arms. "You didn't do so badly," he said.

"Don't, please . . ."

"I mean the work—you did good work. You took risks, but they were good risks. Roth made you look bad, and maybe the jury will believe him, but the work you did was good."

"I feel like I was raped," she said.

"I guess you were."

"The worst part is that I asked for it."

When they got out of the elevator and were alone in the apartment and the door was closed behind them, she held on to his shoulders and let the tears come.

CHAPTER 36

"SHE'S GOING DOWN the tubes," Jake said.

A week had passed, and the rest of Mary's experts had come and gone. Dr. David Karlin, in from Chicago, left a message on Claire's machine with his hotel and room number. She erased it instantly. Dr. Peter Brim had come up from Baltimore.

"You mean *he's* going down the tubes," Claire said.

"I mean her reputation."

"Just like mine."

"Listen," he went on. "When Millar got through with the famous Dr. Karlin from the famous Institute for Dissociation, you could have carted the guy away. Then Spicer took on Brim, the great researcher, who came close to storming out of the place in a narcissistic huff. They looked like fools."

"I know you want to help, and I'm grateful, but that doesn't make it better."

They were seated at the kitchen table. Jake had adjusted his appointments so he could leave time in the middle of the day for trips to court. He saw less of Claire than he was used to, and he missed her. "Buchanan looks really stupid," he went on. "It's like she hasn't done her homework. She puts these assholes on the stand and they look good at first, but when the prosecutors question them, they crumble."

"Hurrah for lawyers," Claire said.

"I was watching her, and I had this crazy thought that she was pleased—that everything was going exactly the way she wanted."

"She hates psychiatry," Claire said. "She's happy to make us look like fools."

"I wondered if she really wants to lose."

Claire considered it. "Is there an angle we don't know about? Would she get more money if she lost? Would she control the money in his accounts?"

"I'll ask Spicer." He knew that Claire was going to be upset, but he had to tell her. "You know, he keeps getting these calls from California. They traced Kiehl's links with two of those couples. There isn't any doubt that he knew them well."

She shut her eyes.

"He used different names: Anthony, Andrew."

She kept her eyes closed and then slowly covered them with her hands.

"They still don't have enough to go to trial . . ."

The meeting was in Claire's office. After the fourth call, after Mary used every argument imaginable, including false tears, Claire had finally relented. "I can't believe I'm doing this. I must be sicker than I thought, or dumber."

"I can't tell you what it means to me . . ." said Mary.

"I'm not doing it for you."

"The trial is going terribly. I assume your husband keeps you well-informed?"

Claire said nothing.

"It doesn't take a genius to know how the jury feels. Believe it or not, you were our high point."

"I wouldn't go back there if you had a gun—"

"I'm not here for that. It's way past the point of experts." The lines around Mary's mouth had deepened. She looked worn-out, much older than Claire recalled. "There's just one hope. It's very risky, but I have to take it . . ."

"Why not? Take any risk you want. It's only someone else's life."

She ignored Claire's bitterness. "Have you pictured Alan Maliver in prison? He'd be destroyed."

Claire kept silent.

"I needed your anger," Mary went on. "I might as well tell you the truth—I'm not so impossible to reach. It was more or less a manipulation."

"What?"

"Juries are always skeptical of expert testimony. Everyone knows you can buy and sell those people. I wanted what you had to say to come across as real. I thought, if you were angry with me and you still said those things, you'd be more believable. I put you through some misery I now regret." She waited for a response that didn't come. "All I want is advice. I've made the decision to put him on the stand. It opens the door to all kinds of complications, but we have nothing else. I want the jury to understand what he's really like."

"To put him on the stand? There are risks," Claire said.

Mary missed her meaning: "Huge. They'll be able to question him about anything they want."

"They can ask about California?"

"Probably."

"They can ask about those people who were killed?"

"Probably. John Spicer will come in his pants."

"What do you want from me?"

"Your thoughts on where to go when I get him up there."

"For what purpose?"

"To show what happened in his life. The truth. To show what he's really like."

"He'll fall apart."

Mary shrugged. "They have to see it for themselves. It's the only way they'll ever believe in it."

No matter what Claire felt about Felix Kiehl, this went against the grain. "You want him to fall apart?"

"Not all the way apart . . ."

"This doesn't trouble you? You told me what they'd do to him in jail. This is just as bad."

"Talking about being raped is not the same as being raped."

Claire shook her head. "You can't speak for him. This is rape. The things that happen in the mind can be worse than any other."

"I'm just his lawyer. I don't know about his mind. I'm there to win his case—that's all."

"And it doesn't matter if you destroy him in the process."

Now Mary shook her head. "Look, we basically agree that Kiehl is not criminally responsible. All I'm trying to do is work out a strategy."

"We don't agree at all. He should pay for what he did, like you or me . . ."

"The law says otherwise."

"It's empty words. *Lawyers* wrote it. This whole insanity defense is just a con game that you run. It has nothing to do with people."

Mary shook her head again. "I'd rather not argue. You said you had some thoughts about what really happened, the things his parents really did."

"He'll fall apart," Claire said again. "He can't deal with that. It's what made him crazy in the first place."

"Doctor, with all due respect, I'm the one to weigh those risks."

"You want him to face this on the witness stand? If I did anything like that, it would be malpractice. We're talking about memories that destroy most people. It's crazy! There's a good chance you'd make him a permanent basket case."

"Isn't he *already* a basket case? At least I'd get him into a hospital."

"Destroy him first and treat him later."

"Isn't he already destroyed?"

"He's a human being. I don't care what he did. It's a monstrous idea."

Mary looked at her watch. She'd been there exactly thirty minutes, and she made the decision not to waste a minute more. Her tone shifted suddenly into one of ice. "Dr. Baxter, I am now making a formal request for all records pertaining to your diagnosis and treatment of Felix Kiehl. As you are doubtless well aware, they are his property."

Claire looked stunned. "There are no records. I explained that when we met. I don't show my private notes to anyone."

"Whatever notes you have, Dr. Baxter, I insist that you turn them over to me." Mary opened her briefcase and exposed a small tape recorder. "Doctor, let me state formally, as Felix Kiehl's legal representative, with the power to make decisions on his behalf and the power to take action on his behalf, including the power to sue for damages on his behalf, that you are in possession of records that are vital to the proper conduct of his defense. If you fail to deliver these notes to my office by ten o'clock tomorrow morning—all of them— you will be interfering with this trial." She looked coldly into Claire's eyes. "I want you to understand that I am referring to every single scrap of paper that contains any reference *whatsoever* to my client, including any of the various personalities that inhabit the body of my client."

Mary clicked the machine off and closed her briefcase. "Listen, let me go past the legal bullshit. I want this to be real clear. If you don't deliver, I'll sue your fucking ass so hard you'll never roll back on it again. I will bankrupt you and have your license revoked and make it impossible for you to do anything but drive a cab. Do you hear me? Do you get it?"

Before Claire could say a word, Mary was out the door.

CHAPTER 37

JUDGE PARRISH SPOKE: "Miss Buchanan, do you have more witnesses?"

"Your Honor, we call Felix Kiehl."

The news of Mary's unexpected move spread rapidly through the courthouse, and the reporters who were out for cigarettes and gossip returned to claim their seats. Alan didn't stir. He sat motionless in the way he had for days, taking the words in. This had nothing to do with him.

Judge Parrish called the lawyers into his chambers. Behind the door, he touched a match to the sour butt of the cigar he had started after breakfast, the one a day he still allowed himself. Spicer ventured a cigarette as Mary gave them both a grimace of disgust. She crossed the room to open the window, but it was sealed.

The tone Judge Parrish took was condescending: "I assume, my dear, that you're clear about all the consequences of this move you're now proposing. I assume I don't have to remind you that you put your man at quite considerable risk . . ."

"First of all, Judge Parrish, I'm not your dear."

"I beg your pardon." He smiled benignly.

"Second, I understand the risks."

"Mr. Spicer here would be free to question certain details of your client's history."

"Judge, I'm well aware of that."

"So what's the point? Why prolong the misery? We all see how this charade is turning out. I've been seriously contemplating calling a halt to this waste of time and money after you rest your case."

"That's exactly why I need him on the stand. I know it's going badly. I think the jury needs to see what he's really like."

"How much time will you need?"

"A couple of days. A lot depends on how he deals with it."

"I think this is a big mistake. I want you to know that."

"Frankly, judge, I'm not asking for advice."

Judge Parrish shook his head in obvious disgust. "If it's what the lady wants, it's what she'll get. I'm calling the stenographer. I want it in the record that I've warned you. I want no grousing in the future, no retrospective second thoughts, no spurious appeals. One insanity plea is more than enough for me. I don't need a lawyer to claim it for herself."

He still had his looks, but up close she could see the cracks in the facade. Mary took in his leathery skin, his robe that needed cleaning, imagined his cabinet full of ancient athletic trophies. She could have strangled him. "I don't need this. If I ever do appeal this case, I can base it on the fact that you're a senile asshole."

His jaw dropped, his eyes glazed, the fingers on one hand began to twitch. Judge Parrish looked as if she had slapped him with a two-by-four. But though he had a witness, he took no action. Let Mary Buchanan dig her own grave, he told himself. It wasn't worth his effort. She could put her client on the stand and do anything else she damn well pleased. His retribution would be the fact that no matter how much latitude he gave her, she was guaranteed to lose.

CHAPTER 38

A<small>LAN WAS TERRIFIED</small> when the two men stood beside him. He tried to shrivel, to sink down in his chair, but there was no place to hide. He slid beneath the table, almost to the floor, but they got his arms and pulled them up, and the rest of his body somehow came along.

The room was still.

They all stared at him.

He sat up straight.

"Mr. Kiehl," the lady said, "I recognize that this is very difficult. But as I explained to you, there are certain things the jury needs to know. Do you recall our conversation?"

He did not respond. He did not recall. He wished his doctor was still with him. Why did she leave? Had he been bad? He didn't know the answer.

"Mr. Kiehl, please tell the jury where you were born and where you grew up . . ."

He did not respond.

"Mr. Kiehl, can you hear me?"

Mary didn't mind at all that he was shaken. She hadn't expected things to start this way, but that was fine. The trick would be to build on it, to rattle him in a way that would be useful.

He studied her. Another lady in a line of them. She was not the nicest. He saw the judge and jury and all the strangers. His eyes fixed on the doors, the windows, and then the one who asked the questions . . .

"Mr. Kiehl, are you all right?"

His hands began to shake. He twitched. He looked as if he had just awakened from one nightmare only to find himself in the middle of a worse one. She wondered if he would speak at all.

At just that moment, the man on the witness stand was dramatically transformed.

He blinked repeatedly. He shook his head as if to clear the cobwebs. He sat up straighter. He looked around, suddenly alert. It was obvious before he said a single word that something was very different.

"Mr. Kiehl, are you all *right?*"

He peered at her and then responded with a strong, surprising drawl: "I'm faaahnnn, young lady. You may faaahre away with any questions . . ."

There was nervous laughter and the flutter of pages turning rapidly in reporters' notebooks.

"Are you *sure?*" Mary was stunned. At least on her part, this was no act.

The man in the witness chair leaned back and grinned. "Given where I am, out here in front of all these folks, and I'm a shy boy, I'd say I'm about as fine as it is possible to be."

The room began to buzz. Judge Parrish slammed his gavel to no effect.

There was total silence when Mary spoke again: "A minute ago you looked terribly upset."

"Upset? Ma'am, no offense, you sure you got yourself the right customer? I been called all kinds of things, but 'upset' ain't one of 'em."

She had the presence of mind to ask which customer he was.

"Name is Curtis. Curtis Wade. Folks call me Wade."

"Which folks?"

"The ones that work with me."

"Where would that be?"

He grinned proudly. "Different towns. I work in the rodeo, ride · broncos mostly, rope calves sometimes, pretty damn good at it if I have to say so."

In the unlikely event that there was any ambiguity about what had just happened, Mary lost no time in spelling it out: "Your Honor, I would like the record to indicate that Mr. Kiehl appears to have gone through exactly the kind of personality change that was described by our consultants. I would like to state for the record that his voice and manner are substantially different from what they were a few minutes ago."

The noise in the room grew louder.

It was interrupted by John Spicer: "Your Honor, may I approach the bench." With Mary beside him, he whispered to Judge Parrish, "Your Honor, if this isn't an act, there's no way this man can comprehend this trial. He's manifestly incompetent. There's no way he should be on the stand. It's not humane. It's not ethical."

"Isn't that nice," Mary hissed. "He cares. Your Honor, my client meets all the criteria for competency. I can show you."

"You'd better do it fast," Judge Parrish said.

"Do you know where you are?" she asked Curtis Wade.

"Ma'am, I'm sorry to say I do. I'm in a courthouse. We're on trial."

She smiled at Spicer. "Do you know Felix Kiehl?" she went on. "I'm afraid I do . . ."

"Could you tell us how well you know Felix Kiehl?"

"*Damn* well! I share this old carcass with the fella . . ."

There was more noise, and more futile attempts to quiet it. Curtis Wade looked cheerful and Mary looked triumphant and Judge Parrish looked perplexed. John Spicer looked as if his mind was moving at the speed of light and not getting anywhere.

She went on: "Your Honor, this man knows exactly where he is and why he's here. He understands his connection with Felix Kiehl. I submit—as I have all along—that he is both insane *and* competent."

The noise continued—a persistent buzzing that the judge ignored. With a look of determination, Judge Parrish took the matter into his own hands. He peered at the defendant. "Sir, would you please repeat your name."

"Curtis Wade, Judge."

"Do you have more names?"

"Some call me Felix, some call me Alan . . ."

Judge Parrish nodded curtly. "And how much do you know about this Felix Kiehl?"

"I know the fella's in a heap of trouble."

"Do you understand the kind of trouble?"

"The next worst kind to woman trouble—they say he took money that wasn't his."

"Then why are *you* on trial?"

"Cause not one of them doctors knows how to rope the bastard!"

Even Judge Parrish had to smile. He turned to Spicer. "I see no reason to call a halt."

"I'll let it rest for now."

Mary then asked a series of questions that were meant to probe the background of Curtis Wade. How much did he really know about Felix Kiehl? What did he know about Kiehl's finances? What did he know about his buried childhood? To Jake's satisfaction and Spicer's relief, she didn't get far. The more Mary pushed, the less Wade seemed to know. Like Arthur Moss, he was more veneer than substance.

"Which of the others do you know?" Mary asked eventually.

"Which other what?"

"Which of the ones who share your body?"

With slow, slightly exaggerated, deftly comical motions, Wade patted his arms and chest and opened his jacket to look inside. "No one in there," he said.

There was more laughter.

One thing she couldn't tolerate was a joke at her expense. At just that moment, Mary made another move. *"Listen to me, Felix Kiehl,"* she said sharply, in the sternest voice she could command. "I know you're in there. I want you *out* now."

Curtis Wade started blinking rapidly. He was not in a hypnotic trance, but he behaved as if he were.

She continued speaking in the same stern voice: "I need someone else. I need to talk with someone who knows what's going on."

Curtis Wade faded. The change was obvious to everyone: One minute he was there, cheerful and bright-eyed and proud of who he was, the next minute he was gone. His face and posture looked completely different. Someone new was seated in the witness chair.

"It would help if you introduced yourself . . ." she said.

"They call me The Professor."

She knew all about him. This one was in Claire's notes. It was Mary's chance to show the jury a very different side. "Sir, I would like to ask you, first, if you understand what's going on here?"

He considered the question. She hoped the jurors could see how much his face had changed. "What aspect of what's going on are you referring to?"

"The reason for this trial."

"Of course I understand. They claim that I made money, quite a large amount, through various techniques of data theft and illegal trading. The defense, I regret to say, is insanity."

"You *regret* to say?"

"I'm not insane," he answered calmly. "I think the notion is utterly absurd. Frankly, I find it demeaning and personally offensive."

"What kind of professor are you?" she asked.

"It's an honorary title."

"Who gave it to you?"

237

"It's just a nickname."

She saw jurors glancing at each other and knew she had to face the issue. "What makes you say you're not insane?"

"I don't dispute the diagnosis of multiple personality," he said. "But that doesn't stop me from knowing what I'm doing. I'm in control. In my opinion, the condition does not make anyone less responsible. In my opinion, if they did wrong, they should suffer the consequences."

She didn't blink. "They?" If Mary was one thing, it was resilient. "I'd like to ask, since there are these others, if they all agree?"

The Professor slowly shook his head. "I'm in the minority."

She watched the jury as his words sank in. "What do the others think?"

"The ones that were party to this sordid episode are eager to escape its consequences. They'd all be happy to be judged insane."

"And you think they should not be?"

He nodded vigorously. "Young lady, let's face the facts. They knew quite well what they were doing. They were fully aware their acts were illegal. Like any common criminal, they should pay the price."

Where could she go with this? Was her losing case lost again? A new thought occurred to Mary: "*Which* ones should pay the price?"

The Professor was calm. "I would start with Victor. He's by far the most greedy. Arthur Moss would come next. Then the one they call The Nerd, who knows much more about this project than he admits."

"And what about Felix Kiehl?"

"I don't know him."

"And what about you?" she went on. "Should you also pay?"

The Professor looked puzzled and then annoyed. She knew as soon as he began to answer that she was onto something. "What an absurd idea. I'm not a criminal. There's no reason I should be in jail."

Mary knew at that moment that she really had a chance. Did they see? Could she *make* them see? The buttons were there! All she had to do was find the right one and push it hard. "Let me be very clear. I need to understand and to make sure that I get this right. I'm sure you know that this is important. Are you saying that *they* are guilty, and *they* should go to prison, but that *you* had no part in this and should therefore go free?"

"You have it exactly. Why is that so complicated?"

She made a circle in the center of the room and spread her arms as if about to fly. "Sir. *Professor.* Could you kindly explain, as clearly as possible—we really need to know—how you could separate yourself from the ones you say are guilty?"

"I wouldn't abandon them," he replied calmly. "I'd come to visit." He shrugged with some embarrassment. "To tell you the truth, I guess I should admit it, I wouldn't think of them that often."

At lunch, Mary's staff confirmed the progress.

"The jury is in awe," Jones said. "I can't say they'll let him off, God knows what they're thinking, but they sure do know he's sick . . ."

Mary sipped coffee as Jones and Hilson ate. "If you think he looks crazy now, just you wait! We're on top of the mountain. What we do next is dig down into his past. I'm going to make this bastard look more off the wall than that decrepit judge and that prick Spicer ever thought possible."

The personality who greeted Mary when they returned from lunch was wide-eyed, uneasy, halting in his speech.

"Would you kindly tell us what happened to The Professor?"

He was silent. He looked ten years younger than he had in the morning. He didn't know any professors.

"Please tell us who you are."

"My name is Alan."

"Do you have other names?"

"No . . ."

She started over. She had learned a thing or two, but she lacked the patience of any decent therapist, and she had very different goals. "I know you have secrets. Your head is filled with buried information."

"Your Honor," Millar interrupted, "this is getting farfetched.

239

What is counsel's point in this?" Before he could go on, Spicer restrained him with a touch on his arm.

"Doctor, I don't understand . . ." Alan's skin turned gray, and sweat poured off him.

"I'm not your doctor, I'm your lawyer," Mary said. "We need to know about the things that happened when you were little. I know that you had dreams."

"*Cut it out!* I don't care who you are!" His voice dropped to a growl and his face turned mean. His latest change startled everyone in the room. "We don't talk about that garbage. It's none of your goddamn business."

They were frightened and fascinated. A performance or not, what they were witnessing was incredible. The button she had pressed was exactly the right one.

"Please tell us who you are."

He glared at her with venom. Lines appeared around his mouth that gave him the look of a snarling animal. "You get one guess."

She had Claire to thank again. "Is your name Victor?"

"Congratulations."

"I'm trying to learn about some things . . ."

"Go to school."

Then Mary had her own surprise. "We visited a school. Your school, in fact. In a town named Stirrup, Nevada."

"What?"

She opened a folder that held a pile of ancient documents. "A member of my staff visited the town. He found your records in the elementary school. The teachers wrote about your problems many years ago. We're putting this in evidence. We think the jury needs to understand the life you lived, the problems that you had."

"I fixed the bastards," he said bitterly. "I'll fix you too. I may be little, but I'm smart. Anyone who comes too close gets hurt . . ."

She waited again. He did look insane, lost in memories, fighting battles that had been decided long ago. She gave the jurors all the time they needed for the image to sink in.

"The other children were easy," she said then. "You knew how to protect yourself. You had lived through worse. We need to talk about the things that were done to you before you got to school."

He shook his head helplessly. He turned away from her and wouldn't say another word. He was somewhere else, a place where she couldn't touch him. She couldn't get anywhere close to him. He was up in the sky, beyond the planets, out among the stars. He felt safe, and if he wasn't safe, his fists were ready.

241

CHAPTER 39

The questioning went into a second day.

Spicer let Mary examine Kiehl in any way she chose. He knew by then that he had made a mistake, but it would only make things worse if he tried to stop her now. He let her play her cards. He kept his objections to a minimum and gave her all the room she needed. He was confident that no matter what new stunt Mary Buchanan pulled, the jury would see through it. Kiehl was a good actor, and Mary was capable of all kinds of clever ploys, but he had no doubt that he still held the winning hand.

In response to Mary's persistent questions, without benefit of hypnosis or any drug, the man on the witness stand, whatever his name or incarnation, began to talk openly about his life. Mary was able to accomplish what her psychiatrists could not. The spectators kept silent, the jurors listened intently, and even fading Judge Parrish stayed thoughtful and alert. All around there were looks of compassion and concern.

"Please tell us about the place where you grew up," said Mary.

He was still Victor. "We lived on a ranch up in the hills. They thought it was the promised land . . ."

"Who thought it?"

"My nightmares . . ."

"Who do you mean?" she asked.

"My mother, my father."

"Why do you call them nightmares?"

"You know all about it."

"We need to hear *your* words, I'm afraid."

"Why don't you ask what I need?"

She studied him with an expression of concern. "I think I already know. You need treatment. In a hospital."

"I had a doctor. She was good to me . . ." He looked around, as if Claire might be somewhere near.

"You haven't answered the question that I asked."

"Which question?"

"Why do you call them nightmares?"

The answer came reluctantly: "He tortured me . . ."

"In what way did he torture you?"

He shut his eyes. There was fluttering beneath the lids. The one who opened his blue eyes was The Professor.

"You pick the orifice, you pick the implement," he said.

She didn't wait for explanations. She could only hope the jurors understood. "You were *conscious* while these things were happening?"

"I looked over his shoulder, so to speak."

"What did they do? Was Felix Kiehl the child that they abused? Is that the reason he's in hiding?"

"It wasn't *they*, it was *him*: the father." The Professor's tone was flat; his voice showed no emotion. "He raped the child. He did it repeatedly, on a daily basis, with every extremity at hand, in every orifice that could accommodate him. Didn't you learn this long ago? Why do you press me to repeat these nightmares?"

"Because what's important now is not what I know or what the doctors know, but what the jury knows. They're the ones who need to hear your words and understand your life."

There was a shift in his tone, a softening of his voice. "No one can understand. There's no understanding pain like that." He began to cry openly and there were jurors—the tough black woman among them—who couldn't help but cry themselves.

After a few moments, The Professor regained control. "He was a child. He was bright, perhaps even exceptional, but he had a child's mentality and a child's limited grasp of the world. There was only one question for the little one—he faced it every day."

"What question?"

"The question was, how much pain?"

The tears came again, but Mary kept on: "Did his mother know?"

"No." He shook his head vigorously.

"Is that possible? You lived in such close quarters."

"She had no idea. She would never let harm come to the boy."

They heard the childlike tone that was not there before. His voice had changed. His hands were trembling. Had she found what she was groping for? Was this finally the thing that would split him open and show them what he looked like inside?

Kiehl's voice was an octave higher than before: "She's a good doctor. She didn't know. She couldn't stop him. She had no power . . ."

"I thought you were telling us about your mother."

He was silent and confused.

"Can you tell us when this all began?"

He shook his head.

"Can you tell us how long it lasted?"

He shook his head again.

"We have to know. You have to tell us." She was convinced that he was on the edge of something.

His face was in constant flux. He looked frantic, like a trapped animal desperately searching for an escape. Fragments of personalities flashed on his face like images on a TV screen. He was mournful; he was detached; he was frightened; he was enraged. Someone was flipping channels. There were images of pain and chaos, but no one in the room could turn away.

Mary approached the witness stand. *"It's time. It's time I talked with the one who knows the truth."*

Another shudder rocked Kiehl's body, and with it came another voice. "Mommy, make him *stop*. Mommy, wake up. Mommy, please make him go away."

"Mommy?" She could see the agony. This was it—the thing he couldn't face. His mother failed him when he needed her the most. "Did you hear what you just said? What about your mother? Why won't she help you?"

He was silent, frozen.

"Where *are* you?" Mary asked. She saw the blank look in his eyes and raised her voice. He still hadn't cracked. He was on the verge, but she was losing him. She still hadn't shown conclusively enough that he was insane. "You can't hide now! You have to *tell* us." She felt like grabbing him and shaking him until he answered.

Mary stood beside his chair. She could touch him if she just reached out. She felt like slapping him. She didn't understand that she was living out a scene in his unconscious. "The one who hurt you is your mother. I see it clearly now. Whenever I ask about her, you get upset. I know your father did bad things, but you can handle them. It's when we get to *her* that you always fall apart . . ."

He shook his head and kept on shaking it.

"You keep confusing me with her. You called me 'Mommy.' You did the same thing when you talked about Dr. Baxter."

He mumbled something that she couldn't hear.

She came closer, so close that he could feel her breath.

His words were clear. "You're making a mistake. My mother was good to me." His voice was calm. He liked the way she smelled. He saw that she was pretty. He felt himself harden into an erection.

"Did she do things that she should not have done? Did she do something bad, or did she just let you down?"

"Please . . ."

245

It was Mary's last chance. "What did she do? What made you run away?"

He mumbled something.

She planted herself directly in front of him and held on to the barrier. "You have to *tell*. You'll feel better when you tell. I promise that."

"Please . . ."

She fixed her eyes on his. "The pain will stop. Your suffering will stop. You just have to tell . . ."

With a guttural scream, he leaped from his chair and grabbed her neck with both hands. She tried to pull away, but he held on tightly to her smooth white throat. Her mouth was open, but no sound came, no breath of air. Mary struggled fiercely. She clawed at his face until he bled, but he held her with a pit bull's power. The guards moved fast, but she had come too close and pushed too hard. With one fierce shake, her head snapped back, a loud crack echoing through the room. She went limp, a floppy doll, a thing a child might cling to. He shook her a second time and flung her out, away from him, into the empty space where she once stood . . .

Mary crashed into the heavy oak table where Jake and Spicer and Roth and Millar were seated side by side. Her head hit the corner with a sickly *thwack*. The guards had reached him now, and pulled him down, screaming.

Mary's eyes stayed open. Jake reached her first and saw that she was breathing. She was alive, but her pale green eyes were blank. He knew at once that Mary Buchanan would never cross-examine anyone again.

CHAPTER 40

MOST OF HER former clients sent the requisite flowers, but not a single one made an appearance at the hospital. Not that Mary would have expected otherwise—they were not the kind to wait around for someone in a coma. Aside from Maya, who came every day and sat sobbing plaintively beside her bed, and Wallace, who came irregularly and got out fast, Mary Buchanan had no visitors—no friends, no family, no old lovers. The neurologists got paid to stand around. They shook their heads and shrugged their shoulders as her brain swelled up and squeezed itself to death. They drilled burr holes in her skull to reduce the pressure, but when the swollen tissue oozed up out of them, it was obvious that things were hopeless. Her EEG was flat within a week, and the only question left was when to pull the plug.

Before they did, a doctor on the staff told Maya that Mary would make an ideal organ donor. She talked with Wallace, who tried to expedite the process, but Mary had never signed the necessary papers. There was no will. And Mary's elderly parents, both still alive in Hartford, would not return his calls. For reasons that were never clear, they wanted nothing to do with Mary's body or her estate or her funeral. Hilson's focus shifted then from Mary's body parts to her considerable fortune. If no one could benefit from her corneas or kidneys, at least the firm could keep as much as possible of the money she left behind.

She had taught him well.

She lingered on much longer than anyone expected, but two weeks after they took her off life support, a full month after Kiehl's attack, Mary Buchanan died.

Exactly one week later, Claire got a call. "You were right," Hilson said. "She should have taken you more seriously. We all should have."

"Just tell me what you want."

"I know this will seem bizarre," he went on, "but the firm still exists, and we still represent the man."

"And?"

"You could play a role. I think your history with him could be very useful. We'll need to monitor his stay in the hospital. We're mandated by the court to evaluate him periodically. We'll need to bring in new consultants."

"It's sick. Bizarre would be real healthy . . ."

"But you're completely *vindicated*. Events have shown how well you understood the man. You come out smelling like a rose."

"And you smell like shit," she said.

"You could run the show this time. There could be a lot of money in it—an annuity that will go on for years. There isn't any risk. We know he's never getting out of there."

"Thanks. And please go fuck yourself."

Judge Parrish declared a mistrial. Though he was shaken, almost in need of a doctor himself, he maintained control and dismissed the jury after Kiehl's explosion, while the medical people worked feverishly on the lawyer. It was obvious that Kiehl could not be tried. The question was whether he could *ever* be tried, but there was no need to deal with that for some time—as far as Parrish was concerned, a good long time. Both sides agreed to lock Kiehl away at an upstate hospital for the criminally insane. The only question that remained was whether he could be present in the courtroom when the ruling was announced. Irrational and dangerous as their client clearly was, Hilson and Jones insisted on his right to hear the judge's words in person and on their own right to show everyone concerned that they were in command.

The courtroom was jammed again. The only vacant chair was the empty one next to Maya Jones—a place for Mary.

The lawyers huddled in separate clusters and pretended they were still at war; the reporters made obscene jokes about a secret love affair between Kiehl and Mary; the psychiatrists sat stiffly in their chairs and stared straight ahead. Most members of the jury were also present. Though they had been excused, this was just too good to miss. It seemed that Claire was the only one in town who felt no need to be there.

"Are we ready?" The clerk nodded in response to Judge Parrish, and two huge officers came to stand beside the judge. "Then let's get this over with." The room was silent before he could request it.

A door opened. Standing motionless was Felix Kiehl. He was wearing a dusty canvas straitjacket that was studded with leather buckles. Iron manacles linked his legs, and a chain ran from his ankles to the wrists of the guards beside him.

A loud, collective gasp passed through the courtroom. Judge Parrish called for silence, but the noise went on, broken now into separate sounds of protest and counterprotest: This was inhumane; no one should be treated in this way; this was out of the Middle Ages; this was just what the creep deserved. The judge rapped harder, a series of blows that finally quieted the room.

Felix Kiehl stood frozen. They waited for him, but they could have waited another day and he would not have stirred. Heavily drugged, barely able to hold himself upright, he looked like a pathetic version of King Kong onstage, an impression that grew stronger when

Judge Parrish signaled and the guards tugged his chains, forcing Kiehl to stagger forward.

Judge Parrish spoke. "Please, let's have a chair for this man, we have a sick person here." The officers scurried to find a chair. They finally saw Mary's, and one guard lifted it across the table while the other guard positioned it directly behind Kiehl. "Is that all right?" Judge Parrish asked.

Kiehl made no response, but he didn't struggle. He lowered himself into the chair when the guards pressed on his shoulders.

Judge Parrish shuffled papers and began to read. His expression was serious and filled with compassion. The courtroom artists would capture it well. His voice was resonant and kind. "After extensive contemplation of recent unfortunate events, after consultation with three special court-appointed psychiatrists, after a review of all prior psychiatric testimony, and with the concurrence of both prosecution and defense, it is the ruling of this court that the defendant, Mr. Felix Kiehl, is not competent to stand trial."

The judge read slowly. He couldn't stop himself from glancing at Kiehl at the end of every sentence. "This court remands the defendant to Willingham Federal Hospital for an indefinite period of evaluation and treatment."

Kiehl had no reaction.

"Mr. Kiehl, you're going to remain at that hospital until the doctors decide that you have recovered sufficiently to participate in further legal proceedings." He saw that Kiehl was not about to leap up from his chair. "The federal and state prosecutors are directed to monitor the defendant's condition and to make decisions regarding future prosecution based on the extent to which the defendant achieves a state of competency. Concurring with the opinions of our distinguished consultants, I do not believe that Mr. Kiehl should be considered for future proceedings for a period of at least one year. This, of course, is subject to ongoing review, as determined by law.

"Finally, I believe it appropriate to add that I have never witnessed a more distressing example of that tragic and mysterious condition called mental illness . . ." Judge Parrish spoke to Kiehl directly.

His voice got louder, as if he thought the man was deaf: "Do you understand? *Sir*, are you able to understand what I'm saying?"

The guard beside Kiehl touched his shoulder. When Kiehl turned to look at him, he pointed to the judge.

Alan tried to make sense out of what was happening. He studied the floor, the flag, the guard, the picture of George Washington above the judge's head.

"Sir, do you *understand?*" Judge Parrish asked again.

To the surprise of everyone, Alan answered softly. "I don't. I don't understand at all." His voice was clear, and he seemed completely rational. "I don't know why I'm all chained up like this . . ."

The buzzing began.

Judge Parrish looked helplessly at Spicer and then at Jones and Hilson and finally at Kiehl. "Something quite terrible happened in this room. Do you know what I'm referring to?"

Alan shook his head. "I know that this is terrible. It's terrible to be chained up."

"You're very sick. We're sending you someplace where you can be treated. The doctors will help you understand." The judge's tone turned more condescending: "These doctors are highly experienced. They're trained to help with the problems that you have. If you talk to them and do everything they tell you, and if you do your best, then I have every confidence—"

"I *have* a doctor." He looked around, but Dr. Baxter wasn't anywhere in sight.

"We're sending you to a place where there will be other doctors —good doctors."

"But I *have* a doctor," Alan said. "She takes care of me."

Judge Parrish shook his head.

"Sir?" Alan's voice was stronger. He sounded like any normal person. "You are a judge, is that correct? This is a courtroom?"

"It is indeed . . ."

"Don't I have the right to know what I've done? This is America, isn't it? I can't be tied up like this without a reason. I'm not an animal."

251

"I never said you were an animal. No one said that."

"Did I do something wrong?"

"The doctors will explain," Judge Parrish repeated, making no more sense than he had before. "I promise you that. They understand your illness much better than I do. The important thing is that you talk to them. Listen to your doctors, and one day this will all be clear."

"But sir . . ."

The man was sick—at least that much was certain. His mind was full of holes. How could he forget what he had done? How could he block it out? Judge Parrish had had enough. It was more than he could tolerate. He made a motion to the guards.

A door opened. There were more guards waiting to take Kiehl down a passageway. An ambulance waited in the street.

"But sir . . ." Kiehl looked across the hushed, crowded courtroom. He didn't move. *"Mommy?"* The word came as a shock to all, including Alan. "Mommy? Mother?"

"She isn't here," Judge Parrish said.

"Where is she? What did you do to her? Did you hurt her?"

"I didn't do anything, young man."

"I know she'll come. She'll take care of me. She promised me. She won't let him hurt me . . ."

"No one will hurt you. You're going to a hospital."

"She'll come. She won't let me down . . ."

Judge Parrish signaled to the guards.

To the sound of rattling chains and the pleading questions that no one stopped to answer, they led Felix Kiehl away. It was the fervent hope of everyone inside that room, with the possible exception of his lawyers, that they had seen the last of him.

PART V

The wind blew in ferocious gusts and the house creaked and shuddered as if it were about to topple, but these were not the sounds that woke him. He heard a moan, a groan, a wail. It sounded like a calf or pig was sick, but he knew better. A chill spread over his skin. He was four years old, old enough to know that they would never let an animal inside the house.

A rhythmic thumping that sounded like a loose gate in a storm came from beyond his door. Felix left his bed and crossed the hall. Was the storm inside? The noise came from his parents' room. Was it a fight? The door was partly open, and he pushed it all the way. The lamp beside the bed was dim, but there was light enough to see, too much light—her legs were spread out wide, and the father pounded with his body like it was his fist. Her eyes stayed shut, and her head kept banging up against the headboard the way the father banged it sometimes against the kitchen wall. She didn't scream or make a sound. She looked asleep, though even at that tender age Felix knew that no one sleeps through that.

He stood helplessly beside the bed and smelled the smell that made his stomach sick and saw the bottle on the floor.

The pounding stopped.

"Well, look what we got here." The father grabbed his arm and yanked him hard, and he felt plucked up into the sky, a newborn lamb caught in the talons of a vulture. "We got something here alive . . ."

Before the child knew what was happening, his pajamas had been torn from his body and he was facedown on the pillow and couldn't breathe. The father pounded into him the way he had the mother, and the sharp pain he felt was agonizing. There was no time to struggle, no way to understand. He only knew that something hard was ripping him apart . . .

He thought he was about to die.

He looked up, straining to see the mother. He reached out to touch her, to wake her somehow, but the father held him down with all his weight and he couldn't move.

"Mommy . . ."

Her eyes stayed closed.

"Mommy . . ."

Her eyes fluttered. She looked at him but couldn't focus. He tried to speak, but his mouth was covered. The words were trapped inside his mind: Help me! Save me! Please!

She shut her eyes and was motionless again.

He left his body and looked down from the ceiling of the room. He could see them clearly: the man's hard back and the sweat that glistened on it; the woman's pale, white, naked body, her breasts flopped to either side, her thin arms, her hair in tangles. Then he saw bits and pieces that had once been the boy—an arm, a leg, a disconnected head.

He was not afraid. He knew that he was dead.

On a bed, in a lonely farmhouse, where no one would ever visit, where no one could ever be saved, lay a drunken man and a drunken woman and a helpless child. The people who did these things were not his parents. The boy on the bed was not him. The boy on the bed had died. He felt no pain. He was not afraid. He felt sorry for that child. He wished that he could help, but he could do nothing. He lived in the sky, inside the stars, too far away. He was much too far away. He was somewhere warm. He was somewhere safe.

In the morning, the bed was wet with blood and excrement. He had no memory of what had happened in the night and no idea why he hurt so bad. The mother said that he had caught an illness. She washed him carefully and stroked his head and cried. She said that she was sorry, but he did not believe her. She said that she would not let him be harmed again, but he knew it was a lie. She promised to protect him with her life if it was ever necessary. It was necessary.

He had a dream that came every night. It stayed with him always, his own secret, a dream he never told: A fire came out of his body—a huge, bright, and searing flame. It was hidden in a secret place that no one could ever see or know or touch, but it was there. He was dead, but his fire was alive, and it was always waiting. It kept him warm. It kept him safe. In the center of the blaze, inside a clear blue light that could melt the hardest steel, he could not be harmed. But everywhere he looked, no matter where he looked, the fire spread. It burned houses and people and animals and cars. It burned beds and trees and vultures in the sky. It burned the sky. Even when he was very young he knew it was not possible, that the sky doesn't burn, but it didn't matter in his dream. In his dream, everything was possible.

CHAPTER 41

THE LOVINGLY TENDED grounds of Willingham Federal Hospital, as far to the north as one can go and still remain in New York State, were surrounded by a double row of electronically monitored chain-link fences, topped with neat loops of razor wire. No one could touch the mesh without setting off a computerized alarm. No one could walk the lush grounds of Willingham—or picnic on them or make love in some secluded corner of them—without written permission from Administration and a pass from Security. No one could do much of anything at Willingham without an authorization that was, at least for patients and their infrequent visitors, exceedingly hard to come by.

On the day after he arrived, while housed in Building One and subject to continuous observation, Felix Kiehl received a visit from a psychiatrist named Dr. Carola Borg. She was a hefty woman in her late fifties with acne-scarred skin and a thick Scandinavian accent that would have been hard to follow even if he had his wits about him. As it was, Kiehl was pumped so full of Haldol that everything he heard came from the surface of a pond in which he rested motionless on the cold and murky bottom.

In her own way, whether he needed one or not, she was a breath of air.

"Hello! I am Dr. Borg! I am to be your doctor." She crossed the room, grabbed his flaccid hand, and shook it firmly. "I see they give you plenty medication," she went on cheerfully. "They keep you happy, ha?"

He sat gazing at this woman with his mouth hanging open and a trickle of saliva dribbling down into his lap.

"Soon you will come to my ward," she went on. "I will do everything I can to make you better." She shook his hand again, even more vigorously than before, then left the room, slamming the heavy door behind her. His mouth stayed open, and the aide who watched on the TV monitor outside saw no sign that he understood a word of what she said.

The aide couldn't understand her either.

Dr. Borg returned the following day. She checked his pupils and reflexes and the strength of his grip. "Please, you will squeeze my hand."

He gazed at her, not moving.

"Ya, I know what brings you here. I do not worry. I have much protection. You can show me all your strength. I wish to know how much the medication dulls you."

He did what she asked.

Before she left, she patted his shoulder and wished him well.

Dr. Borg was no therapeutic genius. Willingham was the kind of hospital—in the kind of location, with the kind of unappealing and dangerous patients—where they hired whatever doctors they could get and were grateful for them. Half the medical staff had foreign degrees; three-quarters lacked formal psychiatric training; a third spoke English as a second or third language. Compared with most of her colleagues, Carola Borg was considered a treasure. She was on leave from her professorship at a Swedish university while her husband, a botanist, was studying the effects of acid rain on the Adirondack forest.

Though fully qualified as a psychiatrist, Carola Borg had no interest in the subtleties of psychotherapy or the nuances of establishing and maintaining close relationships with her patients. She was an academic research scientist whose special expertise was the electrical activity of the brain. Her studies in progress were extensions of research she had begun in Europe. Her present focus was a comparison of certain patterns in the brain waves of schizophrenics with those of depressives. She had no interest in that murky and untestable realm—the "unconscious"—in which too many of her colleagues chose to lose themselves. In her view, the ultimate solutions to psychiatric problems were chemical. She liked to remind her colleagues that even their beloved Freud once said that. She thought the job of psychiatry, until the right medications were finally discovered, was to treat all patients as decently as possible.

In practice, her approach was more humane than most.

Dr. Borg had managed, through the two drug companies that funded her work, to obtain brain-monitoring equipment that was far more sensitive than anything ever seen before at Willingham. The hospital provided her with patients and an assistant and the space to house her lab. Her clinical duties were easily managed in less than an hour each day. Unlike the other doctors, when her duties were finished she didn't turn to *The Wall Street Journal,* or to the search for other employment, or to a crossword puzzle. Carola Borg went to her laboratory and what she thought of as her real work.

One week after his arrival at Willingham, a pair of aides led Felix Kiehl through the ground-level hallway that made a long circle through the hospital and connected all the small buildings in which the patients lived. The aides knew what he had done, and they were very careful with him, but there was nothing in his behavior that gave them anything to fear. He was docile and subdued, and he followed their orders completely. Dr. Borg was waiting. The sleeves of her clean white lab coat were pushed up to reveal her meaty forearms, and she looked like a Swiss hotel keeper in the act of welcoming a valued guest to her cheerful, neat abode.

She had managed to infuse Building Six with a quality of warmth and hominess that was missing in every other part of the hospital. The place was clean. It lacked the stench of schizophrenia that permeated the rest of Willingham. Though she'd been in charge for less than six months, it was already considered a model ward, the ward that visitors were brought to see. A simple brick two-story structure of pseudo-Georgian architecture, it housed some forty men, all of whom had committed violent crimes, none of whom was ever likely to see the outside world again.

Felix Kiehl was the first patient with multiple personality disorder ever sent to Willingham. As soon as she knew he was coming, Dr. Borg had used her influence to have him placed in Six, where she would be able to observe and test him on a daily basis. She had read everything in the library on MPD and had ordered a computer survey of the literature from the National Institutes of Health in Bethesda. She sought out studies that found different patterns of brain activity in the different personalities of people with MPD. Even before he got there, she had begun to plan experiments with him as subject.

She had no choice but to telephone the doctor who had the most experience with him.

"Don't ever forget about his violent potential," Claire said. "I'm sure I don't have to remind you that people repeat themselves. He can go along peacefully for a very long time and then suddenly explode. I think he could do *exactly* what he did again."

"Ya, thank you, Doctor, I understand."

Claire went on: "In certain ways he can be quite appealing. It's easy to fall into a maternal role. He's very good at manipulating women. The fact is, he's quite seductive . . ."

There was a pause. It was already obvious that Carola Borg did not think highly of the psychoanalytic approach. "I beg pardon, Doctor. My English is not so wonderful. Do I understand? You say seductive? As in sex?"

"I don't mean it *literally*. I mean he has a way of getting people—women in particular—excessively involved."

"Does the word not connote something sexual?"

"I think it means *exactly* that in his unconscious."

"Unconscious . . ." Dr. Borg pronounced the word as if it tasted bad. "Ya, may I ask now about the *neurological* reports?"

Claire let it go. She wasn't about to argue. She knew it would be hopeless anyway. "There's nothing physical—the lawyer tried very hard to find an organic basis. Felix Kiehl was given every test available, but there was never any hint of abnormality."

"The electroencephalograms?"

"They showed nothing atypical. Neither did the CAT scans or the MRIs."

"Were there cortical evoked potentials?"

"Not that I know of. Does anyone use them clinically? Aren't they for research?"

"Do you know the work of your Dr. Michael Cameron, where he finds the different personalities to show different patterns?"

"I've read about it. But keep in mind—this was not research. I was trying to help the man make some kind of sense out of himself. The lawyer had her own agenda."

There was another long pause. Dr. Borg had no more questions, and Claire had nothing to add. They had reached the dead end that was inevitable.

They hung up amicably, each thinking that the other was a decent, well-intentioned, sadly misguided fool.

261

CHAPTER 42

IN MAY, TWO weeks after Kiehl was sent upstate, Claire and Jake drove out to East Hampton for a week's vacation. They had been away for months—their longest absence since they first bought the house. The place was filled with unfamiliar colors and textures and furniture they hardly recognized. At least the pictures on the walls were their own choices and the trees were in new leaf and they still could taste the ocean in the air . . .

Where were they going? Did they still want this tainted house, this tainted life they more or less still shared? The end of Felix Kiehl made a new start possible. The question was whether they had the energy and feeling for each other to begin again.

Instead of tennis, they went biking. They glided smoothly over the flat, empty back roads of eastern Long Island. Instead of a net between them, there was only air. They spent days talking and reading and sleeping and talking again as the tension of the year slowly drained away. They made love often and found that even that had changed; it was disconcertingly friendly. Was this what it was like to feel married? Toward the end of the week, with only two days remaining, Jake suggested that they see what they could salvage of their beloved garden. It was a clear statement about the future, and Claire happily agreed.

Aside from the symbolism, there was the thing itself to deal with. They walked the little square of land for the first time since the house was vandalized. What had once been a neat and thriving vegetable garden was now a tangled jungle—crammed to the edge of its sagging fence with last year's withered weeds and with the lush beginning of a new season's crop. The fertilizer they once lavished there had created monsters.

"There's tons of work," Claire said. "And even the tools are gone . . ."

"We've done the hard part," he replied. "Anything after this past year will be a breeze."

The following morning, the start of a hot and sunny day that felt like August, they drove to a garden center outside of town. They bought a spade, a rake, a hoe, and bags of fertilizer. They bought packets of seed and a new hose. By afternoon, they had managed to clear a decent square of weeds and brush. It was a much bigger job than Jake had anticipated. The vines that had grown so rapidly had thorns that pierced his cotton gloves and scratched his arms.

"Maybe we should hire someone," Claire said, rubbing her tired muscles. "We could get it rototilled while we're in the city . . ."

Jake shook his head and grinned. "Not a chance! I can't believe you're saying that. You know as well as I do that this has *meaning*! Take a break. I'll call you when it's time to plant. We can make love out here to help the seeds grow."

She looked at him skeptically and grinned. "Any time you want, but let's use the bed. There are ticks and other creatures out here."

Jake had read of an old method to rejuvenate a garden. The idea was to dig a deep trench that he would fill with a mixture of fertilizer and peat moss and soil from a second trench that he dug beside it. Then came a third trench and another mixture to go into the second. One row at a time, one spadeful at a time, he would turn over the entire garden. The thoroughness appealed to Jake. It would be like analysis, only more in his control.

Within an hour, Jake's hands were blistered and his back was aching and he was dripping sweat. Barely into the second row, he needed a break. He cheerfully refused Claire's reminder that they could still call someone. He screwed up his face and gave her a look of mock seriousness: "Ve go much deeper dis vay. Ve get rid of der bad old roots. Ve make new beginning . . ."

"I get the message, Doctor. But maybe saying it is good enough."

It was obvious that the work would take some time. The seeds would not go in the ground on the date the books recommended. Jake and Claire would have to live with flawed reality instead of perfect theory. It might have irked Claire once. She might have called him sloppy. It could have been the start of a major battle. She might have made an interpretation of his willingness to settle for imperfection. In reply, depending on how annoyed she got him, Jake might have called her rigid and tight-assed and gone on to say that her anal quest for perfection was the essence of what he couldn't stand about her. The battle could easily have lasted for a day, possibly a week. But life was different now. For reasons she chose not to analyze, Claire was content to let Jake prepare the garden in any way he wanted. It was his project, his statement about their future, and looking forward to that future was enough to make her happy.

CHAPTER 43

D<small>R. BORG'S FIRST</small> significant decision was to take Felix Kiehl off Haldol.

If he did need medication, she considered it to be the wrong one. She would decide for herself what was necessary after she had a chance to see what he was like in a drug-free state—and after she had the opportunity to collect some preliminary data.

She began to reduce his dosage on the day he reached her ward, and in less than a week he was off it completely. To her surprise, there was no observable change in the patient's behavior. Whatever had turned him into a zombie went far beyond medication. After two weeks, most of it was out of his system, but he still seemed drugged. He sat silently wherever the aides chose to put him, staring into space, as docile as could be, looking like the overmedicated schizophrenic preferred by the Willingham staff.

But he was not a schizophrenic. He had no delusions or hallucinations or any of the classic abnormalities of schizophrenic thought. Nor was he in the least bizarre. His responses to her questions, though limited, were coherent and to the point. And contrary to her first impression, he was not depressed. He was not sad or agitated or consumed by guilt. What he seemed to be, more than anything else, was immobilized—a kind of resting machine. He had not run out of gasoline and his batteries were charged, but in some way she did not understand, the power was turned off.

During the period in which she took Felix Kiehl off Haldol, Dr. Borg studied the reports that had accumulated in his enormous file. She read the notes he made himself and the transcript of Claire's testimony and everything else they sent her from the court. Only after she had finished it all could she devote herself to her own research.

There were all kinds of anecdotes—some doctors thought them myths—about patients with multiple personality and the ways their alters could differ physically from each other. There were reputed cases where an individual had allergies to certain substances while one personality was in control and not another; there were cases in which some personalities were left-handed while others weren't; there were cases in which some could sing in tune while others couldn't. She could hardly hope to study Kiehl in such great depth, but she could at least explore what she considered basic—the electrical patterns of his brain. Could she tell when a change of personality took place? Would there be specific patterns she could connect with specific alters? Her ideas were not original, and she considered them only a starting point, but this kind of research had never been attempted with the advanced equipment in her laboratory.

Felix Kiehl was not distinguishable from a dozen other patients, all on massive doses of medication, who were arranged in sundry static poses in the dayroom of Building Six—a large open area with windows on three sides, lined with plastic chairs, that served as the center of the ward. The space was airy and attractive despite the fact that the windows were protected by dense, impenetrable screens. It was the place patients came when they weren't at some activity—required or voluntary—or curled up, despite the rules, in their own beds. The TV set was tuned to a morning talk show. A lone man paced the room with carefully measured strides. He touched the wall with the middle finger of his left hand and spun on his heel in an odd pirouette. He walked across the open space to the opposite wall. He touched it with his middle finger and spun again and retraced his steps without a pause. Each step was in control; each touch precisely placed on a small, dark spot. The vinyl tiles beneath his feet were worn. No one knew how far he walked each day, how many miles he logged each week and year. He had been at it long before Dr. Borg arrived and would doubtless continue long after she was gone. She knew she could stop him with the right medication, but she was wise enough to know there was no point.

The only person actually watching television was a fat, freckled aide who was seated at a small table beside the entrance to the dayroom. He was immense, close to three hundred pounds, a size unusual even in a region where the fitness fads of the cities had not yet penetrated. He sat with a pad and a stubby pencil, tracking the comings and goings of his charges. He appeared to be hungover.

Dr. Borg smiled cheerfully and patted the aide's fleshy shoulder. She crossed the room and stood beside Kiehl. "Good morning," she said briskly.

He looked at her blankly.

"You remember what I say yesterday?"

He nodded slowly. "The brain waves," he replied.

"Ya . . . good." She touched Kiehl's shoulder. "The memory works better now. I said we go to a laboratory where I have special equipment. I said you had tests like this before."

"Doctor, my mind is still mostly blank."

"The memory returns in jumps and bounds," she said. "You come now. You take first walk outside. You remember your address?"

He looked confused.

"Six. You live in Building Six. If someone asks, you know where you come from." She touched his shoulder again. "We take good care. You don't get lost. I only tell you so you know your home."

Another aide was waiting outside the dayroom. He was short and

267

slender, with red hands and sinewy arms and a deeply tanned face from the farm work that he did on weekends. "This is Walter Harding," Dr. Borg said to Kiehl. "He helps greatly in my work."

They descended a flight of stairs, with Harding unlocking and then locking behind them each of three heavy wooden doors. They entered the long hallway that linked the residential buildings of Willingham. It was a lively thoroughfare, with doctors and nurses and aides and even an occasional privileged patient walking freely. It was only a few steps to the locked door of Dr. Borg's laboratory, which comprised two rooms on the ground floor of Building Six. They entered a room containing an examining table and a wall covered with shelves of electronic equipment. Another wall was fitted with a panel of reflective glass that was obviously a two-way mirror. There was a door to a second room and another door to a toilet. After giving him time to look around, Dr. Borg directed Kiehl to the examining table.

"Your job is not so very difficult." She smiled warmly. "Not at all —your job is to relax." She opened a tube of conductive jelly. The ones who had been through electroshock were always terrified, and the paranoids had their own peculiar fears, but she did everything she could to keep her subjects comfortable. "There will be no pain . . ." She carefully and methodically attached electrodes to his scalp while Harding flipped switches and made adjustments on the equipment.

Felix Kiehl watched it come to life.

He was thinking that she cared for him. He was thinking that the jelly she was rubbing so gently into his scalp was to keep her moist for him. He was thinking that soon Harding would leave and she would make love to him. He could tell how much she cared for him. He could feel it. She treated him differently from every other patient. Better. There was a special warmth they shared.

He was coming to life himself.

Walter Harding didn't leave the room, and Carola Borg made no seductive moves. But she couldn't control the heat her body gave off as she leaned over Kiehl, or the sweet aroma that was all her own. It fed his dream. She wasn't a beauty like Dr. Baxter. She was older than the other doctor, but she was kind and cheerful and he knew that he loved her and that she loved him equally.

"You understand that we make recordings from the brain?"

"Yes, Doctor."

"It will not hurt, not even one bit. You will be wide awake."

"I understand. I'm not afraid."

"All you need do is let yourself relax."

He smiled, feeling content.

"From time to time, I will make a sound or flash a light . . ."

He lay on her table. He had never felt more docile, more devoid of will. He would do everything she ever asked. After a short while, Dr. Borg stepped into the adjoining room to press keys on her computer. He thought he might offer to help her, write a program for her, show her what he knew, but this was not the time. He would have to wait until Harding went away.

He saw flashing lights. He felt comfortable and happy. He felt relaxed and free. A huge burden had been lifted without his knowing it was there. The thought passed through his mind that he liked this better than hypnosis.

While Felix Kiehl lay on the examining table, Carola Borg sat studying the data that was now displayed by her computer. The patient was calm, and her own mind was racing. This was just a trial—a preliminary test of his ability to tolerate the process—but she felt a rush of anticipation. He really was unique, and she was convinced that what she discovered would be equally unique. For the first time in all the years that multiple personality disorder had been known and studied, someone had the tools and the patient to truly understand.

CHAPTER 44

O<small>N THE FRIDAY</small> that followed their week together, Jake and Claire drove back to East Hampton. They arrived in the early afternoon and Jake went directly to the garden, where everywhere he looked there were new green shoots pushing above the ground. The only solution was to go on digging, as deep as possible.

But Claire felt fatigued, not up to work or exercise—not even the bikes. She knew exactly what she did need: to spend the weekend doing nothing more strenuous than turning the pages of the novel she bought the day before—a nineteenth-century epic that had all the earmarks of being perfect. She was happy to leave the garden in Jake's hands. Soon after they unloaded the groceries and she daubed her face with a layer of sunscreen, Claire parked herself in a favorite corner of the deck to catch the last warm rays.

The garden was on the east side of the house, behind a clump of cedars, and Claire couldn't see Jake work, though she could hear the steady *chunk* as he jabbed his spade into the sandy soil.

He dug with a slow and steady rhythm, pausing only to sip the beer he'd brought along. The sun warmed him and the breeze cooled him and the work was a pleasure. He could feel the sweat spread over his body as his muscles loosened.

Claire was so immersed in her book that she didn't notice when the digging stopped. She looked up to see Jake standing next to her with a strange expression on his face. "Is something wrong? Is your back all right?"

"You have to look at something."

She followed him out into the garden, where he had already completed two more rows. "You're really into this."

He poked his spade at a weathered sheet of dark brown plastic at the bottom of a trench. "I hit this thing. I thought you ought to have a look before I dug it out."

"It's plastic mulch," Claire said. "Remember the year we read that book on—"

"That stuff was green. I remember it very clearly, along with all the slimy critters that called it home. It wasn't as thick as this."

"You're not saying we're on a landfill?"

"I don't know what I'm saying." With the tip of his spade, Jake rapped something hard. The sound was hollow. There was something underneath the plastic.

"A little small for a coffin," he said.

"You're telling me you're spooked?"

"You never know. It could be treasure. Captain Kidd once roamed these parts."

"That was Gardiner's Island. Besides, he had a thing against plastic."

Jake dug carefully. The brown plastic was wrapped around a box. He lifted the package above the surface. It was the size of a small valise. The plastic had been sealed with silver duct tape. It was neatly done, with overlapping layers, not easy to rip away. Inside was an aluminum suitcase of the kind used by photographers to protect expensive cameras. "The family Nikons . . ." he said.

They walked back to the house, Jake carrying the case and Claire the plastic bag, as if the bag itself had meaning. "Should we call the

271

police?" she asked. "Don't they look for fingerprints? Could this be evidence?"

"Of what?" He kneeled beside the case and pressed the buttons on the lid, and the latches popped. He flipped the case wide open.

It wasn't a camera or a bomb or a body or any portion of a body. It clearly didn't belong to Captain Kidd, though it was indeed a treasure: the case was filled with plastic sandwich bags, each of which was filled with wads of cash.

Jake opened a bag and saw a stack of hundreds.

"I don't believe this . . ."

"Little treats for lunch," he said.

"You could say that . . ."

"The motherfucker hid it."

There was only one motherfucker.

"He knew we'd never garden. He made sure of *that*. He buried this deep so that even if we did we'd never find it."

"You think he had a plan? You think he thought this through?"

"What else?" Jake opened a bag and then another and another. All the bills were worn, impossible to trace. There were twenties and fifties and hundreds. He paused before he spoke and looked directly into Claire's eyes. "He won't be back to claim this for a while."

She shook her head. "Are you thinking what I think you're thinking?"

"Of course I am."

"It isn't ours."

"There's no way he gets out for a hundred years."

"Even if you're right, which I sincerely hope, it isn't ours."

"It's not his either . . ." Jake went on. "Who owns it? The noble firm of Potter, Weeks? The *IRS*? The fucking lawyers?"

"Not us," she said.

"Then tell me, who does own it?"

"Let's not fight," Claire said. She turned away from him. "I thought we were starting over."

He wrapped his arm around her. "We are."

They sat on the deck and counted the money. The total was two hundred thousand dollars. It didn't change the way they saw things.

"First of all, it isn't his. He's got no claim," Jake said. "Even if he did, he won't be spending it. You can rest assured—they haven't forgotten him out West. Second of all, the money doesn't belong to anyone specific. There's no way to repay it. There's no one to repay it to."

"You sound like a lawyer," she said.

"Let's not get vicious." She eyed Jake carefully as he went on. "The money was here before we found it, right? It would have rotted here, agreed? No one has to know . . ."

"We already know. Are you telling me to *dissociate?*"

"Not such a terrible idea."

"And you're supposed to be a psychoanalyst?"

It was the way it always had been when they went at each other —except for the tone. Neither tried or wanted to strike the crushing blow. They listened to each other. They held each other's hand.

The joke, not lost on either of them, was that in the end they still had to call a lawyer.

CHAPTER 45

WALTER HARDING SAT in the hallway just outside Dr. Borg's laboratory, reading a hunting magazine he had read a dozen times and chatting when he could with the aides who passed. The doctor kept him parked outside while she was testing. Her experiment was under way, and Felix Kiehl was settled comfortably in their routine. The new patient was easier than most. He did everything that he was told. Harding knew the courtroom story and had even read a portion of the file, but whatever anger this one had was gone. This man was dead, burnt out—though it didn't keep Harding from being careful, and it didn't keep the doctor from being totally absorbed. She was aiming for a big discovery. She told Harding that this one's brain would teach her something special. As for himself, Harding didn't think the brain of anyone at Willingham—doctors included—could teach him anything.

Carola Borg's accented voice, a shade too loud, came over the loudspeaker on the wall beside Felix Kiehl. A bundle of wires trailed along the floor from the neat cluster on his head to a receptacle in the wall, and from there to her computer in the other room.

"Please count slowly, in your mind, from number one to number twenty."

She watched the monitor as Kiehl complied, saw the curves tremble on the screen, heard the pens scrape faintly as they etched their jagged patterns on the moving paper. Her equipment was in perfect order—the powerful computer that recorded and analyzed the data and the archaic pens that Harding cleaned and adjusted and kept running perfectly. She was so meticulous in her approach that things were always in order. "We will proceed in the way that we did yesterday. Certain sounds will come, and from time to time there will be the light. Your work is the same. It is better not to talk. All that is necessary is that you relax . . ."

It was easy. He preferred it to occupational therapy, or art therapy, or music therapy, or group therapy, or any of the other so-called therapies they would otherwise require. The weather was warm and her lab was air-conditioned, unlike the patients' rooms. Best of all, he had her to himself. He liked to be near her even if he couldn't speak. He knew that one day they would know each other better. He knew that he had time.

After fifteen minutes of the lights and sounds that had become familiar over the past three weeks, Dr. Borg shifted to a stimulus that was completely different from any she had used before. It was the start of the experimental portion of her research. Without any warning, she played a tape of her husband reading—he had no accent—a section of Felix Kiehl's own diary. It was written by the personality who called himself The Professor, and it was meant to take the man in her laboratory completely by surprise.

She waited expectantly at her computer. She could see the patient through the glass as she watched the monitor. Would there be a reaction? The question in her mind was what it would be like and where inside his brain it would begin. Her hope was that the one who wrote these words would know them and would himself appear. Then she would see, when she met this "Professor," if his brain was different from the others'.

To Dr. Borg's considerable disappointment, none of her questions got an answer. Her equipment failed to register even the slightest change. The patient's reaction to the paragraph was indistinguishable from the way he reacted to stimuli that had no meaning. She knew he wasn't deaf, but she had to wonder if he heard one word of the tape that she had played.

Two days later she tried again with a different paragraph. Now it was writing that had been attributed to the personality named Victor. He expressed overt anger, with diatribes against several people from the past. She was worried about meeting this one—he was, as far as she knew, the one who killed the lawyer—but she had to try. Her husband had attempted a certain expressiveness in the way he read, but it had no effect at all. The patient was unchanged. Her warning to Harding had been unnecessary.

She tried on another day with the writing of Felix Kiehl. Nothing changed. It made no difference if she chose neutral subjects or the painful events he wrote about.

After another week and another frustrating attempt to provoke a reaction, Carola Borg stayed late to ponder the question of why her stimuli had no effect. She had picked them with the goal of arousing his emotions only to find that there were no emotions. She didn't understand. She ran the data through her computer in a half a dozen different ways. She tried different arrangements of variables and different statistical analyses. She studied the patterns his brain produced with methods that would have been impossible before the advent of computers.

And finally, she found something. It needed more work, but she was experienced enough to know that it had meaning. There *was* a hidden pattern. It was masked by surface activity. It was a rhythm buried deep within his brain. There was no way to tease it out without a complex mathematical analysis, but once she got a glimpse, it was unmistakable. To her surprise, it looked like sleep. Slow and steady, of minimal intensity, regions of his brain were in the deepest stage of sleep. It was no wonder he seemed drugged. It was no wonder he had not reacted to her stimuli. The wonder was that he could hear her voice and sit upright and speak at all.

The more she went over the data, the more Carola Borg began to see how much of Felix Kiehl was sound asleep. He had not gone from too many personalities to none. All the other personalities had been sleeping.

She called her husband and told him she would be working late.

She sat beside the computer as it sifted through more data. She watched and waited as the computer worked. Something was happening! She fed in everything she had. The more she looked, and the more information she gave the machine, the more she saw the pattern. He had been asleep from the day they first began.

She called her husband again and told him she was onto something and would be working through the night. She thought of going upstairs to see what Kiehl looked like in a state of ordinary sleep, but she decided it would be disruptive.

Finally, when it was close to dawn, when she was sure that what she had was real, she stretched out on the examining table and did her best to sleep. It was, of course, impossible. What she needed to ponder next was what she could do to wake the man.

CHAPTER 46

JOHN SPICER ARRIVED on Saturday morning.

Jake had tracked him down at an all-night game and said it was important, and that was all he needed to know. He arrived in East Hampton at nine on a huge black Harley—a toy he'd bought with the help of recent poker winnings. Jake had to ride it, despite the fact that he hadn't been on a motorcycle in fifteen years and this monster had the power to spin out on him in any gear.

Claire stood with Spicer in the driveway as Jake roared off, the pounding from the exhaust so powerful she could feel each throb inside her, as every bird within two hundred yards fluttered up into the sky.

"I assume he can handle it."

"*Now* you ask," she said, not smiling.

"He's a big boy, ain't he?"

"Tell me, do you call *yourself* a boy?"

Spicer grinned uneasily in response to Claire's sour expression. Then he looked up at the house. "So this is the fabled retreat . . ."

"Which fable do you have in mind?"

He looked at her cautiously. "I want to apologize for what we put you through. I'm sure you know where we were coming from. I had to put a little doubt—"

"I know all about it," she interrupted. "You were playing out your role, right? You were being a good lawyer."

He stuck out his hand. "No hard feelings?"

"I'm an analyst, remember? I respect my feelings." She took his hand anyway.

They heard the throb of the motorcycle and Jake rode up, intact but shaken. "This thing's incredible. I never got out of second gear."

"There's nothing like a bike between your legs," said Spicer.

Claire looked into Jake's eyes and struggled not to smile.

Spicer saw. "I said somethin' funny?"

"Only to a shrink . . ." Jake said.

"What would that be?"

"You must be hungry," Claire said, pulling Spicer into the house.

After breakfast, Jake went down into the basement for the metal case. He placed it in the center of the table. "We need to know what you think about this."

Spicer sipped more coffee. He may not have slept the night before, but he was never too tired to play his little games. "Wha' chu' got, my man? You dealin' now? You got dope in there?"

Jake opened the case. "This has nothing to do with drugs."

"*Jesus!*" Spicer reached for a plastic bag, looked closely at the bills, then took another and another. "It's real."

"Two hundred thousand," Jake said.

"You didn't *declare* this? Man, one place I can't do *anything* is the IRS."

Jake shook his head again. "It was in our garden. Someone planted it. Maybe they thought it would grow into a tree."

"You fucking with me?"

"There's only one possible suspect . . ."

Spicer slammed his fist into his open hand. "I *knew* it. I knew that fucker was a con."

279

"It doesn't prove anything," Claire said.

"Let's not go back to *that*," Jake said.

They sat in silence. Spicer's wheels were turning rapidly and coffee was no longer necessary. "So what do you want from me?"

"You get one guess . . ." Jake said.

"Who knows you found this?"

"Not a soul."

"Not even your shrinks?"

"We're done with shrinks," Jake said. "We don't need them anymore."

"I'm not so sure of that," Claire said.

Spicer kept looking at the money. His eyes were glazed and his mouth was open slightly and his pink tongue glistened. He could have been a bullfrog waiting patiently for a fat fly to land. "I take it you folks would like to keep this little stash."

"We know we can't. We're not naive—at least I'm not," Claire said. "You should explain things to your brilliant buddy."

Spicer went on as if he didn't hear. ". . . Like you want to know what the le-*gal*-ities might be?"

"You could put it that way," Jake said.

"Like you wonder what would happen if you spent it carefully, like on trips to Europe and Mexico and Vegas, and maybe you bought some fancy toys and you paid only cash."

"You get the picture, more or less."

"Are you sure *he* put it there?" Spicer asked.

"Who else is possible?"

"The last time we were in the garden was the weekend before the house was vandalized," Claire said.

"You *infer* he left it there."

"You have a better inference?" she asked.

Spicer studied Claire. "Who told you to infer?"

She shook her head. "You know, Mary Buchanan once said something like that."

Spicer covered his face. "I'm in big trouble."

"You're not in trouble; you're just a lawyer," Claire said. "Unless you're all in trouble."

"It could be . . ."

"Can it be that simple? We come to no conclusion?" Jake went on. "We pretend that we don't know? You think that would protect us?"

With a look of sadness and affection, Spicer reached across the table and grabbed Jake's shoulder. "I'm puttin' you on, my man. The lady's right—you're back in dreamland. Didn't you forget one thing?"

"That he may be a fraud? We've been over it, believe me. It may or may not prove that. For all we know, it was put there by one of the personalities. It could be a dissociated act . . ." Jake could see how pleased Claire was.

Spicer kept fondling the bags of cash. He shook his head. "Did it not occur to you that one way or another, con job or not, crazy or not, you would always worry? Some part of the creep—the one that buried it—would still remember. If he ever did get out, he'd damn well show up here."

"You think he could get *out?*" Claire looked sick.

"I think it's an imperfect system."

"That much I know," she said.

By early afternoon, after Spicer made the necessary calls, four agents from the FBI arrived to take custody of the money. They agreed that Spicer would call a press conference on Monday morning and get as much publicity as possible. Along with any points that he would score—and doubtless he would score a few—they had to make absolutely sure that the news got up to Willingham.

By evening, Spicer was totally exhausted. Jake and Claire wanted desperately to be alone, but there was no way that they could send him out into the night. They gave him a large glass of Scotch and sat in the living room with him until his eyes began to close. Then he staggered off into the guest room for a long sleep.

Claire was eager to make love, but Jake was unable to become aroused. "I think I need a bike between my legs," he said.

"Just go to sleep. I'm sure tomorrow you'll be fine."

She was right again. By Sunday afternoon, after Spicer zoomed off toward the city, the problem was easily and satisfactorily resolved.

CHAPTER 47

AFTER TWO MONTHS of daily meetings, Felix Kiehl had still not manifested any of what Dr. Borg now thought of as his *so-called* personalities. He never changed. The only thing she knew was that she could not jar the man. No matter what she tried, his brain continued its long sleep.

Now she had a stimulus that might have a real effect. There was no way he could be prepared, no way he could have thought about it, no way that he could know what was about to come, no way that anyone could sleep through *this*.

The session began like all the others: She attached her electrodes to his scalp and chatted briefly with him about superficial subjects. Then, for a five-minute period, she exposed him to the familiar lights and sounds and made baseline measurements. The results could have been superimposed on those that had come each day before. Instead of what she once expected—a lively patient with a lively, active brain —he continued to hibernate.

She inserted a cassette into the tape machine. It was her husband reading from the local newspaper about a school-board meeting. If Kiehl wasn't already asleep, the article was dull enough to bring sleep on. But the patient remained predictably the same, his pattern unvarying. He just did not react. Then, after a second five minutes, without any warning, without any introduction, with her own heart pounding rapidly, she inserted a second tape into the machine and pressed the button to start it playing. It was the article from the *New York Post* that reported on the buried money:

> The plush East Hampton home of Dr. Claire Baxter, the psychiatrist who testified about her treatment of Felix Kiehl, the notorious computer manipulator and courtroom killer, was the scene of the latest development in this strange man's tormented tale. A box containing two hundred thousand dollars in cash was found buried in the doctor's garden. A spokesman from the U.S. Attorney's office speculated that the money was stashed by Kiehl as insurance against the possibility of future need. Mr. Kiehl is currently an inmate of . . .

She was well prepared. As usual, Harding was seated in the corridor outside her laboratory door. She had alerted him and she had a nearby alarm if there was any need. But there was nothing. Not a sound came from Felix Kiehl—not even a grunt, not even a sigh.

To Carola Borg's huge disappointment, there was not the slightest hint of any reaction to her latest effort. The patient lay there motionless. His breathing stayed regular and his brain was unchanged. If there *were* other personalities, they sent no signals to her computer and left no tracks on her roll of paper. Could he have blocked out everything about those people and that house and all that money? Could anyone be so dissociated? It was too much for her to believe. More and more she wondered if the personalities were creations of the psychoanalysts and lawyers.

She got up from her seat at the monitor and entered the room where Kiehl lay quietly. He gazed up at her as she checked connections. She knew the problem could not be so trivial as wiring, but she methodically followed each electrode, one by one, from the place where it was attached to the patient's scalp, to the place where it exited the room.

He saw the pink strap of her bra and the soft skin of her arms as she leaned over him. Her blouse was modest, but it revealed the outline of her large breasts. Her arms were bare and covered with fine, blond hair. He sucked in her aroma. It had a delicious ripeness one might not expect in a woman of her age and matronly appearance. She smelled faintly of the love she'd made that morning . . .

Kiehl smiled up at her.

"This is better than the ward," she said. "Not so hot. You prefer the air conditioning?" Whatever the problem was, he couldn't be blamed for it.

"I like to help you, Doctor."

"I do appreciate." She was nowhere close to giving up. She had other methods that were worth a try. There were drugs. She might even explore hypnosis.

"I want to be like Walter," he went on. "I want to help. I could do chores."

"You help in your own way," she said. "The work would not be possible without you."

The electrodes were attached correctly, as she knew they would be. The useless results were valid. Then she went back for a check of her monitor, and she was stunned to find that now there was a change. As she watched in amazement, the intensities ran off the screen. The shapes were very different from any she had seen before. Something new was happening inside his brain.

"Are you all right?" she asked through the speaker.

"I'm fine, Doctor." His voice sounded the same.

"Do you feel different in any way?"

"I feel fine, Doctor."

Was it real? Could something she just touched have thrown everything awry?

She went back into the room where Kiehl was lying motionless. He did not look different, but she needed to examine the connections again. She patiently began where the wires left the room and worked her way back to the table. Everything looked exactly as it had before, and she began to hope that the new results were real. The last thing to check was the attachment to his scalp. As she leaned close, as she looked into his dreamy gaze, Felix Kiehl sprang to life. With one smooth motion, his hands were at her throat.

"Wha—" was the only sound she managed.

"Do you love me?" he asked softly, pulling her face up against his own. "This is all for you, isn't it?"

She could not answer.

"You're only using me. It's for your pleasure." She struggled helplessly as he held her close. He ground his pelvis into her. She couldn't move his hands. They squeezed steadily as she flailed, choking under the pressure of his grasp. Then Carola Borg saw black.

Her body was sprawled on top of him, her head pressed close against his own. He could smell her perfume and her sweat and something he remembered vaguely but could not identify. The tracings in the other room had spiked in a burst that corresponded to the moment of his ejaculation. Then he did remember: She smelled of semen, not his own.

He waited for several minutes to be sure that they had not been overheard. He peeled the electrodes off his scalp. He rolled her on her back. Now he had to wait. He crouched in a corner like a frightened child.

Half an hour later, when his shift was done, Walter Harding unlocked the door to the laboratory and pushed in slowly. The room was dim, but he saw the doctor instantly. Was she asleep? Did she get the patient back upstairs without his noticing? Had he been asleep himself? Before he could reach the lights, a metal stool crashed down on his head. He lay on the floor unconscious as Kiehl knelt over him. When Kiehl withdrew his hands, Walter Harding was no longer breathing.

Felix Kiehl's own breathing continued slow and steady. First he pulled Carola Borg's skirt above her waist and then he removed her panties. She was wearing bikini underwear more revealing than he had ever imagined. He thought it was not right for her to wear such things. He told himself that it was further proof of how bad she really was. He stripped the clothes off Harding and lifted his body up onto the cot. He pulled her legs apart and wrapped them tightly around Harding's hips. He knew that anyone who came in now would back out instantly.

Then he removed his own clothing and dressed himself in Harding's shirt and trousers. The clothes were small, but they would have to do. He found keys and a wallet and the registration for Harding's car. He had the urge to light a fire, but he knew it would be unwise.

At exactly four-thirty in the afternoon, Felix Kiehl stepped out of Dr. Carola Borg's laboratory and walked through the corridors of Willingham. The day shift had just ended, and large numbers of hospital employees were heading for the parking lot. He knew the pattern. He followed a chattering group of nurses who were complaining about the recent dry weather and its effect on their gardens. No one paid the least attention to him. They all prayed for rain.

He found Harding's brown Plymouth without any difficulty. Though the car was old, it started smoothly. It needed gas, but he would worry about that later. He followed a line of cars down a one-way road to a gatehouse and a heavy steel barrier that blocked the world outside. He knew he had reached the hardest part. He had never seen this place and had no way to plan. But he knew about faces. He had studied Harding for many weeks. The age and hair were close enough. The height was wrong, but seated in a car it would not show. Now he did his best to imitate the worried look that was always on Harding's face. The most they could do was lock him up again.

The farm boy in the little booth never looked up. The television set that kept him company showed a weather report that he watched anxiously. Like Carola Borg, like Walter Harding, like all the others who ever befriended Felix Kiehl—in California and Nevada and

287

wherever he would be going next—the people who worked at Willingham were subject to benevolence and cloudy judgment.

They were not like him. They needed to feel those maudlin emotions in order to make their lives worthwhile. He had rid himself of foolishness when he was very young.

CHAPTER 48

Claire arrived at her office at seven A.M. to find a message asking her to call a number with an upstate area code. It had come in during the night, and she knew instantly that it had to do with Kiehl. After she saw her two early patients, she gritted her teeth and dialed.

"Doctor, I'm *so* glad to hear from you." The woman who answered sounded very young. "I'm with the North Country Press. We're doing a piece about yesterday, and I was hoping to get some background—"

"Yesterday?"

"You haven't heard?"

Claire had been asleep at ten and up to jog at dawn. "Heard *what?*"

"That Felix Kiehl escaped from Willingham . . ."

"I don't believe this."

"I'm really sorry. I had no idea I'd be the first."

"How could he *escape?*"

"It's kind of ugly. Is there someone with you?"

"I'm a psychiatrist," Claire said. "Just tell me . . . ."

A few minutes later, Claire called Jake and left a message on his machine.

"The son of a bitch," he said when he called back.

"She said he strangled them."

"The son of a bitch."

"Both of them."

"I get it," he said softly.

"He stripped off their clothing. He arranged their bodies to make it look like they were making love."

"The same old story."

"He could be anywhere," she went on. "He could show up in my waiting room again."

"He doesn't have to play that game. The money's gone."

It was nine-thirty. Claire's most troubled patient was in her waiting room. There was nothing to be gained but hurt feelings and a month of misery if she didn't see the woman. She told Jake she would go on working, and he said that he would come to her at noon. In a little while, when he had a break, he would make some calls.

During the next fifty minutes, Claire received four phone calls. Her machine responded with the clicks and clanks that were characteristic of it, and her patient became convinced that Claire was preoccupied. The woman was right, and Claire decided to admit it. To her surprise, the patient was not upset. They agreed to end the session early. The woman left cheerfully—grateful for the evidence that not everything that came into her head was fantasy.

The first two messages were from reporters. The third was a hang-up. The fourth was from the chief of police of the Town of Willingham.

"Thank God for Spicer," Jake said at noon.

"Did you reach him?"

"At least Kiehl knows we found the money. At least he won't come looking." He was in her office, pacing.

"This is not about money—you know it as well as I do."

"He may be crazy," Jake said, "but he's not a fool."

"I don't know what he is."

"Why would he bother us?" Jake went on. "He can't use us anymore."

"There are lots of ways of using people."

"You have one in mind?"

"The way he used those two upstate. The way he used the others . . ."

Claire looked so sad and frightened that Jake put his arm around her. "I see it differently. My bet is that he's in Canada by now. I think he's got a Swiss account and a Cayman Islands account and a ton of money stashed. There are millions unaccounted for."

"But look at how he killed them," she said. "You can't say it has no meaning."

"I'm sure it does. It could prove all kinds of theories." He held her tight. "I don't care what it means. I want you to know I've learned a thing or two. I swear that if he comes, I'll deal with him."

She didn't argue. She didn't say that Jake was crazy or impulsive or too macho. She wrapped her arms around his waist and let him hold her. The longer they held each other, the more obvious it became that something had really changed. She was willing to let him give her comfort. And Jake, in his own way, was learning how to give it.

Eventually, a peculiar thought occurred to Claire. She had her doubts, but she had a funny feeling something was happening. Later in the afternoon, she stopped at a pharmacy and bought a kit. Her period was only two days late and a negative result would not have been conclusive, but that was one uncertainty they would never have to face. In the evening, to their shared awe, the test came up pink— confirmation that Claire was pregnant.

Even more amazing was the fact that she felt no ambivalence at all. They held each other in bed and, for the first time in a long time, they both felt the same emotion—joy. For at least a little while, the nightmare of Felix Kiehl was not the only thing that filled their thoughts.

"Forget the creep," Spicer said on the telephone. "The man's no dummy. He's *gone*. You can bet the farm he had another stash."

"How do you know?" Jake asked.

"Cause it always was a con. Cause he's got no reason to stick around."

"You're not dreaming, are you?"

"I told you I don't dream."

"You go with logic."

"You're goddamn right I do—and with where they found the car."

"*Where?*"

"Niagara Falls. Half a mile from the border."

"Maybe he went swimming," Jake said. "Maybe he tried a barrel."

"Maybe you'd like to put him in one."

"Hey!" Jake said. "Stick around with shrinks and you get to talk like one."

"There are tours," Spicer went on. "People cross the border by the thousands every day. The Canadians are looking for him. The people on our side will be looking too."

"You'll call if you get word?" Jake asked.

"I'll come right over. I'll move right in that pretty house and take care of both of you."

The weeks went by. Jake made daily calls to Spicer, but there was no news—no signs or sightings, no hints or rumors, not a trace. They began to hope that he was right.

Nevertheless, Jake took measures he did not discuss with Spicer. Every Friday afternoon, before the drive out to the beach, he took the gun out of his cabinet and wrapped it in a rag and stashed it in the bottom of his briefcase. When they reached the house, he put the gun into a kitchen drawer that held waxed paper and aluminum foil and was strategically close to the living room. At the end of every weekend, he put the gun back in the briefcase and returned it to the hiding place in his office.

On a rainy Saturday, after Claire drove off to visit a friend with a newborn baby, Jake took the gun into the basement and fired a round into a target he improvised out of a stack of firewood.

He was amazed by the ringing in his ears and by how much damage that single bullet did.

CHAPTER 49

As SUMMER WENT on, they gradually relaxed—or at least became less terrified. Felix Kiehl was not forgotten, but he seemed more and more remote. July arrived; warm and clear and every weekend a time of joy. The house began to feel like it belonged to them again, and life seemed almost safe. The pregnancy kept going well. Claire was round and luscious and felt sexier than ever. She gained ten pounds, but said she felt lighter than air. After the first few weeks, she felt no fatigue. The same mysterious change in her physiology put an end to every ache and pain. She was full of stamina and grace and a glorious intensity that brought her tennis to a level it had never reached before. Everything she did felt effortless . . .

And then came blessed August. The month had special memories and charms. Augusto, Augusta—names they laughingly considered. A year ago, in Italy, it had been the best month of their marriage. This year, in a different way, was every bit its equal. It was calm. They felt connected with each other and with their house and with the land and ocean and the new life growing inside her.

The return to work after Labor Day was less agonizing than in the past. New things kept happening. There were doctors to visit and classes to attend and changes to make in the apartment. They started to plan the baby's room. It wasn't too early to think about the help that they would need, and about switching offices so that Claire could be closer to the baby when she went back to work. She was ready— even happy—to give up her retreat. And though the pregnancy was barely visible—it was just the beginning of her fourth month—on the very first day of Claire's return, two patients, both single women in their late thirties, became obsessed with the idea of becoming pregnant.

October. The East End of Long Island was at its most appealing. The leaves had turned, and everywhere you looked there was brilliant autumn color. It was the best time of the year, the most peaceful, the month when it was possible to imagine what the land was like a hundred years ago. The farm stands beside the highway were piled high with broccoli and Brussels sprouts and pumpkins. Claire's belly began to show in earnest. Like every couple they knew, they shared fantasies of finding a way to live out there full-time.

After years of seeing locals with surf rods mounted on their jeeps and pickups, Jake was inspired to try fishing in the ocean. He read a book on surf casting and spent a Saturday morning at the tackle shop, where he bought a rod and reel and a supply of lures and a portion of the local wisdom. The man who owned the place said his timing was perfect. It was the season when large schools of bluefish and striped bass migrated along the ocean beaches, and the month when fishing reached its peak.

Everything else was at its peak, he thought, why not this too?

The surf was warm as he waded into it, and the beach was empty except for Claire, who sat in a canvas chair, wrapped snugly in a blanket, watching, reading, sleeping, while for the third weekend in a row Jake heaved silver lures into what seemed an empty ocean. She was there because she loved the waves. She was also there because she still wasn't ready to stay in the house alone.

The fish didn't leap into his pail. Casting the heavy lures sometimes hurt his back. But after he reconciled himself to the fact that fishing in the surf is a low-percentage enterprise, Jake had a moment that all surf casters dream about—the good luck to be on the beach when a school of feeding fish moved in between the shoreline and the breakers. Beyond the sandbar, out where the big waves crashed, the water was rough and wild, but in close it was crystal clear, and he could see it all unfold.

At first there were just the little ones: a school of bait fish milling in nervous circles, in danger, more or less helpless, more or less knowing it in whatever way fish know these things. He got out of the water. He called to Claire, and she stood beside him. The bait fish were trapped. The water was crammed with millions that had no place to go. They had been herded into shore by larger fish and were being compressed into a tighter and tighter mass. "The poor little things," she said. Large fish then made rapid sweeps through the clustered school. It started methodically, one big fish at a time, a vicious pass that left a trail of death. It quickly became a frenzy—the bait fish leaping everywhere, even up onto the shore, the big fish pursuing them relentlessly. "The poor little things," she said again.

They were giant bluefish, the piranhas of the ocean, more vicious than sharks at a time like this. Jake and Claire were close enough to see the open mouths, the razor teeth, the bait fish bitten into quivering halves. Then the gulls arrived, in a frenzy all their own, more excited than they ever were at the landfill. They swooped down for scraps, as vicious in their own way as the bluefish.

"I thought we came to catch a fish," Claire said.

With one easy motion, no need to try for distance, no need to wade barefoot in the teeming water, he flipped his lure into the middle of the school.

The rod dipped sharply when Jake pulled back, and he felt a tug more powerful than he had ever dreamed. He had to struggle just to hold the thing. It was more than a fish. It was more than just alive. His reel gave line and he let it run. He felt intense excitement and a powerful erotic surge. He felt no eagerness to land this thing—it was too wild, too alien. He didn't see it as a meal or a trophy or as an enemy. All he wanted was to hold on. He had not tasted blood; he was still a cat who has not learned to kill.

Claire stood beside him. "My God, I can't *believe* this."

"If you felt this bastard, you'd believe him."

Jake's rod absorbed the fish's power. When it tired, he reeled in steadily. When it sensed the shore, it struggled toward the depths and he gave it line. When it tired again, he brought it closer. And throughout the struggle, utterly indifferent to it, the school continued feeding. The unhooked bluefish and their helpless prey drifted down the beach in the direction of Montauk Point.

Five minutes later, the school was gone and the birds were gone and Jake and Claire were alone with what was now a solitary bluefish. It struggled on, perhaps more desperately than before, pulling line out toward the breakers where the waves would amplify its strength. Jake tightened the drag, and the fish's run soon slowed. He gained more ground. Then the fish was truly exhausted, limp in the water, and he pulled it up onto the sand with the assistance of a gentle wave. The bluefish lay there, a gorgeous silvery creature that weighed at least fifteen pounds.

"My hero," Claire said.

They kneeled together to look more closely at the gasping blue-fish. The fish's sides were shimmering with blues and grays that looked illuminated. Fragments of its prey were still in its mouth, along with his lure, hooked firmly into its lower jaw. Its cold eye looked some-where, not at them.

The fish was dead when they got home. The glow was gone, and it had turned slate gray. It was still a perfect thing, more beautiful than any shark, though as much a machine for killing. Now came time for a break. Claire had gone up for a nap. Jake wanted a drink, a little celebration as he relaxed out on the deck. He wanted to see what the cookbooks had to say about the best way to prepare a blue-fish.

Before she got into bed, Claire looked herself over. Her belly was coming along—round and solid, a wonder and a joy, even though she sometimes felt like she had swallowed a cantaloupe. She stepped out of her slacks and stood in front of the mirror in her T-shirt and panties. She ran her hand across her abdomen—hoping, as happened more and more these days, to feel the fluttering of her baby.

"Oh my God—"

The mirror showed the reflection of Felix Kiehl, standing behind her.

"Please . . ." He smiled tentatively.

Her knees began to wobble, but she had the presence of mind to get her slacks back on. "What do you want?"

"I didn't mean to frighten you."

She needed to sit, but she fought the feeling off. "What do you *want?*"

He was polite. His voice was new. He tried to sound benign. "I had to see you, to meet you, to show you who I really am."

The room began to spin, and she had no choice but to reach out for the bed.

CHAPTER 50

A BEETHOVEN STRING quartet echoed through the empty woods as Jake sat on a deck chair in the autumn sun and leafed through sections of three different cookbooks: French; Cajun; Southwestern. They all were wrong, not good enough for food as fresh as this. He narrowed the choice to baking his bluefish whole—they could make salad of the leftovers—or cutting filets and broiling them with herbs. He'd see what Claire preferred. He went upstairs to shower. It was the perfect moment to make love.

She was lying on her back with her eyes wide open. She didn't move. Her skin was ashen.

Beside her, not touching her, curled on his side and gazing at her with a rapt expression, was Felix Kiehl. He looked like a little boy, innocent and worshipful except for his gun. The weapon was black and oddly shaped, like a plastic space-age toy. He sat up slowly and pointed the thing at Jake's abdomen. "Don't make sudden moves. You know how dangerous I am."

"He was waiting here," Claire said. She looked into Jake's eyes, as if he needed to be warned. "He wants to show us who he really is. He said, if we do everything he asks, he'll treat us well."

Kiehl smiled benevolently.

"Then we'll treat *him* well," Jake said. It helped to mask his fear. "You picked the perfect day. We have fresh bluefish—too much for just the two of us. You'll *have* to stay for dinner."

Kiehl's response was friendly. "I accept with gratitude, old man. I haven't had a decent meal in the longest time. My only regret is that I brought no wine."

Who the hell was he? What the hell was he after? What kind of crazy game was this?

"No problem," Jake said. "The liquor store is just a mile away."

"I'm terribly sorry, but the car is in the shop. I had to come by cab. You must have *something* fit to drink." He got off the bed and stood facing Jake. Despite the pleasantries, he aimed the gun.

"Nothing really *right*," Jake went on. "After all, this is a celebration. You're welcome to take my car."

"What are we celebrating?"

"Old times."

"Nice try. I'll pass anyway," Kiehl said, and the game was over. His eyes were more focused than the bluefish, but every bit as cold. With his weapon still aimed at Jake, he directed them down the stairs and into the living room. He gently pushed Claire toward the couch. "Have a seat, my love. I'm sorry to have startled you so badly. I thought you knew that one day I'd return. Dr. Silver, you may sit as well. Please don't get up unless I ask you to."

"The money's gone," Jake said. "Didn't they tell you? It was in the papers. We called the FBI. They still check in on us every once in a while."

"They don't get *The Times* at Willingham. They don't even get the *Post*."

"You didn't see television?"

Kiehl contorted his face bizarrely. "Enough to make you crazy." Then he grinned. "I know all about that cash. A little lady whispered it into my ear."

"A lady?"

"In a moment of passion . . ."

Claire stifled a moan, and Kiehl looked at her with real concern. "Dr. Baxter, please don't be alarmed. There's nothing to fear."

She couldn't help but stare at his weapon.

"I mean no harm. I mean no one harm unless they harm me first." Kiehl circled the large open space that made up the living room, dining room, and kitchen of the house. He looked up at the skylights, where the sun still cast its orange glow. He ran his hand across a smooth new granite countertop, above the drawer where Jake's gun was hidden. "You've done a nice job. I think the place is much improved."

"Are you the one who did the damage?" Jake asked.

Kiehl looked closely at the antique maps that hung on a wall in the dining area. They were of Florence and Rome. "You'll have your answer in due time."

"I take it you didn't care for Willingham," Jake went on. "I hear the place is not too wonderful." He had to keep on talking. He knew they had to come across as real. If they became the fantasy this man was playing out, then they were dead.

"I was treated well. The staff was more humane than the people in New York."

"I take it they didn't cure you," Jake said.

A sly smile crossed on Kiehl's face. "What makes you think there was anything to cure?"

"Are you saying there wasn't?"

"I always thought you were among the doubters."

"You didn't answer," Jake went on.

"Are you playing therapist? Or is it lawyer?"

"It's time we all stopped playing."

Jake's words just hung there, and the silence was enough to bring Claire back. She looked into Kiehl's face. "Have we met? Who *are* you?"

"You know my name."

"I do?"

301

"You've been wanting me as much as I've been wanting you."

She glanced at Jake and their eyes met briefly. "Are you Felix Kiehl?"

His smile was warm. His face appeared to glow. "Of course."

"The real one?"

"There's only one . . ."

"Why didn't you speak sooner? Did someone stop you?" she asked.

"Only myself."

"You've been *conscious?*"

"To the extent that anyone is conscious."

"Meaning what?" she asked.

"Think, my dear . . ."

"Are you saying you don't have MPD, that you never had it?"

"The light bulb lights!" His face was filled with pride.

Could it really be? Claire had trouble grasping this. She shut her eyes.

"It was all a sick, outrageous lie . . ." Jake said.

"Not sick; not outrageous; just smart." He kept smiling tenderly at Claire. "My love, I hope you understand."

"I don't." She was angry and ashamed and oddly sad. "The ones I knew, are they all gone?"

"They exist in memory."

"I was used by you," she said.

"I'll make it up. I promise that. What I want most of all is to make you happy."

"If you want me happy, don't do us harm."

Kiehl crossed the living room and stepped into the kitchen. He opened the refrigerator and found an open bottle of white wine. "You taught me how to live," he said as he poured the wine into three of their best glasses. "I'm deeply grateful. The least I can do is repay your kindness." He tucked the gun into his belt and brought a glass to Claire. He motioned Jake to get his own.

Didn't he see? Hadn't he seen when he looked at her upstairs? Was he crazy? Did he think she would even drink one drop?

Kiehl raised his glass. "A good meal, good company, delicious wine. Isn't that the only thing in life one really needs?"

"I have this feeling you have more in mind," Jake said.

"How insightful of you, Doctor."

"What was your goal?" Jake continued. "This thing you did was such a huge ordeal."

"To be rich. What other goal is there?"

"There must be more."

"To win. To show I'm the best. To escape the past."

"How can anyone do *that?*"

"Do you know what they would do to me in prison? No one can touch me now, no matter what I did, no matter what mistakes I made. They can say I'm crazy. They can put me in a hospital, but not in any jail."

"You can get away from lawyers and rapists," Jake said. "I think the past may be more difficult."

"You sound like a shrink," Kiehl replied.

"I guess it's what I am. I guess I know it."

"No!" Kiehl's anger burst into the open. "You're not what you think you are. We don't need your useless words. Your job will be to cook our meal."

The look on Kiehl's face was all Jake needed. He stepped into the kitchen area and began the task that only a little while ago had been so appealing. He stayed close to the drawer in which his gun was hidden, but he didn't open it. He had to play his cards carefully. The weapon in Kiehl's hand was much more powerful than his revolver. He wouldn't make a move until the odds were better, until Claire was out of danger. For the time being, no matter what Kiehl said, Jake would use words.

Kiehl pressed buttons on the stereo. He found a station that played soft music—the kind of pap that Claire and Jake despised. He took a seat on a chair where he could keep his eyes on Jake. He registered Claire's disgust and fear. "My love, I'm deeply sorry if I upset you. I don't mean you harm. I want you to know the man I really am." He sipped his wine as Jake kept working. "I'm not a bad person. I'm not even violent. I know that will be hard to believe, but I was young when certain things occurred. I was impulsive and I lost control. I did things that I know were wrong. But it was long ago. I'm not who I was then. I'm not the same person—what use is there in my suffering for the past?"

He sat across from her like an old friend who had come for dinner early and just happened to have a weapon in his hand. "I've changed. I've learned from you. I know things I didn't know before. I could help people if I got the chance. I can do good things now."

"Me too. I can do good things." Jake opened the oven to a blast of heat. "I'm going to set the table and in about ten minutes, I think this should be ready."

Kiehl took the place that Jake meant for himself. He sat at the head of the table, with Claire across from him, and he raised his glass to her in a silent toast. He never seemed to notice that she didn't drink at all.

Jake served large portions of bluefish filet, along with a salad and fresh bread they had bought that morning from a local baker. He wanted to dump the sizzling platter into Kiehl's lap, but the man's watchful eyes studied his every move. Jake and Claire ate slowly, forcing the food down only because it made more sense to eat than not to. Kiehl ate huge quantities. Claire shot Jake a look when he reached for his wine. He sipped often, but hardly drank at all.

They worked together to keep Kiehl talking.

"The way you managed it, all the things you made those computers do, it still amazes me," Claire said.

"I knew a long time ago that I was very smart. I knew that there was more to life than a godforsaken ranch."

"Did you really hate it there?" she asked.

"I didn't hate it. They were good enough to me. I just knew that there was more." He looked at Claire with an intensity that made her squirm.

"They were *good* to you?"

"Who doesn't have complaints?" he asked.

"There was no abuse?"

Kiehl shook his head. "It was part of the picture I needed to create."

"What picture?" she asked.

"If you have multiple personality, or want to pretend you have it, you need to be abused. You can spend five minutes with the books and learn that much."

She shook her head. She was out of questions.

"How did you choose the personalities?" Jake asked.

"I knew people like them. I read about others. I made things up as I went along . . ."

"An analyst would say that they reveal important things."

"I'm lucky, then, that I don't need an analyst."

"I'm not saying you need one," Jake went on. "I'm saying it could help you understand yourself."

"Do you drum up business that way?"

"I'm trying to be helpful," Jake said. "You spent a lot of money on treatment. Maybe you should get something out of it."

"I got exactly what I wanted out of it."

The telephone rang. Kiehl made a sign that they were not to move. After the fourth ring, their machine picked up. He crossed the room and turned the volume up so they all could listen—they heard a voice with a familiar accent: "Good evening. Here is a ghost you may not wish to hear. If that is your preference, I will understand. It would sadden me, but there are many things that sadden me. I have apologies to make. In the event that it is possible to talk, I would like to speak with you—both of you. I am sober. I now live full-time in this blessed village. If there is any possibility that the three of us might meet, would you kindly call?"

"Who is this fool?" Kiehl asked.

"Max Dorfmann. An old friend," Claire said.

"Is he a drunk?"

"He used to be."

"Did he let you down?"

"I don't know what you mean."

"Did he make you suffer?"

"Well . . ."

"Will you see him?"

"That depends . . ."

"On what?"

"At the moment, I'd say on you."

"Then you won't see him."

He motioned them back into the living room. He turned on the television set and handed the remote to Claire. They spent the remainder of the evening watching television. He chose a series of sitcoms they would never have looked at without a gun aimed at them.

At eleven o'clock, he turned the set off. "It's time for bed." He looked from one to the other and seemed not to notice the terror in Claire's face or the helpless rage in Jake's.

"You can have the guest room," she said firmly. "There's fresh linen on the bed. I'm sure you'll be very comfortable." She started up the stairs, and Jake followed behind her.

"I don't think so."

They kept going.

"Please *stop* where you are."

They both stood motionless.

"Dr. Silver, come down."

Jake didn't move. "There are limits . . ."

"You're not the one who sets them."

Claire began to cry, a plaintive weeping that Kiehl responded to: "My dear, I made a promise. No harm will come. I only want you to have peace and quiet."

She looked at Jake. "And him? Will he have peace and quiet?"

"He won't disturb you."

"I need to know he'll be all right."

"If he doesn't make trouble."

"Is that a promise?"

"Yes."

She went up the stairs as Jake stood watching. She closed the door and they heard her lock it.

"The guest room will be yours," Kiehl said. "Fresh linens, you know." When they were inside the room, he took handcuffs out of his trouser pocket.

"Is this necessary? You know I'm not going anywhere. I won't take a leak without asking your permission."

Kiehl studied him carefully. "You'll be a good boy?"

"Yes."

"This will help." He tossed the cuffs onto the bed. "Attach one hand to the headboard." It was wrought iron and a perfect place. "I'll unlock you in the morning. We'll both sleep better that way."

"Where do you sleep?"

Kiehl pointed into the living room.

"And your name is really Felix Kiehl?"

"I told you that."

"And you don't have other names?"

"Not one."

"And you'll let her sleep?"

"I keep my promises. It's more than most people do."

"There are no more surprises?"

"No more tonight." Kiehl smiled. "Are you done? Is there something else you want?"

"A glass of water and a bedtime story . . ."

The look he gave Jake was almost tender. "Who knows? Maybe, if you're a good boy, I'll tell you one tomorrow."

CHAPTER 51

IN THE MORNING, when Claire unlocked her door, Kiehl greeted her cheerfully. He had been outdoors in the cool clear air to collect dried flowers and golden leaves for the center of the table. The rich aroma of the coffee he had brewed filled every corner of the house. He had unlocked Jake, who was seated in the chair he had last night and looked like he hadn't slept at all.

"I hope you're well," Kiehl said.

"What's the point of this charade?" she asked as she came down the stairs. "If you really cared about the way I feel, you'd put that gun away."

"But I *do* care . . ."

He poured Claire's coffee. He somehow knew she drank it black. She took the cup, though she couldn't get herself to look at him. She took her seat. They sat in silence and sipped their coffee and gazed out through the sliding glass doors into the autumn morning. The sky was dotted with small puffy clouds, and the light kept changing from gray to yellow. The leaves still filled the trees, though their colors had faded. One good storm and they would all be down. There were no signs of life. It was as if the birds and rabbits and dogs that sometimes came to beg all knew to stay away.

It was obvious that there was something on Kiehl's mind. There was nothing to do but wait for him to say it. But before he could, a small red convertible turned into their driveway and came up the little dune with its engine over-revving. There was a loud screech as the car pulled up beside their Saab.

Jake spoke calmly: "It's pathetic how he drives. Every six months that thing needs brakes and a new clutch." It was the expensively restored MG Max called his "toy."

"Who?" Kiehl held the gun between both hands. His eyes were wild.

"It's only Max," Claire said. "The man who called last night. You don't have to worry. Either he's lonely or desperate or on the bottle again."

Kiehl turned to Jake and motioned toward the front door. "Get rid of the drunk. Fast! If you make one mistake, you're dead—you'll both be dead."

Jake stepped barefoot onto the chilly deck. The top of Max's car was down, the way he always drove it, and he looked up sheepishly from behind the wheel. He had on the beret he wore for effect, and a white silk scarf was wrapped loosely around his neck. His style was rakish, but his words were desperate: "We have to talk. I can't live like this. I want you to know I am not the same person. My heart is bad. I gave up alcohol. I even gave up tobacco."

He got out of the car awkwardly and stood beside it with the door hanging open. He was holding a paper bag. "Please invite me in. I brought fresh bagels. It was all *craziness.* It was my unconscious and her unconscious. Accept my most profound apology. Accept the fact that it involved no ego."

"This is not the time," Jake said. "You have to leave."

"Please . . ." Max went on. "I *need* you. Both of you."

"We'll talk another time. I promise. It can't be now."

"Is something wrong? I heard about the pregnancy. I congratulate you both—"

"I really mean it."

"I have to see her. Just for one minute. Just to say I'm sorry. I'm imploring—"

Kiehl stepped onto the deck and pointed his gun at Max. "The lady is fine. You're the one who doesn't look well."

"Who is this?" Max leaned against his car.

"You shouldn't crash a party if you're not invited," Kiehl said.

"A party?" Max was totally confused, an old man out of his familiar territory.

"You shouldn't go inside a room when the door is closed."

"A room?"

"Get in the house," Kiehl snapped. "Both of you. Now!"

Max took two steps up onto the deck and started breathing heavily. His face was puffy, as if an ambitious plastic surgeon had filled the wrinkles with too much collagen.

"This is Felix Kiehl," Jake said, "our guest . . ."

"Your *patient?*" Max's mouth opened and closed like that of a dying fish.

Jake led the way indoors.

"Take a seat," Kiehl said to Max. "You look like you need one."

He sat heavily on the couch, his mouth still working as he looked across the room at Claire. "I'm sorry . . ."

Kiehl's tone was menacing. "Who knows you've come?"

"I live alone. I went out to buy the paper, and I saw their car."

"Answer me! Who knows?"

"No one. I wouldn't tell anyone that I was coming."

"Why wouldn't you?"

"I would have been ashamed."

"Ashamed?" If Kiehl had learned one thing, it was the way that therapists ask questions.

"I came to apologize. I'm a sick man. I'm trying to straighten out my life. I need to make amends . . ." He was telling the truth and trying frantically, exactly like Jake and Claire, to make some kind of sense out of what was happening.

"Amends for what?"

"My good man, I don't know you. I don't consider that your business."

Kiehl slowly raised his gun. It was obvious that he could use it.

"All right." Max looked at Claire and spread his hands apologetically. "I had a relationship with Dr. Baxter that should have ended . . ."

"What kind of relationship?"

"That is not your business."

"We didn't ask you here. You had to stick yourself into a place you don't belong."

Max's eyes widened. Something began to register. He glanced at Jake and Claire and then back at Kiehl. "Young man, I said I came to make amends, not to relive the past."

"You won't have any future."

"I don't have one anyway," Max said. He seemed revived. His confusion and his fear were gone. He was calm and dignified, and he seemed less ill. He was an analyst again—and a good one. "What is this secret you need so much to know? What makes it so important?"

Kiehl aimed the gun. "Just answer me."

"Isn't the answer obvious? Must I say the words? Can't you tell that we made love?"

Kiehl shook his head vigorously. "I don't believe you. That isn't possible."

"I am sometimes capable of the unexpected," Max said. "Perhaps you are as well?"

"Why would she?" Kiehl asked.

Max's memory worked better than it had in years. They had discussed this man in detail. He made the interpretation long ago, and now he had his evidence. "Have you heard of the Oedipus complex?" he asked Kiehl.

"Of course."

"What I told the lady's husband, and what I'll say to you, is that

311

our relationship was a form of madness. It was our fantasy, only our fantasy. Do you understand? We were in pieces, and we thought we could be whole." Max waited for some response, but Kiehl was silent. "The lady had the sense to end it. She loves her husband, who deserves her love . . ."

Kiehl stared at him in disbelief. There were deep furrows in his brow, and his voice was strained. "You forced her. She would never touch you if she weren't forced. You did it against her will. It was rape."

"Don't be ridiculous. It certainly was *not*. I'm an old fool, but I'm no monster."

"That's *exactly* what you are."

Max spoke slowly and very carefully. He was an archer with one last arrow, and he had to place it perfectly: "Young man, please listen to an old doctor who has failed in many ways but who knows a thing or two about the mind. What you are feeling now has very little to do with me or this good woman. We are merely the stimuli. Your reaction is rooted in your past. What disturbs you now are things you felt when you were young."

Kiehl shook his head again. "I had a happy childhood. I pretended to be a multiple. I wasn't abused by anyone. I made that story up. My parents were good to me and kind to me. This stuff you're hinting at is all a lie."

"Stuff? Hinting?" Max didn't argue. His tone stayed calm and his manner clinical and gentle. He knew better than to clash head on. "You're an intelligent man. Surely you know there must be meaning to the things you do. Haven't you wondered why you sought treatment from a married couple?"

"I didn't seek treatment. I picked people who were useful—like the ones I picked in California. I needed a place where I could hide some money. I chose these doctors because they had this house . . ."

Max fixed on Kiehl with a thoughtful gaze. "Do you really believe your motives are so simple? I think you are too intelligent to be so naive. Why is it always married couples? And why, after you meet them, do they always die?"

"People die when they don't treat me right!"

"Is that a reason to *kill?*"

"Yes!"

"Who were the first you hated? Was it your own parents? Did they—like everyone's parents—set the pattern?"

"My parents were good people! They treated me well. They never hurt me. They never used me. They never made me suffer."

"I think you made that up," Max said flatly. "I think you are telling us about the parents you wished for. Your real parents were not so kind. I think your real parents did you great harm . . ."

The gun cracked once. A small, neat hole appeared in the center of Max's chest. The impact pushed him back against the couch. He looked surprised. His mouth opened, closed, opened again, and then stayed open. His eyes stayed open wide. Just the smallest trickle of blood—as if it was all he had to spare—oozed out beside the polo player stitched onto his shirt. He looked oddly happy.

"Oh my God . . . Oh my God." Claire began to weep.

Kiehl looked at her with tenderness. "My love, don't worry. He won't hurt you again or force you into anything again. You're free of him. I'll take good care of you. I can make you happy. I'll *prove* to you I can . . ."

"But—" She turned from Kiehl to Max and then back to Kiehl again. Max was right. The theory was right. It was all Oedipal.

There was no time to cry. She used every drop of the strength she still had left to keep herself from looking at Jake.

CHAPTER 52

KIEHL ORDERED THEM out onto the deck behind the house. He put his handcuffs on Claire's wrists and locked her arms around the rail. He gently squeezed her hand as he pressed the mechanism closed. "This will take a little while."

Should she scream? Was there anyone to hear? "Please . . . You made a promise . . . Haven't you done enough? You made a promise," she repeated helplessly.

"I will not harm you."

"And *him?*" She reached out to Jake, but the handcuffs stopped her.

"That depends on him." He turned to Jake. "We're going to do some gardening, old man."

"It's the wrong season."

"No more jokes. No more games. No more pretending."

Jake walked around the house to the garage, where Kiehl ordered him to raise the overhead door. In the corner, beside a pile of firewood, lay the small collection of garden tools they had bought last spring. He told Jake to pick up the spade. Then Kiehl noticed the bag of charcoal and the fluid used to start the coals. He carried the plastic bottle in one hand and his weapon in the other as Jake led the way out to the garden.

The sound of a spade striking sandy earth went on and on, much longer than Claire thought possible. She began to tremble uncontrollably. She couldn't see them. Was it Jake's grave? Would all that they had struggled through just end like this? The sun disappeared behind a cloud, and a cool wind blew against her. She thought about the life inside her. For its sake alone, she had to live. Then she thought of Max, poor sad old Max, still upright on the couch. He did his best, and it got him killed, but his words were still the only hope they had.

"It's gone," Jake said. "I told you. It went to the FBI." He stood in the shallow hole that once held Kiehl's case.

"Let's go deeper," Kiehl said. "Isn't that what shrinks do? You never know what you can find."

The one thing left was to play for time. Jake had the spade. If Kiehl dropped his guard, he would get one swing. Just one. The trick would be to find a way to make it possible.

He dug down into the sandy earth. The weeds and roots had taken over. Next summer there would be few signs there was ever a garden here. The spade was sharp, and his back felt strong. He would just keep going. He had to. He dug into the hole where the case had rested. He dug down through the tangle into a layer that looked like it had never been disturbed. The ground was sterile; devoid of roots; just sand and stones left by a glacier twenty thousand years ago. The digging became more difficult. The sides kept caving in, and the center of the hole kept filling with debris. "What's the point of this?" Jake asked. "The police will find it anyway. Whatever you bury here will be dug up the day you're gone."

"You think I'm putting something *in*?"

Jake looked up. "I guess I should be relieved."

Then his spade hit something hard.

The sun stayed hidden behind the clouds. Claire felt the handcuffs cutting into her wrists. When the men returned, the sweat was dripping off Jake's forehead in muddy streams. He was carrying a metal trunk that made her think of a coffin.

Kiehl handed Claire a tiny key and watched as she unlocked herself. He continued to hold the gun in one hand and the plastic bottle of fluid in the other. "I said I could take care of you. I always tell the truth."

"The man has layers under layers," Jake said.

"I don't let people down. That's the bottom layer. I don't make promises that I don't keep."

Jake carried his load inside. It was the kind of trunk one sends off with a child to camp, neatly sealed with the same silvery tape that sealed the first case. It was coated with a layer of moist sand that fell in gritty clumps onto the floor. Jake put it on the rug in the center of the living room and spoke to Claire: "This box was out there—six feet under, more or less. The other was just a decoy."

Kiehl pointed at Max's body. "Now get rid of *that*."

"You're the boss and I'm the boy . . ."

"You could put it that way."

Claire watched as Jake dragged Max's body into the guest room. Kiehl placed the bottle on the floor beside the case. She saw him hold his gun as he peeled the tape away with his free hand. She saw him motion Jake to a seat on the couch. He was proud and happy, and he had good reason. He opened the lid of the case that held his treasure.

The trunk was full, its contents neatly organized. The absconding president of some raped S&L could not have hoped for more. There were packages of bills in every denomination from thousands down to twenties. There were packets of bonds and negotiable securities with elaborate printing and exotic colors and face amounts in the tens of thousands. There were bundles of British pounds, French francs, Swiss francs, marks, Canadian dollars, Australian dollars, yen. There was a package of passports: U.S., Canadian, Australian. There were dozens of credit cards. There were plastic garment bags containing clothing. There was another automatic pistol and more ammunition. And finally, at the very bottom, were plastic bags containing precious stones and jewelry. Kiehl reached for one of these after he jammed the new weapon into his belt.

"This is for you," he said to Claire, "to make up for the pain I caused." He leaned toward the couch and placed a small plastic bag on the cushion next to her. It held a pair of diamond earrings of extraordinary clarity and brilliance. The stones were huge. They were set simply and tastefully in platinum.

Jake eyed the drawer where his gun was hidden. Could he make it? Too far . . .

Claire's response was automatic: "I'm sorry. I can't take gifts from patients. No analyst can ever—"

"But I'm *not* your patient," Kiehl interrupted.

"Once you are, you always are."

"But I'm not! *Not me!*"

She saw the look that came into his eyes. She knew the anger that could follow. She saw Jake's expression. She knew his thoughts exactly. No matter what the rules, she had to play this game. She couldn't be detached. It wasn't enough to make interpretations. She had to be what Kiehl needed her to be and see where it would lead. "May I hold them?" she asked.

"Of course."

She extended her hand. "Have you seen my ring?"

He smiled as he nodded. "I did enjoy hypnosis, even if I was never in a trance. I thought of it as a form of making love."

She held the earrings near the lamp. "I do admit you tempt me. Could I wear them for a while? They really are exquisite."

"It would make me happy."

As Kiehl gazed tenderly at her, Claire put on the earrings. Large as they were, they were not gaudy. They dangled gracefully, exactly right. He had chosen them with her in mind.

"At least I understand why you came back," Jake said. "With a stash like this, you'd be crazy not to."

"I came for various reasons."

"I assume you have a plan."

317

Kiehl looked at him. "You lost the game already. I'm being kind because the lady asked and because I promised her."

"All I did was ask where you were headed."

Contempt was in Kiehl's voice: "Let's see how well the shrink can read my mind."

"I was fired, remember? I'm off the case."

"I'll let you redeem yourself."

"I only read minds that I get paid to read."

Kiehl reached into his case and tossed Jake a wad of hundred-dollar bills. The package bounced off Jake's chest and came to rest on the floor in front of him. It was at least ten thousand dollars. "We'll play it your way. For the next ten minutes, I'll be your patient . . ."

"I don't take ten-minute patients," Jake said calmly.

"It's more than you were ever paid."

Jake paused. Then it came to him . . . "I don't do chores or run errands or sweep shit out of barns. I'm not your little boy—I follow your orders only because you have a gun." He spat the words like ammunition.

Kiehl stood abruptly. He aimed the gun at Jake. "That's it. I've had enough. Put my things in the car. We're getting out of here. Don't push your luck."

"Please. You *promised* me." Claire touched both ears. "I could never wear these if he was hurt."

The elements were in the open, the pieces all in place. It happened in every treatment—no matter who the therapist, no matter what was the theory. Jake saw it clearly. It didn't matter if Kiehl was or was not a multiple. It didn't matter what he faked. What mattered were his acts. He had picked Jake and Claire—knowingly or not—to relive his past. The things he did were real. They were in the same place all the others had been, caught in the same morass, repeating the nightmare Kiehl was doomed to repeat forever. The only hope was to see the pattern and then break out of it.

Jake spoke with as imposing a voice as he could muster: "She won't go. Your time will come. Some day you'll find a woman of your own—it isn't now."

"Maybe *your* time has come . . ." Kiehl held the plastic bottle between his legs and unscrewed the cap. He squirted the liquid in oily spurts around the room. It dripped off the walls and onto the floor and furniture. Their eyes watered from the fumes.

Jake carried the case through the front door and out of the house. Claire followed behind, with Kiehl beside her.

"Put it in the car."

"It'll never fit."

Max's little car sat beside their own.

"In the *big* car," Kiehl said.

Jake lowered the case to the ground beside the Saab. "You can take my car. It's a gift."

"Open it! The trunk!"

Jake stood behind the car and tapped his pockets with both hands. "I left the keys inside . . ."

"Get them!" Kiehl stood on the deck, his weapon ready, his shoulder touching Claire.

As Jake passed by, Kiehl sprayed him with the fluid. "No bright ideas."

"You're the only one allowed? Is that the way it is?"

Kiehl tossed the empty bottle into the house and reached in his pocket.

"No!" Kiehl held the same brand of plastic lighter Claire recognized from the hospital.

Kiehl stood in the doorway with the lighter in one hand and his gun in the other.

"Give him a chance," she pleaded. "Let him look. We can't get out of here unless he finds them."

"I always lose the goddamn keys," Jake called out from the kitchen. Kiehl watched as Jake opened drawers.

"Let me jog your memory."

Kiehl pressed the lighter and a large flame shot out.

Jake talked as fast as he could: "You know, I disagreed at first, but Max Dorfmann was absolutely right. You think you're smart, you think you've got it all worked out, but you miss half of what goes on in front of your eyes. You're crazier than you imagine—much crazier. You block reality. This is a *fantasy* you're living out. It isn't just some act, some game. You really are insane." Jake pulled the gun from the drawer and held it below the counter.

"Doctor, you have my permission to say anything that comes into your mind." Kiehl kneeled and touched the flame to the puddle at the door. "But if you don't find the key—and soon—you won't get out . . ."

A bright yellow flame spread quickly across the floor. It reached the couch and went up one wall.

Jake had to jolt the man, distract him somehow, get him away from Claire. He had one last weapon—the one he got from Max: "You know, she's not your woman. She never will be. Don't you see it yet? Don't you see her belly? Can't you see she's *pregnant!*"

Kiehl stood in the doorway. His eyes went from Jake to Claire and back and forth again. The couch began to burn.

"She won't stay with you," Jake went on. "She's carrying my child. I'm the father—the *real* father, not the one in your sick fantasy."

Kiehl's eyes locked onto Claire's abdomen.

"It's the truth," she said. "I'm due in four months. I do love him. I'll always love him."

"And me? What about *me?*" Kiehl shook his head. He seemed confused. His face was changing. "Dr. Baxter, what *happened?* Have you been keeping secrets? Did you lie to me?"

Flames crept up the stairs. It was more than the fluid—the wood itself was burning.

"She's *pregnant,*" Jake went on. "Do you get it? Does someone in there get it?"

Kiehl's voice turned harsh: "That little bastard! I'll show him who gets what. I'll rip his heart out! I'll cut his balls off . . ."

"Victor? Is it you?" she asked.

"You said you would be *mine.* You said you would take care. You never meant a word! You lied!"

She backed away. There was space between them.

And in that moment, Jake brought his gun into the open and pulled the trigger. The first shot missed, but the second caught Kiehl in the throat, the third hit his chest, and the fourth his abdomen. Kiehl dropped his gun and fell writhing on the deck.

Jake ran out of the burning house toward Claire. His skin stayed cool. The fluid that soaked his shirt escaped the flames.

Arterial blood spurted from Felix Kiehl's neck, a huge, unstoppable amount. He looked up, searching for Claire, and raised an arm. His face had changed again and all the rage was out of it. Was he Alan? Was he The Professor? Was he someone new? He reached out for her. His mouth moved, but no words came. His arm fell back and his eyes glazed over . . .

She put both arms around Jake and held on tight.

A wave of hot air hit them. The house filled with flames. Black smoke poured out of the open door. Jake dragged Kiehl's body off the deck and out beside the cars. Kiehl's case lay at their feet.

An odd smile crossed Jake's face. He looked down at the case.

"You don't give up, do you?" Claire said.

"We deserve something . . ."

"We deserve it all. That doesn't mean we get a dime."

He reached out and touched her belly. "A present for the baby?"

She had to smile. "Such as?"

"The earrings were a gift."

She touched an ear. She was still wearing them. She took them off and held them in her hand. "Are you assuming, then, we have a girl?"

"I could live with that." The first faint feeling of real relief began. "They could pay for tennis lessons—unisex."

"More likely for analysis . . ."

"*Our* kid won't need a shrink."

"I'm not so sure."

There was no wind. The plume of smoke went straight into the sky. They heard distant sirens.

The earrings caught the yellow flames and sparkled brilliantly as she held them in her hand. "We could call them a legacy," Claire said.

Jake kissed her cheek. "Let's call them a gift from Max."

She took his hand. "Let's say they come from us—a gift from you and me. Let's say they celebrate the fact that we're together."

ABOUT THE AUTHOR

LEONARD SIMON is the author of two novels, *The Irving Solution* and *Reborn*. He is in private practice as a clinical psychologist and psychoanalyst in New York City.